A QUIET DEATH

A QUIET DEATH

A Hannah Ives Novel

Marcia Talley

This first world edition published 2011
in Great Britain and in the USA by
SEVERN HOUSE PUBLISHERS LTD of
9–15 High Street, Sutton, Surrey, England, SM1 1DF.
Trade paperback edition first published
in Great Britain and the USA 2011 by
SEVERN HOUSE PUBLISHERS LTD.

British Library Cataloguing in Publication Data

Talley, Marcia Dutton, 1943–
 A quiet death. – (The Hannah Ives mysteries series)
 1. Ives, Hannah (Fictitious character) – Fiction.
 2. Railroad accidents – Fiction. 3. Love-letters – Fiction.
 4. Maryland – Fiction. 5. Detective and mystery stories.
 I. Title II. Series
 813.6-dc22

ISBN-13: 978-0-7278-8041-3 (cased)
ISBN-13: 978-1-84751-350-2 (trade paper)

All Severn House titles are printed on acid-free paper.

Severn House Publishers support The Forest Stewardship Council [FSC],
the leading international forest certification organisation. All our titles that
are printed on Greenpeace-approved FSC-certified paper carry the FSC logo.

Typeset by Palimpsest Book Production Ltd.,
Falkirk, Stirlingshire, Scotland.
Printed and bound in Great Britain by
MPG Books Ltd., Bodmin, Cornwall.

Acknowledgements

On June 22, 2009, Metro train no. 112 pulled out of Takoma Station, Washington, DC, heading for Fort Totten, Maryland. At 5:02 p.m., it plowed into the rear of another train standing in the Fort Totten station, killing nine people, making it the deadliest crash in DC Metro history. I've never been in a train wreck, thank goodness, but wish to acknowledge the eyewitness accounts told by survivors, rescue workers, and good Samaritans in the days following the disaster that helped inform Hannah's story.

In addition, I want to thank:

My husband, Barry Talley, who puts up with my absences, both physical and mental, whenever I get lost in my writing.

My daughters, Laura Geyer for 'John Chandler,' and Sarah Glass for the broken arm, and for being a Mawrter, too.

Rick 'Ike' Iacangelo, DCFD Engine Co. 13, #2 Platoon, wagon driver, retired.

Capt. Donald Jensen, MC, USN, aka 'Mr X-ray.'

My Sisters in Grime, including Carol Chase, Terri Ryburn, Toni Tucker, Laurel Anderson, Jo Mink, Joan Hubbs, Kathi Davis, Vicki Hill, Peg Shea, and Carolyn Paullin, who will know why.

My amazing editor, Amanda Stewart, my can-do publicist, Michelle Duff, Piers Tilbury and Claire Caswell, who design the most eye-catching book covers ever, Edwin Buckhalter, and everyone else at Severn House who makes it such an incredibly supportive place for a mystery writer to be.

And, once again, my fellow travelers at various stations on the road to publication, the Annapolis Writers Group: Ray Flynt, Lynda Hill, Mary Ellen Hughes, Debbi Mack, Sherriel Mattingley, and Bonnie Settle.

And to Kate Charles and Deborah Crombie – Plot fest forever!

For reasons of national security, the Library of Congress Office of Security and Emergency Preparedness has requested that I alter certain details concerning security screening procedures at Library of Congress buildings within the District of Columbia. Not really, but if I got it wrong, that's my story.

At three and twenty I am left alone, and what more can we be at seventy? It is true, I am young enough to begin again, but with whom can I retrace the laughing part of life? It is odd how few of my friends have died a quiet death; I mean in their beds. But a quiet life is of more consequence.

Lord Byron (George Gordon),
Letter to James Wedderburn Webster, August 24, 1811

ONE

Once upon a time, I worked in Washington, DC. Then, in an extreme case of downsizing, I lost my job to the recession and a breast to cancer – both in the same year.

Now, I was back, threading my way through a knot of entrepreneurs at the McPherson Square Metro station – a sad-eyed Korean girl selling roses, a ukulele-playing panhandler, and some guy pimping Krispy Kremes – and it occurred to me that I didn't miss the job or the commute one little bit. The breast? Well, that was another matter. Reconstructive surgery had worked its magic – my husband thinks I look hot in my red and white tankini – but the fact remained that *Sports Illustrated* magazine wouldn't be featuring me in their annual swimsuit issue any time soon.

A swimsuit, I wish! What better attire for sweltering in a Washington, DC subway station on a busy Tuesday afternoon? For three thirty, the platform was unexpectedly crammed. Tourists drooped, still jabbering about their tour of the nearby White House. School kids sagged under the weight of their backpacks. Other commuters in sweat-stained cotton shirts loafed about, mopping their collective brows, enjoying a temporary respite in the underground tunnel from the relentless triple-digit temperatures. An early-September heatwave had swept over the eastern seaboard, breaking all previous records. When I left Annapolis earlier that morning, the thermometer on my shaded patio had already read eighty-nine degrees. Now, even in the air-conditioned station, I could feel sweat beading along my hairline and trickling down between my breasts.

A blue line train slid into the station and carried some of the wilted passengers away, but by the time I pushed my way on to the lead car of an orange line train heading for New

Carrollton, and the parking garage where I'd left my Volvo, it was still standing room only, so I planted my heels firmly on the floor and grabbed on to a pole as the train picked up speed.

At Metro Center, more people got on than off, squeezing damp bodies, bags and backpacks into the overcrowded car, and squashing me against a guy who, according to his Hoyas T-shirt, was a student at Georgetown University. As my hip ground into his, I readjusted my shoulder bag so it hung in front of me – pickpockets were not unknown on the DC Metro system – and looked around somewhat desperately for a seat.

Several stops later, at L'Enfant Plaza, I was eyeing a vacant seat toward the front of the car, when a teenager muscled by, tethered to an iPod Nano by white ear buds screwed in tight, a scratchy *boom-chica-boom-chica-boom* leaking out of his ears. He beat me to it. I scowled in his general direction, and at the sign on the bulkhead behind his seat that stated in bold, black letters: 'Priority Seating: Reserved for the Elderly and Handicapped,' not knowing whether to feel outraged by his discourtesy, or secretly pleased that I didn't appear to be all that elderly.

At Eastern Market, I plopped myself down gratefully at the rear of the car next to a young businessman cradling a shopping bag in his arms like a newborn, closed my eyes and inventoried the contents of my freezer, trying to decide what I might throw together for dinner. When the train popped out of the underground tunnel into the blazing sunlight after the Stadium Armory station, I used my iPhone to call my husband, who was probably still grading papers in his office at the Naval Academy.

Paul answered right away. 'Hannah.'

'Caller ID never ceases to amaze me.'

'How was the fashion show?' Paul was referring to the fund-raising luncheon I'd just attended, sponsored by a prominent DC law firm in partnership with Nordstrom in order to raise money for breast cancer research.

'Gorgeous. There was this Eileen Fisher beaded wool cardigan. Only three hundred bucks. You're lucky I left my checkbook at home, Mr Ives.'

'How can you seriously look at sweaters in all this heat, Hannah?'

'You forget. I'm a trained professional.' I shifted the phone from my left ear to my right and relaxed into the vinyl upholstery, deliciously cool against the tepid dampness of my favorite knee-length, black and white paisley dress. I adored that dress, purchased at a boutique on Fosse Street while on vacation in Dartmouth, England, the previous summer.

'Crossing Eye Street was a hazard, no surprise. You know those cute little Prada slingbacks I slipped into this morning?' I asked, knowing he wouldn't. 'I thought I was going to lose them, sucked into the tarmac like the La Brea Tar Pits, not to be rediscovered until late in the thirty-first century.'

On the other end of the line, Paul chuckled. 'I didn't jog today either.'

'Sensible lad.' I checked my watch. 'Look, I'm running late. Would you mind swinging by Whole Foods on your way home from the Academy? Pick up something interesting for dinner?'

'Not exactly on my way, is it, but I'm happy to oblige. What are you in the mood for?'

'Anything but poultry,' I said, remembering the chicken salad I'd had for lunch that had all the taste and consistency of a minced dishrag.

'Cuisine?'

'Anything but fried.' I mentally reviewed the items on offer at the numerous prepared foods bars of the upscale supermarket, factored in the heat of the day and concluded, 'Salads! That's the ticket.'

'Will do.'

'And wine. I could use some right now, in fact. A bottle of Sauvignon Blanc. Well chilled. With a straw.'

'Hold that thought,' Paul said, and rang off.

I stared at the screen on my iPhone for a moment, wondering if I had time for a game of Bejeweled, when the guy sitting next to me stirred. 'You like it?'

I turned to face him. 'My iPhone, you mean?'

He laid his bundle across his knees. 'Been thinking about getting one, but I've got Verizon.'

'Apple's working on that,' I said, noticing that his shopping bag carried the Julius Garfinkel & Co label, a landmark Washington, DC department store that had gone out of business more than twenty years before. 'My mother sent me off to college wearing clothes we bought at Garfinkel's,' I told him, indicating the bag. 'Back when dressing for dinner meant something more refined than pushing a tray through a cafeteria line while wearing clean jeans and an Eminem T-shirt.'

'I know what you mean,' he said, dark eyes serious under pale, shaggy brows that marched across his forehead like caterpillars. 'Nobody's got standards any more. Although I can't wait to get out of this suit.' He plucked at his shirt collar, open wide at the neck. His tie, navy blue with minute red and yellow stripes, had already been removed, rolled up and tucked into the breast pocket of his jacket, where it peeked out like a plump sausage. 'Jesus. If the heat doesn't break soon, people are going to start going postal. Is it always this hot in September?'

'Rarely,' I chuckled. 'Usually we go straight from summer into winter, skipping the business of fall altogether, except for a few perfectly splendid days in mid-October which make one ridiculously happy to be alive.' I paused for a moment. 'Do you sail?'

'Me?' He managed a smile. 'Never. Boats don't agree with my stomach.'

'Cruising the Chesapeake Bay in October is one of life's greatest pleasures. We don't have a sailboat,' I added, 'but my sister-in-law does, and she's always looking for crew. I provide ballast,' I said with a grin.

'How long is this heat supposed to last?' my seat-mate wanted to know.

I shrugged. 'Couple of days? Wait a minute.' While he observed over my shoulder, I tapped the weather app on my iPhone. When the five-day display appeared, I turned the tiny screen in his direction. 'Looks like we're back to normal on Friday.'

'What's normal?' my seat-mate asked as he watched the Cheverly station roll by outside the window.

'Low to mid-seventies,' I informed the back of his head, which was covered with a tangle of sandy curls.

'Huh,' he replied.

The four o'clock Acela Express screamed past on its way north, sucking the air out of our car in one greedy, pneumatic gasp. My seat-mate jumped like he'd been shot, then settled back into his seat and continued staring silently out the window, our deeply intellectual conversation about the weather clearly over. I zoned out, mesmerized by the blur of passing scenery and the comforting *chubunk-chubunk-chubunk* of the wheels along the tracks.

As we pulled into the station at Landover, my seat-mate stood, tucked his package under his arm, and eased past my legs into the aisle. I thought he was preparing to get off, but when the train rolled out of the station again, he remained standing in the aisle near the door, grasping a metal pole with one hand and his Garfinkel's shopping bag with the other.

My iPhone peeped. A text message from my daughter, Emily, asking if I'd RUN C'PL TOM. I was mentally rearranging the next day's schedule so I could drive my grandchildren to school, when a voice from the front of the car screamed, 'Oh, no!'

Startled, I looked up just in time to see my seat-mate vanish into a cloud of dust, glass, seats and carpeting that rolled up the aisle toward me in an undulating wave – ten feet, five feet, four, three – before sucking me into the undertow.

The squeal of metal against metal, a teeth-rattling jolt. The train rocked once, twice, before settling nose up and tilted to one side with a mournful, metallic groan. For a few moments, there was utter silence.

And then the chaos began.

TWO

What had just happened? Stunned, I lay on my side in a bed of debris and broken glass and tried to make sense out of it. The train must have hit something. Had we derailed?

Dust filled the air, thick as smoke. I coughed and tried to roll over. Why was I looking up into a cloudless blue sky?

When we left the Landover station there had been no more than a dozen passengers remaining in our car; New Carrollton was the end of the line. Now they all seemed to be crying out:

Help me! Please! My foot's stuck!

Baby! Where are you, baby? Are you OK?

Jessie! Jessie! Oh my God!

Somebody open the door! Get us out of here!

I eased myself into a crawling position and tried to move toward the nearest exit, but when I pressed my left palm against the carpet, a lightning bolt shot up my arm and across my shoulders, a pain so intense that I fell sideways against what remained of one of the seats, now lying bottom side up, blocking a pair of exit doors. I didn't have to look to know my left arm was broken, but I inspected it anyway, fearful I'd find bones sticking out through my skin. There was no blood, thank goodness, but my arm was bent in a way Mother Nature never intended: I appeared to have a second wrist midway up my forearm. 'This can't be good,' I muttered, drawing the damaged arm closer to my body.

'Do you need help, ma'am? I heard you scream.'

I was eye-to-eye with a pair of combat boots that I'd last seen jutting out into the aisle from the seat behind me. I looked up, way up, into the face of their owner, a lanky black man who appeared miraculously uninjured, save for a one-inch gash on his stubbly chin. Sweat glistened on his cheeks, beaded his forehead. He wore a green, tan and gray camouflage uniform, and the Velcro patch on his chest told me he was a staff sergeant. A second patch over his right pocket said: Boyer. I tried to answer, but dust seemed to be coating my vocal cords. 'Broken arm,' I croaked.

'Can you walk?'

'I think so.'

Sergeant Boyer bent down, extended his arm. Using my good arm, I grasped his forearm tightly and held on while he stood, pulling me gently to my feet. 'I'm Will,' he said. 'Anybody with you?'

Struggling for balance, my fingers dug into his sleeve while I bent double, coughing until my lungs burned. The sergeant waited me out.

'There was a guy sitting next to me,' I wheezed. 'He was standing up when the train . . .' My voice trailed off as I took in the condition of the front end of our car. The impact had savagely twisted seats, doors and windows, compressing them into a mountain of wreckage that spanned the entire width of the car.

The dust was beginning to settle when another man staggered out of the debris field, dragging a young woman by the hand. Strands of hair had escaped her bun and hung lifelessly around her face which was bloody and pocked with glass. 'Get me out of here, baby,' she wailed as she limped along behind him. One of her shoes had gone missing.

'The side doors are jammed,' the man called Baby reported, waving vaguely. 'And the windows won't pop out like they're supposed to. How about the rear door?'

'I just tried,' Sergeant Boyer informed him. 'No joy. You can see that the bulkhead's collapsed.'

The woman began to wail like a professional mourner. 'Oh, God, baby, we're trapped!' She shook her hand free of his, staggered over to a twisted window and began pounding on the glass with both fists. 'Help! Help! Get us out of here!'

Sergeant Boyer watched her performance for a second, then grabbed the hem of his uniform jacket and, in one swift move, pulled it off over his head. 'I guess we'll have to make an exit, then.'

I watched in awe as he marched on the rear door in his olive green undershirt, solid and determined as a Sherman tank. As he moved, he wrapped the jacket around a tattoo on his forearm that said, in gothic script, Psalm XXIII. 'Stand back,' he ordered.

Boyer cocked his padded arm and took a swing at the door. He cocked his arm and swung again. And again, and again. The door stood firm.

'Sergeant! Stop! You're going to hurt yourself,' I yelled as Boyer hauled his arm back to take another swing.

'Shut up, bitch!' someone behind me snarled. 'Who else

gonna get us outta this mess!' The potty mouth belonged to another survivor who had staggered up to join us, a twenty-something thug wearing a wife-beater tank and a pair of shredded, low-rider jeans. Earlier, he'd been sporting a ball cap worn backward and to one side, gangsta-style, but his cap had disappeared in all the confusion.

Boyer shot shrapnel out of his eyes. 'Watch your language, asshole. You in such a hurry to get out of here, grab something and start pounding.'

I scanned the floor, looking for ammunition, and spotted a fire extinguisher next to a crumpled bulkhead, near what had once been my seat. 'Sergeant Boyer! Use this!' I nudged the extinguisher toward him with my bare foot. Bare foot? Where the hell were my shoes?

Boyer picked up the extinguisher, flashing me a wan grin. Holding the extinguisher like a battering ram, he hammered the base of it hard against the glass. He brought his arm back and swung again.

A small crack appeared.

'Go, go, go!' the man called Baby chanted, as Boyer continued hammering away on the door.

His girlfriend had abandoned her histrionics and rejoined our little group, yelling encouragement from the sidelines as the crack spread, creeping with snail-like speed up the glass. 'You've got it! You've got it! Keep going! Keep going! You are the *man*!'

I found I was chanting, too – Go! Go! Go! – each time the base of the extinguisher made contact with the glass. The crack was gradually widening, expanding, spreading like a spider web.

Boyer delivered a final savage blow, and the glass popped out.

We all stood there for a moment, silent, not quite believing that we'd soon be free, leaving the devastation behind us. Still holding the extinguisher, Boyer fell back against the bulkhead, breathing heavily, trying to catch his breath. Sweat beaded on his forehead, ran down his cheeks, saturated his T-shirt, turning the underarms dark. 'Out!' he ordered, then slowly uncurled his hand and let the extinguisher drop to the floor.

The man called Baby helped his girlfriend through the opening, then scampered quickly after her. The foul-mouthed thug was next in line, hopping from one foot to the other, raring to go, but Boyer grabbed his arm, held him back, taking the time to lean out the opening he had created in the door and yell to Baby's departing back, 'For Christ's sake, tell someone to turn off the third rail before some idiot gets electrocuted!'

Then the thug, too, slipped away to join a steady stream of walking wounded, limping along the tracks outside, dragging their possessions behind them like zombies in a B-movie.

Boyer offered me his hand. 'Time to go.'

'Is that all of us?' I choked. 'Only five?'

Boyer sucked in his lips, looking grim. 'I think we have to leave it to the paramedics now.'

I had started toward the opening in the door when somebody called out, 'Hello? Can anybody hear me?'

Even though I'd had only a brief conversation with him, I recognized the voice: the guy who had been sitting next to me nursing the Garfinkel's bag.

'Did you hear that, Sergeant?' Cradling my injured arm, grinding my teeth against the pain, I inched toward the front of the car and began a surreal climb through an alien landscape strewn with familiar objects, distorted, like in a Halloween funhouse mirror. 'I'm here. Where are you?'

'I don't know.'

'Talk to me!' I yelled.

'My legs are trapped.'

Thankfully, Sergeant Boyer had followed me forward and was standing just three feet away. 'Sergeant! Can you get some help? Quickly! There's someone still alive up there! I'll see if I can find him.'

'Keep talking,' I called out to my former seat-mate as Sergeant Boyer hurried off to do as I asked. Feeling increasingly desperate, I scanned the wreckage. And then I saw him: a head of curly hair, a shoulder and one arm. But his body from the chest down had disappeared. It took me a moment to figure out what had happened. As the floors heaved up, the seats had folded down, trapping his body in their cruel jaws.

With my good arm, I reached out to see if I could shift one of the seats holding the man captive, then thought better of it. He could have a spinal injury. If so, I would only make a bad situation worse.

'I'm coming,' I called out as I scrabbled over shifting debris – shattered glass, scraps of advertising posters, the Life section of *USA Today*, a dusty Kindle, shoes. His Garfinkel's bag was in the way, so I moved it aside, sat down in the aisle, or what was left of it, so that I could look directly into his face, pale and etched with pain.

'Hold on,' I told him. 'Help is on the way. One of the passengers just busted through the door.'

His eyes were white with panic. 'Don't leave me.'

'I won't.'

'Are those sirens?'

'Yes. Help is coming.'

He closed his eyes. 'I'm dying,' he whispered.

'No, you're not. My name's Hannah. What's yours?'

'They call me Skip.'

'What's your last name, Skip?'

He moaned. 'Sweet Jesus, I can't feel my legs.'

'You're gonna be OK, Skip. Keep talking to me.'

Skip's eyes rolled back, his head lolled.

'Skip?'

His head jerked up, he whimpered in pain. Then his eyes found mine, locked. 'I've done a terrible thing.'

'You have?'

A gurgling cough. 'I think I killed somebody.'

I caught my breath, tried not to gasp. I wasn't trained in deathbed confessions, and wasn't sure I wanted to take on the responsibility for the disposition of this man's soul when it showed up in the afterlife. I glanced around the car, looking for support, but the sergeant hadn't returned. For all I knew, Skip and I were the only two people left alive in the car.

'Do you want to tell me about it?' I asked quietly.

'Are you Catholic?' His voice trembled.

'No, but I'm Episcopalian. That's a Catholic of sorts.'

'Rosary,' he sighed. 'My pants pocket.'

I couldn't even see Skip's legs, so there was no way I could retrieve a rosary from his pants pocket. I broke this news to him as gently as I could. 'But I'll be happy to recite the rosary with you.'

'In the name of the Father, and of the Son, and of the Holy Spirit, Amen,' he began, crossing himself.

Skip's voice remained strong through the Creed and the first Our Father, but by the time we got to the Hail Marys, it began to tremble, then falter. 'Hail Mary full of grace,' he began, his voice barely audible.

'The Lord is with thee,' I continued, inclining my head towards his and taking his hand. 'Blessed are thou amongst women, and blessed is the fruit of thy womb, Jesus.'

'Holy Mary . . .' A shuddering sigh, then silence.

'Mother of God,' I prompted, but Skip's lips were no longer moving along with mine. 'Mother of God. Skip? Stay with me, Skip!' I eased my hand up to his wrist, wrapped my fingers around it and felt for a pulse. It was there, slow and weak. 'Holy Mary, Mother of God, pray for us sinners now and at the hour of our death,' I rushed on, then began the cycle again.

With the dying, I had read somewhere, hearing may be the last of the senses to go. *Now and at the hour of our death.* I hoped Skip heard and that the words would be a comfort to him.

'Skip?' I asked after a while. 'Are you curious about how I can recite the rosary, not being Catholic?' His hand was still warm, thank God, but his fingernails looked pale, bluish. 'My dad was in the navy,' I rattled on while gently stroking his hand, desperate to restore circulation. 'When I was in the third grade, we were stationed in Norfolk, Virginia, and my best friend was a girl from New Orleans. I sometimes went to mass with her family.'

The tension had drained from his face. He looked relaxed, completely at peace. Was Skip sleeping, in a coma, or had he died? I shivered and tore my eyes away. Outside the window, police cars, fire trucks and ambulances were lining up, lights flashing red and orange and blue. While a bone-thin stray watched warily from a patch of weeds, a cutter like a Transformer toy began to chew through the chain-link fence that bordered the tracks.

It seemed like hours before our first rescuer appeared, climbing through the makeshift window that Sergeant Boyer had created. He wore blue coveralls, a fluorescent green reflective vest, and a yellow helmet. Another firefighter followed. Then another. 'Let's get to it!' one of them yelled.

'They're here now,' I told Skip, squeezing his hand reassuringly. 'Hang on.'

To the firefighters, I mouthed, 'Hurry!' then moved out of their way as quickly as I could so they could get to work. I slumped, relieved but exhausted, against a crumpled wall, totally defeated by the oppressive heat.

While I tried to remain invisible, two firefighters concentrated on freeing Skip, using prying tools and hacksaws to saw through the twisted metal that imprisoned him. Before long, they were joined by rescuers from other companies, some wearing brown pants held up by suspenders, and jackets with reflective stripes. The men swarmed over the car, calling out, prying up seats to look for victims.

'Are you hurt?'

I opened my eyes. The firefighter asking the question had 'DCF & EMSD' scrawled across the entire expanse of his black work shirt. You need a bigger shirt or a shorter name, I thought to myself, feeling giddy.

I held out my arm, winced. 'It's throbbing like a son of a gun.'

'That's a broken arm,' he said, after a brief examination.

'I sorta thought so.'

'How many people were on the train with you, do you remember?'

'Four people already got out,' I told him. I rubbed a hand over my eyes. Oh, God, who was missing? 'There was a couple in front, looking at a map,' I continued. 'A kid listening to a Nano. A woman in a floppy hat. Maybe three or four others.'

He patted my hand. 'Thanks. Now stay put. I'm going to get a splint for your arm. I'll be right back.'

I was light-headed, exhausted. I leaned sideways against what remained of a seat cushion and closed my eyes. I found my mind drifting, floating, rising above the heat and the pain, until something wet and warm began sliding down my cheek. I wiped it away, then, curious, opened my eyes and examined my hand.

Blood!

My heart flopped, quivered, then flopped again. I glanced in confusion from my hand down to my chest. A circle of blood was slowly spreading across the front of my dress. I reached up and touched my head, running my fingers through my hair, feeling for the wound. 'Oh, God, I'm bleeding, but I don't know from where.' I took one unsteady breath, then another. My head swam. I bit my lower lip, hard, trying to hold on to reality. The last thing I wanted to do was pass out.

In with the good air, Hannah, out with the bad. In with the good . . .

Feeling helpless, I stared at the blood on my hand as even more blood trickled warmly down my neck.

'I'm bleeding,' I called out to one of the firefighters. 'Can you help?'

Suddenly, two firefighters loomed over me, superheroes in hardhats and suspenders. 'I think she's shocking!' one of them said. He peeled off his gloves and kneeled in front of me, taking my chin firmly in his hands, his eyes boring into mine. With his other hand, he smoothed back my hair. 'Don't move!'

'I'm bleeding,' I sobbed, 'and I don't know where it's coming from.'

The firefighter's eyes drifted from mine to the roof of the ruined car. Following his lead, I looked up, too, to a ragged gash where the ceiling had been sheared back, as if a giant can opener had peeled it open. 'It's not yours, ma'am,' the firefighter said.

Staying awake suddenly seemed too hard. Everything was closing in – screaming sirens, bullhorn blaring, the shouts of rescuers as they pulled and sawed and pried. Nothing this man was saying made any sense.

Blue sky . . . and . . . and . . . somebody was lying on the roof of the car. Through the jagged opening, a pair of white ear buds dangled, and as I watched in growing horror, a rivulet of blood began a slow descent down the thin, white

cord, collected for a moment on the earpiece, then dripped
warmly into my hair.

Darkness came roaring down a long, narrow tunnel, and I
welcomed it in.

THREE

I awoke to singing.

Sometimes I feel like a motherless child . . .

I squinted into the glare of a powerful light that seemed
to be floating in front of my face like a disembodied eye. I
raised a hand to shield my eyes, but was brought up short
by an IV that snaked into my wrist.

'Ouch!'

'Lie still now, sweetheart.'

I tried to turn my head in the direction of the voice, but
something was preventing it. I could hear water running.
Seconds later, a nurse's aide appeared at my side, holding
a washcloth which she used to wipe off my face and forehead, gently and methodically, as if I were a small, muddy
child. She wore lavender scrubs with cartoon cats printed
on them. A laminated photo ID tag was clipped to her
pocket.

'You look better than your picture, Andrea,' I told the aide,
whose long, apricot-colored hair was swept up in a twist held
in place by a tortoiseshell claw.

'Surprised they leave me alone with patients, a mug shot
like that!' She worked the cloth around the creases of my
nose, laid it for a moment – warm, wet and soothing – over
each eyelid. 'That feels wonderful,' I told her.

'We're just cleaning you up a bit, sweetheart, so the doctor
can get a good look at you.' Her smile dazzled, even in a room
she shared with a 1000-watt light bulb.

'What's your name, sweetheart?'

'Hannah, Hannah Ives. Why can't I move my head?'

'It's in a brace.' Andrea left for a moment, presumably to

rinse out the washcloth, because I heard water running again. 'Not to worry, sweetheart. It's just a precaution.'

'My arm's broken,' I told her when she came back with a freshly dampened cloth. 'I'm pretty sure about that.'

'Does it hurt badly?'

'Only if I . . .' I shifted my arm experimentally and the pain travelled up my arm in a white-hot flash, searing into my brain. Somebody had taped my forearm into a metal splint padded with cotton in order to immobilize it, but clearly the temporary measure wasn't working that well.

Andrea laid a comforting hand on my shoulder. 'Don't *do* that, sweetheart. Just lie still. When the doctor comes, he'll give you something for the pain. Just hold on.'

'Do you know what day it is?' she asked conversationally as she washed dried blood off my good hand.

I had to think. It seemed like a week had passed since the fund-raising luncheon, but it had probably been only a couple of hours. 'It's Tuesday,' I said.

'Do you know where you are?'

'Actually, I don't. In a hospital, of course, but I don't know which one.'

'Prince George's Hospital Center. You've been in a train crash.'

A cold fist of fear square in the solar plexus. A wave of images: panicked survivors, frantic rescuers, the injured, the dead. Blood everywhere.

Somebody else's blood.

'There was a guy on the train with me,' I shivered. 'Named Skip. Is he here?'

'Sweetheart, they've carried victims of that crash to ERs all over the metropolitan area. Here, Med-Star, Shock Trauma in Baltimore. Was your friend hurt bad?'

I tried to nod, but the straps under my chin prevented it. 'He was trapped under some seats. It didn't look good, I'm afraid.'

Andrea had finished with the washcloth. She stood next to the examination table, holding the stained cloth in one hand, her other hand still resting on my shoulder. 'We're a regional trauma center, so he *could* have been brought here. Tell you what. I'll look around. See what I can find out.'

'Thank you.' I shifted on the examination table and regretted it immediately. A lightning strike might have been less painful. I winced, blew air out through my lips twice, three times.

'They're going to be taking you for a CAT scan soon. In the meantime, let me see if I can get you something for the pain.'

'Bless you. Then maybe I'll have the strength to reach into my pocket and get out my cell phone.'

She patted my knee. 'Sweetheart, there aren't any pockets in that dress you've got on.'

Designer dresses, designer handbags, designer shoes. Well-kept women nattering over curried chicken salad and lemon-lime sorbet about escalating private school tuitions and how hard it is to keep good help. It seemed like a century ago in another world, maybe even on another planet.

And none of those women had been wearing . . . somebody else's blood.

Hot tears began to roll sideways down my cheeks and into my ears.

'I need my cell phone,' I sobbed. 'I have to call my husband. He'll be worried.'

'You had a shoulder bag when you came in. Would the phone be in there?'

'It's . . .' I began, and then I remembered. I'd been texting a reply to Emily when the train crashed. My iPhone had gone flying. 'Never mind,' I quickly added. 'I was holding it when . . . I'm afraid it's still on the train.'

Even though we shared a tiny room, Andrea suddenly disappeared from view. 'Now don't go telling anybody,' she said when she popped back into my line of sight, 'because you aren't allowed to use cell phones in here, but . . .' She flipped open her phone. 'What's your husband's number?'

I gave her our home phone number and she punched it in. She listened for a long while, then said, 'Dang! Voicemail.'

'Try his cell,' I suggested.

This time, Paul answered on the first ring. 'Ives.'

'Mr Ives, I have your wife here. She'd like to speak to you.'

'Thank God!' Paul exclaimed, so loudly that I heard it all the way across the room. Andrea punched the speaker button, then set her open cell phone on my chest.

'Talk to me, Hannah,' Paul ordered.

'There was a train crash.'

'Jesus, I know. It's all over the news. I tried to call you, but when you didn't answer, I feared the worst and decided to come looking for you. I'm on Route 50 now. Are you all right?'

'Well, I won't be playing tennis any time soon.'

'Damn it, Hannah, don't joke. Over the past two hours, I've been out of my mind with worry. Besides, you don't play tennis.'

'I know. I'm sorry. It's just . . .' Hearing my husband's voice, so calm and reassuring in spite of the seriousness of the situation, sent me off on another crying jag. 'My arm's broken,' I snuffled, 'but otherwise I think I'm OK.'

'Where did they take you?'

'Prince George's Hospital Center. I'm not sure where that is exactly.'

Andrea leaned forward, cutting in. 'In Cheverly, near the intersection of 202 and the BW Parkway.'

'Got it. I'm almost there, Hannah. Ten minutes, max.'

'Paul,' I sobbed, 'I love you.'

'I love you, too, sweetheart.'

When the doctor popped his head into the examination room two minutes later, I was still bawling.

He grabbed my chart out of a box mounted on the wall next to the door, scanned it quickly. 'Hannah Ives?'

'Uh, huh,' I sniffled.

The doctor approached the examination table, studying me over the rims of a pair of clear, plastic-framed reading glasses. 'I'm Doctor Vaughan, and I'll take that as a "yes."' Dr Vaughan turned to the nurse's aide and asked, 'Has anybody done a neurological?'

'Yes. Other than the broken arm, she seems to be fine.'

Dr Vaughan checked my eyes, ran his hands along the length of both legs, squeezing gently, then pressed the fingers of both hands into my belly. 'Take a deep breath,' he instructed as he felt around my waist and abdomen. 'Another.'

I didn't scream in agony, which I imagine he took as a good sign. 'All seems to be normal in that department.'

After he listened to my heart, the doctor said, 'I've ordered a CAT scan – cervical, lumbar and thoracic. Nothing to be worried about, Hannah, we just want to make sure there's no contusions or hairline fractures.' He patted my leg. 'You OK with that?'

I nodded.

'We also have to X-ray that arm. Would you like something for the pain before we proceed?'

I nodded again. 'I was at Woodstock, doctor. I'm one hundred percent in favor of good drugs.'

Dr Vaughan grunted, scribbled something on my chart, then turned to go.

'Doctor?' I asked. 'When will I be able to go home?'

'One step at a time, Hannah. One step at a time. We're pretty slammed here, as you can imagine, but if the CAT scan turns out negative, once we get your arm set, we'll be sending you home.'

'With a supply of good drugs, I hope.'

Vaughan grinned, made a 'V' with his fingers. 'Peace now,' he said.

By the time Paul caught up with me, the CAT scan was over, perfectly painlessly, as it turned out. They'd rolled me down the hall and into an elevator, hauled me out on another floor, then pushed me into a chamber where a huge white donut of a machine loomed, pulsing with energy, like a transporter on the Starship Enterprise. The gurney, with me on it, slid slowly in, slid slowly out, while I hummed my way through as many Beatles songs as I could remember.

'How long did the CAT scan take?' Paul asked me later as my fingernails were digging into his arm against the pain while they X-rayed mine.

'Two "Hard Day's Night," one "Ticket to Ride" and a chorus of "Michelle,"' I told him, wincing, wondering when the pain meds the doctor had given me were going to kick in.

'Good to know,' he grinned.

The X-raying of my arm took longer than I expected – above

the joint, below the joint, now ninety degrees to the right, if you please. To the left, to the right again. Thank you. Sheer agony, and more tears.

"'It Won't Be Long,'" dum-dum-dum, "'It Won't Be Long,'" Paul crooned in his gravelly baritone, trying to distract me while a nurse got permission to up the dose.

By the time Dr Vaughan got around to setting the bone, I was feeling no pain. I hadn't been so high since . . . well, never mind. What happened in the 1970s stays in the 1970s. Applying the cast was a breeze, too, efficient and painless, requiring no Fab Four diversions. While I perched on the end of an examination table holding my arm steady, a physician's assistant, wearing purple gloves, wrapped it up to my palm in long strips of what looked like white, self-adhesive bubble wrap. Then she applied layer upon layer of fiberglass cast tape, thin as gauze and watermelon pink. 'The warmth you're feeling now will go away in a couple of hours,' she told me as she snipped the tape half through with a pair of blunt scissors and threaded it between my thumb and forefinger, adjusting it to fit. 'Spread your fingers for me, now, please.' She glanced up for a moment. 'The cast will need to stay on for about four weeks.'

'Your wife should see an orthopedist,' she advised Paul a few minutes later. 'Do you need a referral?'

'No, thank you,' I interrupted, mildly annoyed that she was talking to my husband as if I were his elderly mother, or had suddenly left the room. 'My husband's taught at the Naval Academy for years. There are a number of sports doctors among our acquaintances.'

'That's good,' the PA said, wrapping both of her hands around my colorful cast and pressing gently all along its length to seal it. That done, she straightened, stripped off the rubber gloves and tossed them into a trash receptacle. 'You're good to go.'

'Thank you,' I said. 'Everyone here's been great.'

'It's been a difficult night,' the PA commented, glancing up from the sink where she was washing her hands. 'We're lucky, in a way. There were hundreds of injuries. Minor things, mostly – cuts, broken bones like yours, mild concussions – things we can fix. Have you watched the news?'

I shook my head. 'Been kind of distracted.'

The PA smiled wearily, tucked a strand of her pale, shoulder-length hair back behind one ear. 'They're reporting seven fatalities, all in the first car.'

'That's where I was sitting,' I said with a quick, sideways glance at my husband who visibly blanched at the news.

'Then you have an angel in your pocket, Mrs Ives.'

'Somebody was watching over me, that's for sure.' A vision of that empty seat and the youth sauntering past me to claim it shimmered hauntingly in my brain. I shivered, then swung my legs around, ready to hop down from the table.

The PA laid a restraining hand on my leg. 'Not so fast! We need to put you in a wheelchair.'

'Why? I can walk.'

'Hospital policy.'

I rolled my eyes, but was secretly relieved. It was nearly midnight and I felt like a zombie, sleepwalking my way through what little remained of the day. While Paul trundled off after the PA to fill out some paperwork and pick up my prescription for hydrocodone tablets, I leaned my head against the paper-covered headrest and dozed.

At one point, the nurse's aide, Andrea, popped in to report that, alas, nobody with a name resembling 'Skip' had been brought in as a patient that day. 'It would help if you had his last name,' she said, but I didn't, of course.

Andrea was still with me, speculating cheerfully on what name 'Skip' could be short for when Paul returned, pushing an empty wheelchair.

'Your chariot awaits,' he quipped. Andrea helped me down from the table and got me comfortably settled in the wheelchair while Paul went off to fetch the car.

'Where are my things?' I asked as Andrea pushed me down the hallway like an invalid, through a pair of automatic doors into the humid night air.

'Don't worry, they're right here,' she said, indicating a large plastic sack hanging by its drawstring from the back of the wheelchair.

After Paul pulled up, she waited until I got settled in the front passenger seat, then leaned across me to fasten the seatbelt.

'Bye, and thanks,' I called after her through the open window as she pushed the chair back toward the hospital entrance. She turned and gave me a wave.

Paul slid into the driver's seat. I suddenly remembered my car, sitting in the parking garage at New Carrollton where I'd left it, oh, sometime in the last century. 'What about the Volvo?'

'Later,' Paul sighed, sounding exhausted, too. 'We'll deal with that later.'

'Good,' I said as he pulled out of the hospital drive and headed east on 202 toward Route 50. 'The only thing I can deal with right now is home. And sleep.'

The next morning, I popped a pain pill in the upstairs bathroom, then staggered down to the kitchen a few minutes before eight thirty, lured by the aroma of freshly brewed coffee that had wafted its way up, tendril-like, to the bedroom. I found my husband sitting at the kitchen table, the front page of the *Washington Post* spread out in front of him.

'Hey,' I said, making a beeline for the coffee pot, holding my throbbing arm aloft. Paul had set a clean mug out on the countertop for me, and I filled it gratefully.

When I joined him at the table, he folded the section over on itself and pushed the newspaper aside.

'Why'd you do that?' I asked, indicating the banished *Post*.

'Do you think you're ready to read about the accident?' he asked.

I usually wrap both hands around my mug, appreciating the warmth, but that morning I could only hold on to it one-handed. 'Someday, but maybe not today.'

'Ruth's driving me to retrieve the car,' he said, changing the subject. 'Can you tell me where you parked it?'

Yesterday seemed like forever ago. In that distant past, I'd driven in circles inside the multi-story parking garage, twice, maybe three times around. 'A couple of floors up in the garage nearest the Amtrak station,' I said at last.

Paul groaned. 'That certainly pinpoints it nicely.'

'Aim the keys and push the button,' I said, pumping my thumb as if I were holding a keyless remote. 'You'll find the car eventually.'

'Where *are* the keys?'

I had to think for a moment. The keys had been in my handbag, and my handbag was now . . . where? Through the fog of the previous evening, I suddenly remembered something about another bag. 'Didn't the hospital give you a plastic sack with all my stuff in it?'

'Oh, you're right. When we came in last night, I set it down in the hall.' While Paul went off to retrieve my handbag, I slid the *Post* toward me and opened it up.

They'd identified the first victim, the driver of the train. His picture stared out at me from the right-hand column of the front page: Walter Kramer. A pleasant-looking, bald-headed man with fair skin, smiling green eyes and a spotless, ten-year driving record.

Just above the fold was a chilling picture of our train. Just short of New Carrollton, it had smashed into a stationary train, climbed up its rear, gnashing and grinding, disintegrating along the way.

I stared at Kramer's photograph. Were you responsible for this carnage, Walter? Surprisingly, I felt no anger, only sadness that this man – who had a wife and two young children – had lost his life, like the other victims, in such a tragic way.

Had he had a heart attack? Autopsy results were not yet available.

Had he been texting on a cell phone? The investigation was continuing.

Was there a system failure? NTSB was on the case.

I heard Paul padding back down the hall, so I shoved the paper aside.

'Here you go,' he said, tugging open the plastic drawstring and upending the sack on the table in front of me. Out tumbled my handbag, a clip-on name-tag, a canvas tote of freebies from the fashion show luncheon, and a shopping bag from Julius Garfinkel & Co.

FOUR

'**O**h. My. God.'

Still holding the sack by a bottom corner, Paul gaped at me as if I'd lost my marbles. 'Is something wrong?'

'That Garfinkel's bag. It isn't mine.'

Paul balled up the plastic sack Prince George's Hospital Center had provided and tossed it into the trash bin under the sink. 'Whose is it, then?'

'Skip's. The guy on the train I told you about.'

'Damn! So how did it get in with your stuff?'

'It was probably lying on the floor next to me when I passed out. The paramedics must have assumed . . .'

'Garfinkel's.' Paul picked up the bag and peeked inside. 'I haven't thought about them for years. They're out of business now, right?'

I nodded. 'Late nineteen eighties or thereabouts. What's inside?' I asked, my curiosity piqued.

Studying me over the edge of the bag, Paul grinned impishly. 'What's in it for me?'

'Oh, for heaven's sake,' I laughed. 'Tell me what's *in* there!'

'A box.' He spread the opening wider, peered down into its depth. 'Looks like one of those cardboard boxes that Christmas shirts come in.'

'May I see?'

'Sure.' Paul slid the cardboard box out of the Garfinkel's bag, brought it over to my side of the kitchen table and set the box down dead center on my placemat, like an entrée.

'Do you think it will be OK to open it?' I wondered.

'Why not? Could be something. Could be nothing. You won't know until you look.'

I nudged a corner of the box top with my forefinger, raising it about half an inch, teasing him. Another nudge, a quarter inch more.

'Hannah!' Paul tousled my hair playfully. 'It's not a bomb, for heaven's sake! Open the damn thing!'

Thus, led by the man I married into a life of petty crime, like so many women before me, I whipped off the top of a box that didn't belong to me.

The first thing I saw were three packets of letters, each neatly tied around the middle with pale green ribbon. I picked up one of the packets and thumbed through it clumsily with my one good hand. The letters all were postmarked in the early 1980s.

Beneath the letters I found a white envelope with a metal clasp. I opened the clasp, raised the flap and peeked inside. 'Photographs,' I told my husband, before laying the envelope aside.

The only item remaining in the box was an expired United States passport in the name of Lilith Marie Chaloux, who had been born April 4, 1953, in San Francisco, California. On the day she sat for her passport photo, Lilith Marie had worn a school uniform – plaid jumper, white blouse with a Peter Pan collar – and had drawn her dark hair up into a high ponytail. She looked about sixteen, but wise for her years, gazing seriously at the photographer with delicately arched brows over dark, intelligent eyes, the merest hint of a smile tugging at the corners of her lips.

Paul had been kibitzing over my shoulder. 'A rare beauty,' he said. 'A heartbreaker.'

I had to agree. Lilith was one of the most beautiful young women I'd ever seen, like Audrey Hepburn before she cut her hair in *Roman Holiday*.

'How old would she be now?' I wondered.

'Fifty-seven,' Paul declared without hesitation. He was the mathematician in the family.

I set the passport down on the table and picked up a second packet of letters. The one on top was addressed to Ms Lilith Chaloux at an address in the *17e arrondissement de Paris*, and although the postmark had badly faded, I could tell it had been mailed in September of 1976 from New York City. There was no return address in the upper left-hand corner of the envelope, so I peeked at the back flap. No return address there, either.

'I wonder who the letters are from,' I said, flipping through the second packet without untying the ribbon, and then the third. 'They're all in the same handwriting, but there's absolutely no clue on the outside who sent them.' I gave my husband a look, and waggled my eyebrows mischievously. 'Maybe they're *love* letters!'

Usually my husband is Mr Proceed With Caution, so it surprised me when he said, 'Open one up, read it and see.'

'No. I can't.' Using my good hand, I shoveled the passport, photos and letters back into the box. 'Help me put the lid back on,' I said.

'Don't you want to know . . . ?'

'*Of course* I want to know. Who wouldn't be curious? But these letters are not mine, and it seems like an invasion of someone's privacy to go reading them without permission from either the recipient or their current owner.'

'Who is?' Paul inquired reasonably.

'Lilith Chaloux.'

'Or . . . ?' Paul prompted.

'Well, I suppose they could belong to Skip, the guy sitting next to me on the train.'

'Whose last name is?'

I had to admit that I didn't know.

'I can't simply *assume* that Skip died in the crash.' I insisted, slipping the shirt box back into the Garfinkel's bag. 'When the paramedics arrived, I was holding his wrist. He still had a pulse. I have to make *some* effort to find him and return the bag. If these letters belonged to *me*, I'd certainly want to get them back.'

Paul poured himself a second cup of coffee, leaned back against the kitchen counter and sipped the hot liquid noisily. 'What do you think Skip's relation is to Lilith?'

'She is, or was, his mother, would be my guess.'

'Could his last name be Chaloux, too?'

I tapped the passport. 'Unless she was married at sixteen, Chaloux would be her maiden name, Paul.'

'Whatever,' he said, 'but it wouldn't hurt to Google her.'

'Brilliant idea, Professor Ives.'

Carrying our mugs, the two of us trooped down to Paul's

basement office, where we powered up his computer and learned that, alas, Lilith Marie Chaloux had no Internet presence at all. 'At least she's not dead,' I commented wryly. 'Or at least, she didn't die spectacularly.'

'What the hell is that supposed to mean, Hannah?'

'When Skip thought he was dying, he told me that he'd killed somebody. If this woman had been a recent murder victim, surely there'd be something about it on the Internet somewhere.'

'Did Skip say *who* he was supposed to have killed?'

I shook my head.

'Did Skip look like a soldier?'

'No, not at all.' I said, wondering where Paul was going with this line of questioning. 'He's the right age, mid-twenties, I'd guess, but he looked like a stockbroker to me, or an accountant. An attorney, maybe. Why do you ask?'

'He could have served in Iraq, or Afghanistan,' Paul said reasonably. 'He could have killed somebody over there, and be wracked with guilt. Shit happens in wartime. You said he was Catholic?'

I nodded. 'He carries a rosary.'

Paul raised an eyebrow. 'How old did you say this guy was?'

'Twenty-four, maybe twenty-five.'

'Aren't rosaries hopelessly old-fashioned? Something only wimpled nuns and great-grandmothers still do?'

'They're contemplative, Paul. Praying the rosary has a quiet rhythm to it, like meditation. Or, Skip may have been carrying it as a kind of good luck charm.'

Paul grimaced. 'As a good luck charm, it certainly fell down on the job.'

'Speaking as someone who still wears her mother's St Christopher medal whenever she flies, I don't find the fact that Skip was carrying a rosary in his pocket strange at all.' I had a sudden thought. 'Search for Skip Chaloux.'

Paul tapped a few keys, stared intently at the screen. 'Nothing. There's a fitness model named Chaloux, and somebody who makes corsets. Otherwise it's "Skip to Main Menu" or "Don't skip breakfast!"'

'That's what I was afraid of.'

We tried a simple search on 'Chaloux.' 77,000 entries, plus or minus. After paging through half a dozen screens, I called it off.

'So, what's your next step?' Paul wondered as he powered down his computer.

'Without a last name, I'm dead in the water. As soon as I feel up to it, I'm going back to the hospital, and see if I can track Skip down. PGHC is a regional trauma center. If they pulled him out of the wreck alive, that's probably where they would have taken him.'

'Seems like the logical place to begin.' Paul flipped off the desk lamp and followed me back upstairs to the kitchen. 'But if you don't find him there, what then?'

I smiled. '*Then* I open the letters and start looking for clues.'

FIVE

Sitting next to me on the sofa Wednesday evening, Paul scrolled through the channels – WRC, WUSA, WJLA, not to mention CNN, FOX, MSNBC and LYNX. I snatched the remote from his hand, aimed, and turned off the TV.

'I'm sorry, darling, but I just can't deal with it. Blah, blah, blah, twenty-four seven. You'd think that absolutely nothing else was going on in the world except for this Metro disaster. They're running the same footage, over and over again.'

I covered my eyes with my hand, but the images still burned on the inside of my eyelids. The twisted wreckage. The walking wounded. The orange, basket-like stretchers. The yellow body bags.

Indeed, the crash and its aftermath had pushed everything else out of the headlines. So what if fall elections were nearly upon us and the Republicans were likely to take over the House? Who cared if wildfires were burning out of control in the Rockies? A damaged oil rig was still spewing crude into the Gulf of Mexico, an intern at Lynx News had gone missing, and widespread flooding continued in Pakistan. Reporting on these events had been relegated to the inside pages of the *Post* and the *Times*, or reduced to television crawls, while full-blown coverage of the Metro crash went on and on and on.

One by one, the names of the victims were being released. So far, in addition to the train driver, whose name had been announced almost immediately, the victims had been identified as a sixty-three-year-old rabbi from Alexandria on his way to spend a week with his grandchildren in Lanham, a German couple in their early seventies who were vacationing in the United States for the first time, an elementary school teacher, thirty-two, on her way home after work to Cheverly, a forty-year-old unemployed computer programmer heading to CSC for a job interview, and Tashawn Jackson, sixteen.

When pictures of the victims were published in the *Post*, I remembered the German couple. They'd been sitting at the front of the car, gray heads together, consulting a Metro map, but I didn't recall seeing any of the others. Except for Tashawn, the boy who died because he'd been too busy listening to his Nano to give up his seat to me.

Tashawn Jackson, the boy who unknowingly saved my life.

SIX

*D*o not drive or operate heavy machinery while using *this medication.*

Great. It was either the pain or the pills. Not a choice I was prepared to make.

Caution: May cause drowsiness. Alcohol may intensify this effect.

I carefully considered this warning while standing in front of the medicine cabinet several hours before my usual bedtime. Then I popped a pain pill and headed down to the kitchen to fetch a glass of Sauvignon Blanc from the Box-o-Wine we kept on tap in the fridge. The pain was getting easier to deal with, but the nightmares were another story. Over the past two days, even my doctor-prescribed naps had been interrupted by dreams, grotesque variations of the crash that jolted me awake, heart pounding. I chased the pill with half a glass of wine topped off with crushed ice and club soda, then padded back up to bed. For the time being, at least, drowsiness definitely needed to be intensified.

The next morning, I lay awake in bed trying to figure out what day it was – Friday – while communing with a pair of cardinals peeping sweet nothings to one another from the tree outside my open window. The telephone rang, interrupting my reverie. I waited for Paul to pick up, but when he hadn't by the third ring, I figured he'd already left for work, so I fumbled for the telephone myself.

'Hannah, it's Connie. I've been wanting to call, but Paul said you needed to rest. How are you doing?'

Connie is Paul's sister. She lives on the Ives family farm down in Chesapeake County, thirty miles or so south of Annapolis.

'Battered and bruised,' I told her. 'Creeping around like an old lady, but at least I'm creeping. Others weren't so lucky.'

'Paul filled us in. It must have been horrible.'

'Horrible doesn't begin to describe it, Connie. It'll be a long time before I get back on the Metro.'

'Is there anything I can do?'

'Ah, ha! I was hoping you'd say that.' I explained about the mix-up with the Garfinkel's bag and asked Connie if she'd be willing to drive me back to the hospital. 'Paul's got classes and faculty meetings all day, so I'm on my own. I'm not supposed to drive. Hard to do, even if I wanted to, with this pesky cast on my arm.'

'No problem,' Connie said. 'After lunch, OK?'

'Super.'

The heatwave had broken at last, ushering in a glorious fall. Connie picked me up in her lime-green Volkswagen bug with the top down.

'There is nothing that can't be cured by taking a ride in a convertible,' I told my sister-in-law as I eased into the passenger seat and tried to strap myself in. The effort brought tears to my eyes.

Connie drew the seatbelt across my lap and snapped it into place. 'Happy to contribute to the cure.' She had a scarf tied around her auburn curls and a white swathe of sunscreen across her nose. A lemon-yellow chrysanthemum bobbed cheerfully in the bud vase attached to the VW's dashboard.

'How's Dennis?' I asked as she waited to make the left turn from Prince George Street on to College Avenue. Dennis was my brother-in-law, a Chesapeake County police lieutenant.

'He's got a murder on his hands, I'm afraid. A student at the community college. I wish they'd keep the murders over in P.G. County where they belong.' She clapped a hand over her mouth, blinked innocently. 'Oh, my, did I say that?'

'You did. Bad girl. I should report you to Dennis for insubordination.'

By the time we took the exit out of Annapolis on to Route 50 west, I had told Connie as much as I knew about Skip and explained what I wanted to do.

'So, let me get this straight. You need to find this man and return his property.'

'Right.'

'And the only thing you know about him is that his name is Skip, last name maybe Chaloux.'

'Uh huh. And that he's new to the area, because he hadn't a clue about our weather. And his phone is with Verizon.'

Connie groaned. 'Well, that's really going to help us, isn't it?' She eased the VW out into the fast lane and passed a school bus as if it were standing still. 'What's Skip short for, then?'

'Skipper?' I suggested.

Connie grinned. 'Skipper is Barbie's little sister, Hannah.'

'Or a castaway on *Gilligan's Island*,' I added helpfully.

'I know a Steve who's called Skip,' Connie continued, slipping into the HOV2 lane and pushing the little Bug up to seventy. 'And isn't that guy Skip, who fixes your car, really named Wilfred?'

'Nobody's named Wilfred.' I laughed. As Connie sped on, I stared at the cars we passed, silently counting the number of people driving while talking on their cell phones, making the most of the risky practice before Maryland's ban went into effect in a few weeks' time.

'Could he be a third?' Connie said brightly.

'A third of what?' I asked.

'A third. Like Alfred P. Newman the Third, named after his grandfather Alfred P. Newman the First. In other words, the name skips a generation.'

'In that case,' I said sweetly, 'he'd be a second.'

Connie stuck out her tongue. 'Picky, picky.'

'Whether he's a second, third or even a fourth isn't going to help us much if we don't know whether the namesake grandfather was a Charles or a George or, God help him, a Wilfred, is it?'

When we got to the hospital, Connie dropped me off at the main entrance under the portico while she sped off to park. To my left, a row of ambulances stood backed into emergency-room bays, their crews waiting for their ill or injured passengers to be admitted before driving the vehicles back to the firehouses where they normally lived. I stared at the ambulances for a moment, wondering if any of them had delivered me there.

When Connie caught up with me, I was making zero progress with the staff at the information desk in the hospital lobby. 'We can confirm whether or not someone's a patient here,' the gentleman who was helping me said, 'but you have to know his name.'

'Skip,' I said. 'His name is Skip. His last name could be Chaloux.'

'We don't have any Skips on the patient list,' he explained for the second time. 'How do you spell Chaloux?'

'C-H-A-L-O-U-X.'

He tapped a few keys, shook his head. 'Nope, no Chaloux either.'

'Look,' I said, waving my fluorescent cast under his nose as Exhibit A. 'I was a patient here on Tuesday. I think Skip was a patient, too. We were both involved in the Metro crash,' I added, hoping to earn a sympathy vote. 'The hospital, i.e.

you, mixed up some of his belongings with mine, and I simply want to return them.'

The volunteer fixed me with a steely glare. 'Ma'am, I will explain it to you once again. We are required by federal law to protect the privacy of our patients. Unless you are a family member, or a designated person, even if you knew the name of this Skip person, even if you are telling me now that he's your very best friend in the whole wide world, I couldn't tell you a single thing about his condition.'

My sister-in-law stood at the counter next to me, wisely staying out of the discussion. I leaned in her direction. 'I should have lied,' I whispered. 'Said I was his aunt or something.'

'In that case,' Connie whispered back, 'you would have known his last name.'

I felt my face flush. 'Duh.'

'I'll tell you what,' the staffer began again. Maybe he was softening. 'Why don't you leave whatever the mixed-up thing is with me, and if this fellow called Skip is in the hospital here, surely he'll notice that it's missing and ask about it. Then, we can make sure it gets back to him.'

I tend to get huffy when thwarted, so I fixed the volunteer with a steely gaze of my own. 'I'm sure you'll understand that unless you can confirm or deny the presence of a patient nicknamed Skip in this hospital, I can't return the items now in my possession to you directly, only to Skip himself, or to a designated member of his family.'

The old guy smiled. He actually smiled. 'OK. Point taken. Why don't you write Skip a note? If it turns out he is, or was, a patient here, I can see that it gets to him. If, regrettably, he's passed away, I'm sure his next of kin would want all his effects returned and they'll get in touch with you. How does that sound?'

I faced Connie. 'I don't have anything to write on. Do you?'

Connie pawed through her handbag, then shook her head.

'There's a gift shop,' the staffer pointed out helpfully.

I popped into the gift shop and purchased a greeting card – a cocker spaniel holding daisies in his mouth on the outside, blank on the inside, where I wrote:

'Skip. I hope this finds you recovering from your injuries.

I have your Garfinkel's bag. If you get this note, please telephone me at . . .' I turned to Connie who was inspecting some stuffed bears. 'Home or cell, do you think?'

'Both, I imagine.' So I wrote the numbers down, signed the note 'Hannah (the woman on the train),' stuffed the card into its envelope, scribbled on the front and handed it to the staffer behind the desk.

He raised an eyebrow. 'Skip. Parens. Garfinkel bag. Not a lot to go on.'

I shrugged apologetically. 'It's all I know.'

'What now?' Connie asked as we strolled back to the spot where she'd parked her car.

'Now?' I asked.

Connie pressed the keyless remote and the car beeped. 'Yes, now.'

Using my good arm, I reached for the door. 'Nothing to do but wait.

Later that afternoon, when Paul came home from class, he found me sitting in the dining room, the contents of the Garfinkel's bag spread out neatly on the table in front of me, a photograph in my hand.

After Connie dropped me off, I'd untied the letters, carefully preserving the pale green ribbons that had held them together for so long. I'd arranged them in chronological order – 1976 through 1986 – like a game of solitaire.

I held a pencil, freshly sharpened, with an eraser on the end. A spare pencil, equally sharp, was tucked behind my right ear.

I had a notebook in which I had already written '#1, Sep 15 1976 New York' and the address of the apartment in Paris where Lilith had been living at the time.

A cup of tea sat at my right hand, the bottle of pain pills at my left, but, surprisingly, I'd been so engrossed in what I was doing that I'd missed the last dose and hadn't even noticed.

'Hannah, what on earth are you doing?'

I looked up at my husband and grinned. 'Isn't it obvious? Research.'

'Well,' Paul said as he set his briefcase down on one of the dining-room chairs, 'so much for your protestations about invasion of privacy.'

'I feel like a voyeur, I admit. But I've promised myself that I'll read only enough to help me find out who these letters belong to.' I tapped the letter dated 1976. 'There have to be clues in the letters somewhere.'

Paul dragged a chair over from the wall next to the buffet and sat down at the table across from me. 'What progress have you made?'

'Look at this picture,' I said, sliding it toward him across the polished mahogany.

Paul studied the black and white image carefully. It showed a young man in his twenties with dark fluffy hair, long in back and trimmed to just cover the tips of his ears. Sunglasses dangled by one earpiece from the three-button placket of his Izod polo shirt. He was perched on the lip of an ornate fountain and smiling broadly for the photographer.

'Who's this, then?'

'His name is Zan.'

SEVEN

Sometimes my husband has a one-track mind.

'What's for dinner, or dare I ask?'

Abandoning the photograph, he had come around behind me, kissed the back of my neck, then begun to massage my aching shoulders with his thumbs. I rotated my shoulders against his hands. 'Um, that feels good.'

'Pizza?' I asked him after several more minutes of bliss. 'Chinese carry-out? Or . . . do you fancy a stroll down to Galway Bay?'

Galway Bay won hands (and pink fluorescent cast) down, so we set out into the deliciously cool evening for the short walk up the street and around the corner to our favorite Annapolis hang-out.

'What happened to you?' Fintan wanted to know when we appeared at the door.

'Metro crash,' I told the restaurant owner simply.

'My God,' he said, fumbling the pile of menus he was carrying. 'Tonight, drinks are on the house. The usual?'

Fintan seated us in a quiet, two-table alcove near the front of the popular neighborhood restaurant, then, after admiring my eye-catching cast, went off to fetch our drinks – a frozen margarita for Paul and a mojito for me.

Paul spread a napkin in his lap. 'So, his name is Zan. What's Zan short for? Alexander?'

'I don't know. He just signs the letters Zan.'

'Zandros,' Paul mused on. 'Zander. Maybe even Zane. Last name?'

I shook my head. 'Never. The man was married, I discovered very early on, and not to Lilith.'

'Aha! The plot thickens.'

Just then, a waiter appeared with our drinks. After he took our dinner order, Paul tested his frozen margarita, licked salt off his lips and pronounced it good. 'Without a last name to go on, it's going to be pretty tough tracking this Zan person down.'

'I know. We're back to Mr Skip No Last Name again,' I complained, taking a sip of what turned out to be a very tasty mojito, heavy on the lime and crushed mint, just the way I like it.

'Speaking of Skip, how do you think he's going to feel if he shows up asking for his Garfinkel bag and finds you've gone pawing through it?'

'Well, I hope he'll understand that the only reason I was pawing through it, to use your term, is so I could find out who to return the bag to. Besides, you encouraged me to do it, if you recall.' I stared at the decorative window etched with a map of Ireland that separated our table from the hostess station on the other side of the wall. 'If only Skip had told me his last name, instead of . . .' I took another sip of mojito. 'Well, that's water under the bridge now. But, oh my God, Paul, he was so horribly injured, I can't believe he would have survived.'

'Doctors can work miracles, Hannah.'

'I just wish certain hospitals wouldn't be so close-mouthed about everything.'

'Would you want just anybody prying into your medical history?'

'No, but . . .'

'I rest my case.'

'One thing I don't get,' Paul said to me a few minutes later as he cut my portabella burger into pieces I could eat with one hand, while I tried to keep my left elbow elevated above my heart, as per doctor's orders. 'Why didn't this guy, Zan, simply divorce his wife and run off with Lilith? She was single at the time, wasn't she?'

'As far as I know.' I speared a wedge of mushroom and popped it into my mouth.

'It's nuts,' Paul continued. 'The two were obviously crazy about one another, and, according to the letters, the affair went on for over a decade.' He shoveled a forkful of mashed potatoes into his mouth. 'Maybe the wife was rich, and he couldn't divorce himself from her money?'

I shook my head, chewing thoughtfully. 'Somehow I don't think so. In one of the letters Zan beats himself up because even during mass, when he should be thinking pure thoughts, visions of what they did, and the times and places that they did it were running like a movie through his head. I'm one hundred percent positive that Zan was Catholic. In that case, divorce would have been out of the question.

'In any case,' I continued, 'Zan seems to be one of those high-principled "till death us do part" sort of chaps, although he never talks about that, or much about his personal life in any of the letters I've read so far. It's like . . .' I paused to wipe greasy fingers on my napkin. 'I'm sure Lilith and Zan discussed these things when they were together, but in his letters it's like their own private little world.'

'Are there any letters from Lilith to Zan?'

'Not a one, but I know she wrote him.'

'How?'

'Well, he'd respond specifically to something she'd written to him earlier. Curiously, he seemed to know and be accepted by her grandmother and her uncle. When Lilith's grandmother turned eighty, for example, Zan asked Lilith to pass on his birthday wishes. There's nothing about Lilith's parents, though.' I waved a French fry. 'And before you ask, I don't know their names either, although her parents were most likely Chaloux, too.'

'You are a poet, and didn't know it,' Paul wisecracked.

'Ha ha ha. After they'd been together,' I went on, 'Zan would spend half the letter reminiscing about what they did during their time together, the rest of it anticipating their next rendezvous. I suspect they spent a lot of time in hotel rooms.' I grinned and waggled my eyebrows. 'If it weren't for the postmarks and the letterhead he sometimes used, I wouldn't have a clue where he was writing from.'

'Like where?'

'He used hotel stationery, mostly, so I figure his job – whatever it was – kept him moving. Omaha, Chicago, Dallas, Rome, Mexico City, Paris. I'm trying to put it all together, looking for a pattern.'

I reached into the pocket of my jacket for the vial of pills, shook two out on the table, popped them into my mouth and chased them with a swallow of mojito.

Paul looked up from his shepherd's pie and gaped. 'Hannah! Doesn't the label warn you not to take those things with alcohol?'

I coughed modestly. 'Of course it does, silly, but they work much better on the pain part if you do. Besides . . .' I winked. 'I don't have far to drive.'

After we finished our main courses, I threw caution to the wind and ordered dessert – bread pudding with Irish Mist custard sauce – and two spoons. By the time I scraped the bottom of the bowl and licked the last of the custard off my spoon, I was feeling no pain. Paul and I walked home slowly, arm in arm, stopping now and then along the way to admire the Halloween displays that were beginning to crop up in some of the shop windows.

Back home, while Paul cleaned up the dishes I'd left soaking in the kitchen sink since lunchtime, I climbed upstairs and sat on the edge of our bed to undress. I managed to remove my shoes, socks and jeans, but discovered that, no matter how hard I tried, I couldn't wriggle out of my shirt. I was able to slide my right arm out of its sleeve and ease the shirt over my head, but the logistics of threading the cast through the left-hand sleeve had me completely stumped.

'Come sit with me until the news comes on!' Paul called from downstairs.

'The hell with it,' I muttered to myself. Leaving the shirt dangling from my shoulder, I used my good arm to squirm my butt into some drawstring pajama bottoms. Then I grabbed an XXL navy 'Fear the Goat' T-shirt from Paul's bottom drawer and padded downstairs to join my husband.

When he caught sight of me in the doorway wearing nothing above the waist but my bra and a T-shirt flapping from my shoulder like a flag of surrender, he grinned. 'Need help?'

'Got scissors?'

Paul fell back against the sofa cushions and dissolved in gales of laughter. 'That's the most pathetic thing I've ever seen!'

I stood in the doorway and drooped. 'I know. I managed to get into the shirt this morning, so I simply don't understand why I can get out of it now.'

Paul unfolded his long legs, stood, and crossed the room in a couple of long strides. He drew me into his arms, resting his chin on the top of my head. 'Poor Hannah. I'm not hurting you, am I?'

'Oh, no. Just the opposite. I'm medicated, remember?'

He lifted my chin and kissed the tip of my nose.

I smiled into his eyes. 'Thanks, I needed that.'

Paul's lips found mine and I melted into him, pink fluorescent cast, uncooperative underwear and all.

'I gather you need help,' he whispered against my ear.

'I do.'

Keeping one hand on my waist, his other hand crept around my back, found the hooks on my bra and flicked it open.

'Clever boy!' I whispered against his neck. 'But then, you've always been skilled at one-handed bra removal.'

'Practice makes perfect,' he said. Still holding me close, he duck-walked me over to the sofa. Soon it was just Paul, me and my pink fluorescent cast. He kissed my forehead, eyes, nose and mouth, then pressed his cheek against mine. 'God, Hannah, I was so frightened. I don't know what I'd do if I lost you.'

I wrapped my good arm around his waist and drew him even closer. 'Turn out the light,' I ordered as I shimmied along the upholstery until I was lying down.

Paul slipped a pillow under my head and asked, 'Sure you're OK?'

'I'm perfectly OK. Just elevating my arm,' I said, holding it over my head and out of the way. 'Doctor's orders.'

And for several long and blissful moments, Paul swept all my pain away.

Later, as we cuddled on the sofa watching the eleven o'clock news, I found myself drawn to, yet repelled by, the images on the screen. At least they were no longer running wall-to-wall train disaster coverage.

Channel Four was reporting that the driver of the train hadn't been at fault. He'd not been texting on his cell phone, as had been earlier speculated. Indeed, his cell phone had been found tucked away in his backpack. Metal-to-metal compression streak marks proved he'd braked, hard, before the crash.

A news anchor spent several minutes interviewing 'experts' who theorized that a signal failure had caused our train to plow into the back of another, even though all the circuits had been checked and replaced following a devastating crash in June of 2009. The NTSB investigation was continuing.

Pictures of the victims scrolled by. The driver, the teacher, the rabbi, the programmer, the Germans and the teen. I gulped, thinking how easily my picture could have ended up on the television screen, too.

That was it then. Seven fatalities. And no one who looked the least bit like Skip was among them.

EIGHT

A week went by, and I was functioning well, even without the pills. I'd managed a few short trips to the grocery on my own, and a visit to the Apple Store in the mall to buy a replacement for my iPhone, but most of the time I stayed home, busily reconstructing a decades-old love affair.

Early one Monday afternoon, my sister-in-law Connie popped in, armed with a plate of home-made brownies. 'Dennis is working late tonight. Major case,' she explained. 'So I've come over to help.'

'Help with what?' I asked, lifting a corner of the plastic wrap that covered the brownies. I slid one off the plate directly into my mouth.

'Dinner. You're not taking proper care of my brother, or so I hear. He had to resort to McDonald's the other night. Is that true?'

'Perfectly true, I'm afraid,' I mumbled around a mouthful of brownie. 'A double quarter pounder with cheese and a large order of fries.'

'I'm shocked, shocked!' Connie carried the brownies out to the kitchen, along with a shopping bag she'd brought in with her. I trailed behind her and watched while she began assembling the wherewithal for a steak, salad and baked potato dinner on my kitchen counter.

'So, what are you up to?' Connie asked as she rearranged a couple of mustard jars so she could fit a pint of sour cream into my fridge. 'Any word from Skip?

'Afraid not. But I've been giving the letters a thorough going-over.'

Connie dropped the potatoes into a pot in the sink, ran water over them. 'The potatoes can certainly wait. Tell me about it.'

'I'll do better than that. I'll show you.'

Connie followed me into the dining room where the results of my research efforts were strewn all over the table. 'Whoa! I guess this means we eat in the kitchen tonight.'

I grinned. 'We usually do, now that I've turned the dining room into a *de facto* office.' I performed a broad sweep with my arm in a television spokesmodel way. 'There are fifty-six letters, all addressed to a Ms Lilith Chaloux. She's a lot more well-travelled than either you or I were at that age. The letters were sent to addresses all over the world.'

I picked up a strip of photos that had obviously been taken in one of those Take-Your-Own-Miniature-Portraits-4-Poses-4! carnival booths and handed it to Connie. It showed a fair, dark-haired, doe-eyed woman mugging impishly for the camera.

'Is this Lilith?' she asked.

I nodded. 'I keep assuming that Lilith is the mother of that man I met on the train, but there's no way to know for sure. He was fair-skinned, too, but his hair was light, not dark like hers. I keep trying to imagine his face from . . . before . . . so I can compare it with these photos of Lilith, but all I see now is his face on the train, streaked with dirt and blood and contorted in pain.'

Connie slipped her arm around me and gave me a hug. 'I can't imagine how hard it must have been.'

I swiped tears off my cheeks with the back of my hand. 'Frankly, this project has been a welcome diversion,' I said reaching for the box of tissues on the sideboard, whipping one out and giving my nose a good blow. 'As you can probably see, I've arranged the envelopes in order by postmark. The letters begin in September of 1976, but I know the relationship had been going on for a good while before that. I figure the September letter arrived soon after the first time Lilith and Zan were separated.'

I tossed my used tissue into a trash bin, sat down and motioned for Connie to join me at the table.

'What does the letter say?' Connie asked.

'The usual. My sweet darling. Miss you terribly. Then he enclosed a poem – "Yes, call me by my pet name" – and signs it "Zan," just "Zan."'

'"Let me hear the name I used to run at, when a child,"'

Connie quoted. 'Barrett-Browning. Sonnets from the Portuguese.'

'Exactly. Later on, he sends her the ubiquitous "How do I love thee, Let me count the ways."'

'Always a good poem,' Connie said.

'A very good poem,' I agreed. 'Lilith was living in an apartment in Brooklyn, New York, at the time that first poem arrived. The last letter in the collection was dated ten years later, December 1986. Lilith was staying at the Hotel Simon on García de Vinuesa in Seville. The letter was full of antici-pation for their upcoming holiday. They were spending New Year's Eve together, among other things. And it's signed, "Farewell, you who make me fare well."'

Connie flicked away an imaginary tear. 'Romantic dude.' She fingered the envelope, turning it over. 'No return address.'

'Not on any of the letters.'

'Cautious, too. Married?'

I nodded. 'Bingo.'

'What happened after New Year's Eve 1986?'

I shrugged. 'I can think of several possibilities. The letters stopped because they split up, or the letters stopped because they decided to stay together, or maybe Skip didn't have all of Zan's letters.'

I handed her a packet of photos. 'The photo on top? I figure it was taken about the time Zan's last letter was written. See where they're standing?'

Looking at the photo, Connie frowned. 'I'll need help with that, Sherlock. All I see is a man and a woman standing arm in arm in front of some monument, taken by a third party who wasn't very good at it. Look, the photographer's too far back and he's cut off their feet.'

'It's the tomb of Christopher Columbus,' I informed her. 'I looked it up at the library in a Fodor's travel guide for Spain. The tomb is inside the big Catholic cathedral in Seville.'

In the photo, Lilith didn't look a day older than her earlier photos, although she'd traded in the ponytail for a short, layered do that feathered prettily around her face. She was dressed entirely in black, with a wide belt worn low on her hips. Zan, on the other hand, looked like a prep. He wore a

Polo shirt tucked into the waistband of cuffed khakis. I couldn't see his eyes, hidden behind dark-framed Ray Bans, the kind popularized by Tom Cruise in the movie *Risky Business*. Yet his smile was friendly, open, as if he had no fear of being recognized.

In another photo, possibly taken the same day, the photographer had done a better job. The same outfit, but this time I could see that Zan wore penny loafers without socks. He posed in front of a fountain, his hand resting casually on the head of one of a dozen lions that formed the fountain's base. 'I had to page through all the pictures in the guidebook before I found it. That's the Patio de los Leones at the Alhambra,' I explained.

'What's this?' Connie laid down the photos and picked up a small envelope I'd set aside on the corner of the table.

'Look inside. I found it among the photographs.'

'Gift cards, note cards,' Connie commented, plucking one out of the envelope at random and examining it closely. 'This must have come with some flowers. There have to be fifty of them here!' She squinted at the tiny print. 'Lilies for my sweet Lilith of the valley,' she read. 'How sweet! Dennis and I've been married for, what, seven years, and if I had a nickel for every time he'd sent me flowers, I'd have twenty-five cents.'

I laughed out loud. 'Don't be so hard on the guy, Con. Dennis is nuts about you.'

Connie tucked the flap back into the envelope and set the envelope down on the table. 'Zan really loved her, didn't he?'

'"Soul mates" is a hackneyed term, almost a cliché, but I think it describes the situation perfectly.'

'How old was he, do you know?'

'Hard to say. Older than Lilith, certainly. From what I gather from one of the earlier letters, he was already married with one child, a daughter, when the relationship began. Later, there must have been another daughter, because he refers to them as "my girls."'

'What I can't figure out,' I continued, 'is what Lilith did for a living. She was an artist. I know that because Zan made reference to her "works in progress" and encouraged her to try to get a particular painting into a photorealist show going up at some gallery in Soho, but I see no evidence that she did anything more than paint for her own amusement.'

'It costs money to travel around like that. London, Paris, Hong Kong, Rome,' Connie pointed out.

'Exactly,' I said. 'She spent a lot of time in Zurich, too.' I pawed through the photographs and came up with another picture. 'I think these people may be her parents. It's labeled on the back Schloss Kyburg, Zurich, 1966.'

Connie scrutinized the photo of a sophisticated couple standing arm-in-arm in what appeared to be a castle court-yard. 'I'd agree. There's a strong resemblance between Lilith and this other woman. They're both stunningly beautiful.'

'Another thing I know about Lilith,' I said, 'she was a Democrat, because in one of the earlier letters, Zan mentions how elated she must have been at the outcome of the fall elections when Jimmy Carter defeated Gerald Ford.'

Connie, a lifelong Republican, like her late parents, rolled her eyes. Dennis was a staunch Democrat, and there were some years when neither one of them went to the polls, claiming they simply cancelled each other out.

'By the 1980s, I think Lilith settled down, Connie. Most of the letters from that period were mailed to an apartment at Thirty-nine Fifth Avenue in New York City. The address sounded very posh, so I looked it up on Google Maps. It's medium posh, as it turns out, just north of Washington Square Park, adjacent to New York University. But the letter that I sent to her there boomeranged back "Addressee Unknown. Return to Sender."'

'You actually *wrote* to her?'

I shrugged. 'Why not?'

Connie had picked up my notebook and was studying the handwritten spreadsheet I had made showing where Lilith and Zan had been living at the time each of his letters was mailed. Chicago to Brooklyn. Omaha to Zurich. Mexico City to Rome. The jet-setting pair seemed to have been hopscotching all over the planet.

'Was Zan wealthy, too?'

'Possibly. I'm trying to find a pattern, but so far it eludes me. I wish to hell he'd written more about what was going on in his life, rather than sending her sappy poetry.' I found the envelope I was looking for, opened it and extracted a letter. 'Listen to this!:

"Your skin is so soft
Your face is so fair
I want to touch
Your raven hair.
I will come
To see you soon
And then I'll be
Over the moon.'"

Connie groaned. 'He would have been better off to stick with Elizabeth Barrett-Browning.'

'You'll get no argument from me. When did they repeal the law that said that all poetry had to rhyme, anyway?'

'I don't know, but clearly Zan didn't get the memo. It's that slavish use of rhyming couplets that always slays me.' She looked up from the spreadsheet. 'Did you see *Miss Saigon*?'

'The musical where a helicopter lands on the stage?'

Connie nodded. 'As far as I'm concerned, the helicopter is the highlight of the show. How many hours can you take of doggerel like: "No one can stop what I must do; I swear I'd give my life for you."'

'Thank you!' I made a cutting motion across my throat.

'I really like this picture of Zan, though,' Connie said, handing the short stack back to me. The color Polaroid on top featured Zan – long-haired, bearded, wearing wire-framed glasses – perched on a log and surrounded by dozens of dark-haired, brown-skinned children.

And then Connie said something that had not occurred to me before. 'Say, Hannah. Do you suppose Zan was in the Peace Corps?'

NINE

The Peace Corps has a headquarters building on 20th Street between L and M, a comprehensive library, a website, a blog and a fan page on Facebook. They even Tweet. When you show up with no more than a person's nickname, however, it's one great big Dead End.

Reluctantly, I put Zan on the back-burner.

Besides, I was distracted. My cast – colorful as it was, and decorated with drawings by my talented grandchildren – hearts and flowers, and airplanes shooting down other airplanes with ack-ack fire – was driving me crazy.

'It itches,' I complained to my husband a little over three weeks after the accident as I scrabbled in the utility drawer looking for a chopstick. I was seconds from inserting the chopstick between the cast and my skin so I could indulge myself with a good scratch, when Paul snatched the chopstick out of my hand.

'No, you don't! Technical foul! If you open up the skin under there, you'll be in big trouble, missy.'

The cast cramped my style in the bath, too. No more long, hot, semi-submerged soaks. My cast was supposed to be semi-waterproof, but that didn't mean that I could go deep-sea diving in it.

In desperation, I sweet-talked a receptionist into moving up the appointment I had made with an orthopedic specialist at the sports medicine center favored by a number of Naval Academy athletes. If they could put an injured quarterback back in action in time for the Army–Navy game, couldn't they work miracles for me, too?

After taking some X-rays and clucking inscrutably over the results, the doctor made my day by powering up a cast removal saw and releasing me from bondage. Scratching furiously (but oh so gently!) at the skin which had been covered by the cast for so long, I felt like Scarlett O'Hara being released from her stays. The doctor replaced my cast with a brace similar to those used to treat severe cases of carpal tunnel syndrome. Had I died and gone to heaven? Oh yes, indeed, I had.

'Don't twist your arm,' the doctor warned, 'No screwing, or you'll be back in my office in no time.'

I nearly fell off the examination table. 'What?'

'No screwing.' He demonstrated, extending his hand and twisting it as if working a screwdriver.

I felt my face redden. 'Thanks,' I chuckled. 'I won't.'

Having tabled Zan, I decided to run down every lead I had on Lilith before allowing myself to give up on her, too. She'd stayed in a dozen hotels, at least, and I Googled every one. For those hotels still in business, I jotted down their phone numbers and gave them a call:

Mlle Lilith Chaloux, s'il vous plaît,
Por favor, Señorita Lilith Chaloux,
Fräulein Lilith Chaloux, bitte.

I spent a good five minutes practicing my French on the woman who answered the phone at L'Hotel de la Belle Aurore in Ste Maxime – *une coude maison rêve sur son rocher au bord du golfe de Saint-Tropez. Ooh la la!* I thought I'd hit the jackpot at the posh seaside resort, until the switchboard put me through to a Mlle Lili Charlotte who mistook me for some lackey setting up her photo shoot for a spread in *Paris Match*. '*Mille pardons*,' I groveled, and hung up.

I tried snail-mailing the hotels, too. I included a photo of Lilith and a personal note, asking her to get in touch with me so that I could reunite her with her letters and photographs.

It was early days yet, but no dice.

Still no word from Skip, either.

Reluctantly, I packed everything away neatly in the box it had come in and tucked the Garfinkel's bag away in the closet where I kept my knitting. Winter was coming. If I hurried, the sweater I was working on might be done in time for Christmas.

TEN

I was beginning the collar, picking up stitches around the neck opening on a pair of circular needles, when Emily called, in tears.

'Mom? Can I bring the kids over tomorrow? I have to attend a memorial service in DC, and Dante's got an All-Day Autumn Bliss special going on at Paradiso.'

The following day was Saturday, and I had nothing on my plate, not even one of Dante's Serene Calm half-day spa packages, so I said, 'Of course I can. Who died, Emily?'

The question set my daughter off on a crying jag. 'It's . . . it's . . . muh . . . muh . . .'

'Honey, I can't understand a word you're saying. Do you want to call me back?'

'No, no,' she snuffled. 'It's for Meredith Logan.'

'Meredith Logan? Isn't she that intern who went missing from Lynx News headquarters? She's *dead*? My God, how terrible.'

'I can't believe you didn't know that, Mom,' Emily sniffed. 'It's been all over the news.'

'I'm sorry, sweetheart, but the television has been off more than on in the Ives household lately. I still find footage of the Metro crash a little hard to deal with.'

'Sorry, Mom. I didn't mean to be insensitive. But this is mega upsetting! I've known Meredith since Parade Night at Bryn Mawr. You met her, remember? Meredith was our garden party girl at graduation.'

'Oh my God! *That* Meredith? I thought Meredith's last name was Thompson.'

'Logan is her married name, Mom. That's why I didn't know about it sooner. I saw the news reports, sure, but Meredith changed her hair color, you know, and cut it off short and kind of punk, so it wasn't until I got an email from one of our classmates that I found out that it was *our* Meredith whose body they'd found. I feel like such a shit.'

'Just go, sweetie. Don't worry about a thing. Your father and I will watch the kids. Take them downtown for ice cream or something.'

'Thanks, Mom,' Emily sniffed. 'Oh, damn! Do you think you can handle it with your wonky arm?' she added, almost as an afterthought.

Classic Emily. I could have been trussed up in a full body cast, hanging from the ceiling by weights and pulleys, and she'd still have asked me if I wouldn't mind watching the kids.

After I'd made pickup arrangements with Emily, I looked up the Meredith Logan case on the Internet. When I saw the girl's picture, I remembered her well, even though it had been nearly a decade since Emily's graduation.

Several weeks before, the article said, Meredith's body had been found stuffed behind a fountain in Lower Senate Park by Capitol Hill K-9 dogs on routine patrol. The autopsy showed that she'd been strangled, but there was no indication that she had been sexually assaulted.

I clicked through from the newspaper article to a Lynx News video clip reporting on the case. According to the reporter, Meredith had told colleagues she was going out to meet somebody for lunch, but she never came back. Lynx News security cameras recorded her leaving the building at 12:45 and turning north on Louisiana Avenue. There were several restaurants in the immediate area where she'd been a regular – Art and Soul, Johnny's Half Shell, Taqueria Nacional – but nobody at the restaurants remembered seeing her that day. She could have gone further afield, of course, or disappeared into the great maw of the food court at nearby Union Station, but police could turn up no evidence that she had done either.

Conservative Lynx news commentator John Chandler, every silver hair neatly arranged, accused the police of botching the investigation due to jurisdictional squabbles. Interviewed on the set of his show, *And Your Point Is?*, Chandler hastened to

clarify that Meredith was not an intern, as had been reported
in the media, but a production assistant. Meredith worked in
the *And Your Point Is?* production office, answering phones,
taking deliveries, preparing scripts, picking up lunches, and
performing other tasks related to the show. Recently, she had
been filling in on the physical set of the production, too. She
was a 'company woman' with a promising future, Chandler
reported, a real trooper, regularly the first to arrive and the
last to leave. She would be greatly missed.

Lynx News didn't exactly have a reputation for giving cops
a fair shake, so I clicked over to Channel 4 News where an
archived 'Watch This' video featured a police spokeswoman
responding to Chandler's stinging on-air criticism. 'Policing
in DC is complicated,' the woman explained. 'There are at
least twenty-one police jurisdictions in the district. Some
overlap and cooperate, while others are exclusive. Meredith
Logan's body was found on Capitol grounds by Capitol Police.
The Capitol Police have exclusive jurisdiction within the United
States Capitol grounds, and concurrent jurisdiction with other
law enforcement agencies including the United States Park
Police and the DC Metropolitan Police Force in an area of
approximately two hundred blocks around the Capitol complex.'
According to the spokeswoman, all three agencies were co-
operating to help bring Meredith Logan's killer to justice.

Super.

It had taken over ten years of similar 'cooperation' before
Chandra Levy's killer was finally brought to trial.

When it came to the Meredith Logan investigation, I was
sitting on John Chandler's side of the fence for once.

The next day, my heart ached as Emily stood on our porch
with red-rimmed eyes, her skin so white that her pale
yellow hair shone bright by comparison. Pain washed over
her face, like when she was a toddler and her Raggedy
Ann doll went missing, and the pain was just as real then
as it was now.

Emily reached into her tote and pulled out a miniature
statue. I recognized it at once – the goddess Athena. A seven-
and-a-half-foot tall statue of Athena had graced the Bryn

Mawr campus for over a century, and students frequently made offerings to her, asking for her help with papers or exams, or in dealing with the usual vicissitudes of academia. 'This was Meredith's,' Emily explained. 'She gave it to me, and I'm going to give it to Meredith's mother. Do you think that will be OK?'

I gave my daughter a hug, kissed her cheek and sent her on her sorrowful errand. 'I think Meredith's mother would appreciate it very much.'

ELEVEN

I'd finished the sweater. Blocked the pieces, sewn it together, and attached the buttons. It fit perfectly and had even garnered compliments from Emily, new-age fashionista, when I showed up at Spa Paradiso for the massage she'd arranged to thank me for my babysitting services.

Now I needed another project.

I could rake leaves (would that involve 'screwing?') alphabetize my spice rack, or . . .

'I'm taking the train up to New York City today,' I announced to my sister, Ruth, as we lingered over our two-egg platters at Chick and Ruth's Delly (no relation!), a few doors up Main Street from Ruth's shop, Mother Earth.

Ruth paused, coffee mug halfway to her mouth. 'And you're doing this, why?'

'I considered flying to Paris or Seville, or one of the other exotic locations where Lilith Chaloux preferred to receive her mail, but the most recent address I have for her is in New York City, so I thought I'd start there.'

'Didn't you tell me that the letter you addressed to her in New York City came back, addressee unknown.'

'It did, but Thirty-nine Fifth Avenue is an apartment building. If I'm lucky, somebody still living there now will remember her.'

Ruth set her mug down on the black Formica tabletop,

worry lining her normally smooth brow. 'The train, Hannah? Are you *sure*?'

I shrugged. 'Have to climb back on the horse that bucked you.'

'Does Paul know what you're up to?'

I rested my knife against the rim of my plate. 'No. He fussed that I was obsessing over Lilith and Zan, which is true. I was – *am* – obsessing over their story. Paul put up with it while I was recovering from the accident because it kept me home and out of trouble, but I think he was secretly pleased when I put the letters away and got back to my knitting.'

'So to speak,' Ruth grinned.

'No, really,' I grinned back. 'I actually finished a sweater.'

'Won't Paul notice that you're missing?'

I shook my head. 'Paul's in Colorado Springs.'

'What the hell's he doing in Colorado?'

I tore off a bit of toast and dredged it through the egg yolk remaining on my plate. 'The Navy–Air Force game is today. He's flown out on a party plane with a bunch of his Naval Academy buddies.'

Ruth gave me a look that I'd often seen on our mother's face whenever we were trying to pull a fast one. 'He's going to have a cow when he finds out!'

I shrugged. '"It's much easier to apologize than it is to get permission,"' I said, quoting Grace Hopper.

'So, how come *you're* not going to the game, Hannah?'

'No scientific instrument yet invented is sensitive enough to measure how little I care about football.'

Ruth smothered a laugh with her napkin. 'Want me to come to New York with you? I could get Neelie to cover the store for the day.'

Cornelia – nicknamed Neelie – was my widowed father's girlfriend. The Alexander girls – my sisters, Ruth and Georgina, and I – thoroughly approved of Cornelia Gibbs and couldn't imagine why our father hadn't asked her to marry him yet. It had been almost a decade since our mother's death. But we knew from experience that there was little to be gained from pushing the man. There's not much you can tell a retired navy captain. They're accustomed to being in charge.

'I appreciate the concern, Big Sis, but some challenges simply have to be faced alone.'

The waitress appeared, and Ruth held out her mug for a refill. 'It's your funeral, Hannah, but for heaven's sake, be careful!'

An hour and a half later, I parked my car in the Amtrak garage at BWI and bought a ticket on the next train to New York City. I thought I had the Train Thing under control until the Northeaster actually pulled into the station and it was time to climb aboard.

One step forward, two steps back, the heebie-jeebies had taken hold. Except for the conductor, I was alone on the platform.

'Are we holding you up?' asked the conductor. 'You getting on or just sightseeing?'

I took a deep breath, and dashed up the steps into one of the middle cars before I had a chance to change my mind.

Three hours later, I got off at Penn Station.

Miraculously unscathed.

It's a twenty-five minute hike from Penn Station to 39 Fifth, but cabs can be expensive, so I ruled them out. I had no appointments, no schedule to keep, so I'd planned a leisurely stroll along a route that would take me past Macy's windows and down Broadway. I took my time doing it, too, zigging across town on the numbered streets and zagging down the avenues, enjoying the exercise and the crisp fall air.

Thirty-nine Fifth turned out to be a handsome, seventeen-story apartment building situated between 10th and 11th streets on the edge of Greenwich Village, just a couple of blocks north of Washington Square. Unusual terracotta frescos decorated the façade at the building's third-floor level. I ducked under the fancy green awning that sheltered the entrance from the elements and rang the bell.

When the doorman appeared on the other side of the glass, my heart sank. He was probably in his early thirties. At the time Lilith Chaloux lived here, he would have been struggling with fractions in elementary school.

The door opened a crack, and he peered out, followed by a blast of superheated air.

'Can I help you, ma'am?'

'I hope so. My name's Hannah Ives, and I'm organizing a high school reunion. One of my classmates used to live in this building. Apartment Four-B? Lilith Chaloux?'

'Which high school?' he asked.

'Cardinal Spellman,' I ad-libbed, naming the only high school I knew of in New York City that didn't have 'PS' and a number attached to it.

'Right. Well . . .' He scratched the back of his head, as if actually thinking. 'Nobody named Chaloux in this building now, and there's two women with a baby in Four-B, so I'm afraid I can't help you. When did you say she lived here?'

'In the 1980s.'

'Way before my time, you know?'

I smiled. 'Yes, I guess it was. Well, thanks anyway.'

I had expected to be disappointed, but the news still stung. Thinking that a cup of coffee might improve my disposition, I walked around the corner to University Place where I remembered seeing a Dean and Deluca café. I bought a takeaway cup of the house blend, then strolled back the way I had come.

On the corner of 10th Street and 5th Avenue stands Ascension Episcopal Church, a red stone building surrounded by an iron fence. I crossed to the other side of 5th Avenue and leaned against the churchyard fence, sipping my coffee, observing as residents came and went from Lilith Chaloux's old building.

At a bus stop across the street, someone was watching me, too – a husky guy wearing a New York Yankees ball cap and sunglasses with odd, glacier-blue lenses. He was reading the *Post*, waiting for the bus, glancing up at me from time to time. Did he think I was a bag lady?

His scrutiny, however innocent, was making me nervous, so I wandered halfway down 10th Street, admiring the church's splendid stained-glass windows and lamenting that they had to be protected by Plexiglas sheets, but understanding why.

Back at my station in front of the church a few minutes later, I was relieved to see that the guy wearing the blue sunglasses had gone. I alternated between Googling on my iPhone – the stained-glass windows were by John LaFarge, I learned – and keeping my eye on Lilith's old building. My patience was rewarded (finally!) when a pair of elderly women emerged from 39 Fifth being led by a large German shepherd dog. The women were dressed in nearly identical bulky, oversize cardigans, black ankle-length skirts, and neon-pink jogging shoes. They resembled each other so closely that they had to be sisters.

As I watched, the dog dragged his mistress south along 5th Avenue toward Washington Square, heading, as I soon found out, for a play date with an exuberant young golden retriever at the dog run in the park.

I chucked my empty coffee cup into the nearest trash container and followed.

The sisters had been sitting together on a bench for about ten minutes, watching with wry amusement while the dogs frolicked, before I plucked up the courage to join them.

'I hope you'll excuse me for interrupting you,' I said, 'but I just noticed that you came out of Thirty-nine Fifth. Do you live in that building?'

'I'm sorry, dear, but we don't take surveys. I know you're just doing your job, but . . .'

I raised a hand, chuckled. 'Please, don't worry! I'm not taking a survey. I'm just trying to track down somebody I used to go to high school with.'

The woman glanced nervously at her sister, who smiled, nodded and gave her a light, go-ahead-she-looks-harmless-enough-to-me punch on the arm. 'Why, in that case, yes, we live at Thirty-nine Fifth Avenue.'

'My name is Hannah Ives. I live in Annapolis, Maryland, now, but I used to go to Cardinal Spellman with a girl named Lilith. Lilith Chaloux.'

While I explained about the imaginary reunion, I pulled Lilith's picture out of my handbag and handed it to the older of the two women.

'I'm Elspeth Simon, and this is my sister, Claire.' Elspeth

held the picture close to her face as if she'd forgotten her reading glasses, turning it this way and that in the bright sunlight, then handed it to Claire. 'Yes, that's Lilith all right. Lovely girl. She lived in our building for quite some time.'

I showed them the second picture, the one of Lilith standing in front of the tomb of Christopher Columbus with the man I assumed to be Zan. 'Do you know who this is?' I asked, tapping the man's face.

Elspeth studied the image for a few seconds, nodded in recognition, then shared that photo with her sister, too. 'He was the love of Lilith's life,' she told me, looking wistful. 'Claire, what was that man's name? Something Japanesey, as I recall. Zen?'

'No, it wasn't Zen.' Wrinkles furrowed Claire's brow and she stared up at the massive stone archway that dominated the park, deep in concentration. 'No, it was Zan. Zan something.'

'Did Zan have a last name?'

Elspeth laughed. 'Of course he had a last name, dear! Something foreign with little squiggles on it. Claire, do you remember?' Claire shook her head, her gray curls bouncing against her neck. 'I can't remember if I ever heard her say it. Lilith always referred to her boyfriend simply as Zan.' She handed the picture back to me. 'Lilith kept pretty much to herself. Didn't talk much about her private life, but whenever that man was in town . . .' She tapped the photo with a neatly manicured index finger. 'Well, whenever Zan showed up, that girl simply glowed.'

Claire brightened. 'Lilith had a studio somewhere down on West Broadway. She was an artist, you know.'

'I did know. I have some of her work, in fact. She was into photorealism back then, wasn't she?' I said, drawing on information I had gleaned from one of Zan's letters.

Claire nodded. 'She even had a picture in a group show at the Meisel Gallery on Prince Street. We went to see that show, didn't we, Ellie? It was a painting of sunlight shining on broken glass vases. She was very talented.'

'Is that how Lilith made a living?'

'Oh, I don't think so,' Claire said. 'She was always most reluctant to part with her work. I often wonder what happened to all those beautiful paintings when she moved away.'

'When was that?'

'About the time the building voted to go condo,' Ellie cut in. 'That would have been, let's see, 1986.'

'No, that's not right, Ellie. She moved away in April, or maybe May, of 1987. Remember? They'd just put up the scaffolding in front of the building. The movers had to work around it.'

'I distinctly remember it was 1986, Claire. The year Pedro died.'

'Pedro died in 1987.'

'Oh, well she left in '87, then.'

'Who's Pedro?' I asked.

'Our dog.' The sisters said it in unison, setting off a fit of giggles.

'He was a chihuahua,' Ellie explained. She held her hands in front of her, palms facing, about eight inches apart. 'He was that tiny.'

I pointed at the German shepherd who was lolling in the dirt with his playmate and raised an eyebrow.

Ellie laughed. 'Well, we've super-sized it, haven't we? Meet Bruno.'

Long, lean, strong-boned and muscular, Bruno was my kind of dog. Bruno was a dog's dog. Yappy purse-sized dogs left me cold.

'So Lilith didn't have a job? A real job, I mean.'

Ellie thought about my question for a moment while lacing the end of Bruno's leash around her fingers. 'No. I gather she had money, though. She told me that her parents had been killed in a plane crash when she was still in her teens. She had a trust fund administered by some doddering old uncle in Switzerland. Zurich, I believe. Lilith didn't spend money willy-nilly, mind you, but I don't think money was a particular issue for her.'

'Remember what she said, Ellie? About the magic credit card?'

'What's a magic credit card?' I asked, intrigued that there

might be such a thing and wondering where I could apply for one.

'She'd charge things on it,' Ellie explained. 'And every month it would get paid off by some bank in Switzerland, no questions asked.'

'Where do I line up to get a credit card like that?'

'We'll be right in line behind you!' Claire chortled.

'Do you know where Lilith went when she moved away?' I asked.

'First, she was going to stay with that uncle I mentioned in Zurich. I remember that plainly, because she said she was having her things put into storage for six months.' Claire looked thoughtful, then raised her eyebrows and her hands in unison. 'Until the cottage was ready! That's what she told us, didn't she, Ellie? She was going to move into a cottage!'

'What cottage? Where? In Europe?'

'I'm afraid I don't remember, dear. I'm so sorry. My son says it's CRS. Can't remember shit.'

I handed Ellie one of the business cards that I'd printed out on our home computer, a simple sailboat graphic with my name, address, phone number and email. 'If you think of anything that might help me find Lilith, please give me a call. We're having the reunion next spring. It's our fortieth, can you believe it? I really would love to get back in touch.'

While eyeing my brace, Ellie tucked my card into the pocket of her sweater. 'Can I ask what happened to your arm?'

'Fender-bender,' I fibbed, not feeling up to revisiting the ordeal. 'Airbag broke my arm.'

This launched Claire on a lengthy monologue about the dangers posed by airbags to short, elderly drivers, copiously illustrated with hair-raising examples from among her own circle of friends.

When she wound down, I offered to buy the sisters lunch, but they demurred, claiming they had to get Bruno home for his nap. I bid them thanks and goodbye, then wandered across the park, heading south down West Broadway into Soho proper.

West Broadway between Broom and Prince used to be prime Soho retail space. Sadly, it seemed to have fallen on hard times. Storefront after vacant storefront made my leisurely stroll unexpectedly dreary. RIP Rizzoli's Bookstore, Sigrid Olsen and Té Casan. I poked my nose into a few shops and wondered, as I walked, which of the studios I was passing might have been Lilith's.

On a hunch, I popped into the Louis Meisel Gallery, but the black-garbed *Twilight* wannabe manning the desk had never heard of a Lilith Chaloux, nor was she listed among the artists who had ever shown there. Puzzled and disappointed, I walked a few blocks further and cheered myself up at the Apple Store by taking an iPad for a test drive.

Before heading back to Penn Station, I picked up a carry-out sandwich at Olives – smoked turkey, bacon and avocado on sourdough – then caught a cab that got me to the station well in time to catch the 5:39 back to BWI. I sat in the waiting area, ate my sandwich, powered up my new iPhone 4, and launched the Safari browser.

I was still giving my iPhone a workout three and a half hours later when the train pulled into BWI station. I hurriedly unplugged the charger from the seat-side outlet, snatched up my purse and hopped off on to the platform. When Paul came home the following day, I'd have to confess, of course, but at least I'd have something interesting to report.

TWELVE

Back home in Annapolis, by some miracle, I managed to find a parking spot only half a block from our home at 193 Prince George. After careful backing and turning, made extra challenging by my doctor's instructions not to twist my arm, I successfully squeezed the Volvo into the narrow space left by two of my neighbors, locked up, then hustled along the sidewalk, stepping carefully on the ancient brickwork that edged the darkened street.

I let myself in the front door, tossed my handbag and the car keys on the little table in the entrance hall, and headed for the kitchen. I flipped on the small-screen television that sits on top of the refrigerator and was pouring myself a glass of apple juice when the sports news came on. Out in Colorado Springs, the Falcons had trounced the Midshipmen fourteen to six, snapping the Mids' fifteen-game winning streak against the other service academies, including eight wins against Army and seven against the Air Force.

Damn. There'd be no post-game euphoria to help ease my husband into the confessional.

When Paul came toodling in from the Academy late on Sunday evening, I was already propped up in bed, slogging through the second chapter of *The Girl with the Dragon Tattoo* and wondering what all the fuss was about.

'Sorry about the game,' I said.

Paul kissed me on the forehead. 'Erratic passing,' he mumbled, stripping off his shirt. 'Solid defense . . . failed to execute on the goal line . . . converted only five of fifteen third-down chances.' Snippets of his report drifted from the bathroom as he prepared for bed.

'Did you watch the game?' he asked, slipping under the covers next to me.

'Uh, no. I was doing something else.'

Paul propped his head on his hand, puffed peppermint toothpaste in my face. 'And what was that?'

'I took Amtrak to New York City to check out the last place Lilith lived.'

Paul scowled at me without speaking.

'It was a spur of the moment thing,' I forged on. 'I found the building Lilith lived in, learned that Zan was probably foreign, and that Lilith moved from her apartment in New York City to a cottage, location unknown.'

Paul flopped over on his back, crossed his arms over his chest, glowered at the ceiling. 'You could have told me what you were up to, Hannah.'

'I told Ruth.'

'You're not married to Ruth.'

'I'm sorry, Paul, but I knew you'd worry and I didn't want to spoil your weekend.'

Paul stewed in silence for a few moments.

'I think you'll find it interesting,' I continued.

'Life with you always is, Hannah.'

I took that as a green light and kept driving. 'Lilith's parents were killed in a plane crash when she was still in her teens,' I reported, playing the sympathy card.

'Ah, the proverbial lost-both-parents-in-a-tragic-plane-and-or-car-crash hard-luck story,' Paul commented brightly, his little sulk apparently over.

'Don't scoff. That part of her story is absolutely true. It took me a bit of searching, but I finally found a reference to it on the Internet. On September eleventh, 1968, Charles and Lucille (née Aupry) Chaloux were killed in the crash of Air France Flight 1611.'

'How come that didn't come up before when we Googled Chaloux?' Paul wondered.

'It might have done, on screen nine hundred and seven. But if you add "plane crash" to the equation, the article pops up on the first screen'

'Any details?'

'Hold on.' I reached for the iPhone on my bedside table and swiped it on. 'It says here that Flight 1611 was en route from the island of Corsica to Nice, France, when it crashed into the Mediterranean Sea killing all ninety-five on board.'

Paul sucked air in through his teeth. 'Damn. Lilith would have been only fifteen. What caused the crash?'

'The *official* report said a fire in the lavatory near the galley, of undetermined origin.'

'Do I detect a note of skepticism in your voice?'

'Well, there was a French general on board, René Cogny, so there was talk.'

'And?'

'I was saving the best for last. In 2005, there was a Lynx News white paper on the crash that advanced the theory that the accident was the result of a missile strike or bomb, and that the true cause had been suppressed by the French government under secrecy laws.' I paused, waiting for that to sink in. 'Guess who the reporter was?'

'Who?'

'John Chandler.'

'So?'

'Don't you think it's a little more than a coincidence that John Chandler is doing a story on a plane crash that killed the parents of Lilith Chaloux?'

'And ninety-four other people, I believe I heard you say.'

'True. But the connection made me curious, so I looked up John Chandler on the Internet. I think I've found Zan!'

'John Chandler? You think John Chandler is Zan? Are you out of your cotton-picking mind?'

Now it was my turn to sulk. 'So, are you ready to hear what I learned about John Chandler, or not?'

Paul plumped up his pillow, stuffed it behind his back and sat up, giving me his full attention. 'Shoot.'

I tapped the Safari icon. 'Listen to what Wikipedia says. "John Chandler – born on November fifteenth, 1950 – is a television journalist for Lynx News where he anchors the program, *And Your Point is?* Born Alexander Svíčkář in Brno, Czechoslovakia, he emigrated to the United States in 1956 with his parents, Rubert and Janna (née Cerny) Svíčkář. He became a United States citizen in 1971, changing his name to John Chandler.

'"Chandler graduated from Earlham College in 1972 with a degree in Peace and Global Studies,"' I read on. '"While at Earlham, he was a reporter for the campus radio station, WECI-FM. From 1972–74 he served in the Peace Corps in Guatemala where he acted as liaison between government agencies bringing relief to victims of Hurricane Fifi. Later, he worked as an aide to Jimmy Carter during his successful 1976 presidential campaign.

'"Prior to joining Lynx News, Chandler worked for the Catholic News Service and the Associated Press in Europe.

'"Chandler lives in the Georgetown area of Washington DC and is married to Dorothea Goodrich, a vice-president of the Women's Democratic League. He has two grown daughters."

'There!' I plunked the iPhone down on top of the duvet and took a deep breath. 'Don't you see? It all fits! Chandler's real name is Alexander. Zan!' I ticked the remaining points off on my fingers. 'There's the Peace Corps connection, the fact that he worked for the AP in Europe – no wonder he was mailing letters to her from all over the world – married, two daughters. And finally . . .' I took a deep breath. 'I think I know where he met Lilith! The Democratic National Convention was held in New York City in 1976, and they probably worked together on Jimmy Carter's campaign!'

I fell back against the pillows, triumphant. 'So, what do you think?'

'Compelling coincidences, I have to agree, but I don't think you could use it to prove anything in a court of law. There are a lot of men in the world named Alexander.'

'Ah, yes, but I'm remembering what Elspeth Simon said about Lilith's Zan. She told me his last name had little squiggles on it. Wait a minute.' I retrieved the iPhone and scrolled back to the beginning of the Wikipedia entry. 'There,' I said, aiming the tiny screen at Paul so I could point out the acute accents and upside down circumflexes over the letters 'i,' 'c,' 'a,' and 'r' in Svíčkář. 'Squiggles. I rest my case.'

'*Čárkas* and *háčeks*,' Paul corrected. 'Not squiggles.'

I stuck out my tongue. 'Smarty pants.'

I opened my bookmarks and tapped on a link to a *Times* article I'd saved earlier. 'There's more. Novak was interviewed by the *Washington Times*. He's quoted here as saying that one of his journalism professors advised that he'd never get a job in broadcasting with a name like Svíčkář. Impossible to pronounce, hard to spell. So, he changed it.' I glanced up from the little screen. 'I looked it up. Svíčkář means "candlemaker" or "chandler" in Czech.'

I switched the iPhone off and put it back on the bedside table. 'Seems to me that somebody's repealed that silly law about foreign-sounding names and success in broadcasting. Guillermo Arduino, Fareed Zakaria, and Wolf Blitzer seem to be making out just fine.'

'Mandalit DelBarco.' Paul's pronunciation was eloquent, the syllables of the NPR reporter's name rolling off his tongue like honey dripping from a flaky buttermilk biscuit. He closed his eyes. 'Maria Hinojosa, Christiane Amanpour, Sylvia

Poggioli,' he recited. 'Pah-JOE-lee, Pah-JOE-lee. I could listen to Sylvia Poggioli read the telephone book.'

I had to laugh. 'How about Lakshmi Singh?' I added, 'Or, what's her name, the NPR business reporter, Snick Paprikash.'

Paul snorted. 'You mean Snigdha Prakash.'

'Her, too. Or Ofeibea Quist-Arcton.'

'Simple always worked for Larry King,' Paul mused.

I raised an index finger. 'Ah, but King's real name is Lawrence Harvey Zeiger.'

'How do you know that?'

'I am a font of all wisdom,' I said, hooking a thumb in the direction of my iPhone.

'Squiggles,' Paul repeated with amusement. 'Men have been hung on less evidence.'

'Well, I'm not planning on hanging Mr Chandler,' I said. 'I have no interest whatsoever in the man's sex life.' I paused. 'Do I hear a "but?"'

'*But*, if Chandler can tell me where I can find Lilith Chaloux, no questions asked, I'd be really grateful, and I think she would, too.' I reached out for Paul's hand. 'If these were your letters to me, I'd certainly want them back, bad poetry and all.'

Paul squeezed my hand. 'Roses are red, Violets are blue, If I had some chocolate, I'd give it to you. How's that?'

'Thank you, Mr Longfellow!' I kissed him on the forehead. 'Tomorrow, I'll just take a ride into DC and pay a call on Lynx News.'

I shot my husband an anxious glance, hoping that since my little New York adventure had gone off without a hitch, he'd not pout and get all stroppy with me about a short hop, into the District of Columbia.

Paul squinched up his face. 'On the Metro?'

I pulled the duvet up to my chin. 'No, I've temporarily retired my SmartTrip card. I don't think I'm ready for the Metro yet. Not tomorrow, not the next day, maybe never.'

'Just be careful.' Paul searched out my hand under the covers and gave it a squeeze.

'I always am.'

*   *   *

The next morning, I was sitting at the computer in our basement office working on my second cup of coffee when Paul
staggered down from the kitchen, rubbing sleep out of his
eyes. 'You're up early.'

'I couldn't sleep, so I decided to do a little snooping around
on the Internet.' I handed him my empty mug. 'Fetch me
more coffee, pretty please, and I'll tell you all about it.'

Paul returned several minutes later bearing mugs of steaming
coffee, pulled up his office chair and sat down on it.

'Look what I found in the photo archives at *Time* magazine,' I said after he'd gotten settled. I handed him a printout
hot off the printer. 'The photo's credited to Annie Leibovitz
and is captioned "Jann S. Wenner and Hunter S. Thompson
at a *Rolling Stone* party held for the Jimmy Carter campaign
staff, New York, 1976." The same picture shows up on Jann
Wenner's webpage,' I added, 'but it's been cropped.'

'I know who Hunter Thompson is – that gonzo reporter
– but who the heck is Jann Wenner?' Paul asked.

'How soon you forget. 1967? The Summer of Love? *Rolling
Stone* magazine?

Paul still looked puzzled.

'Wenner founded *Rolling Stone.*'

'I knew that,' Paul said, with a grin that told me that he
hadn't a clue.

'Anyway. Check out this larger version of the photo. Who
is that, there, in the background?' I tapped the image.

Way in the background, her face turned slightly away from
the camera, was a young woman with her hair cut in a Dorothy
Hamill-style wedge, whose profile looked very much like
Lilith. She held a wine glass aloft, as if toasting someone
outside the frame.

'Looks like Lilith Chaloux.'

'I'm almost positive it's Lilith. And who is that standing
next to her, that long-haired guy, looks a bit like John Lennon,
cupping a cigarette like it's a joint?'

Paul leaned forward, squinting. 'Could *be* a joint.'

I bopped him on lightly on the head. 'Be serious.'

'Looks like the guy in those other pictures – Zan,' Paul
admitted.

'Yes indeedy-do. And I found another picture, too, in the photo archives of the Jimmy Carter Library and Museum.'

'My, my, you do get around, Mrs Ives. And still in your pajamas, too.'

I ignored the jab and passed Paul a streaky, monochromatic printout. 'It's a photo of Zan standing in front of a green and white Carter/Mondale "Leaders for a Change" poster, wearing a chocolate brown "Gimme Jimmy 76" T-shirt. Or it would be if your stupid printer hadn't run out of magenta toner.'

Paul handed the printout back. 'Interesting, but what does this tell you that you don't already know?'

'What I said last night? That was all conjecture, speculation based on Zan's letters, Chandler's bio and a handful of pictures. Reading those letters is like wandering around Planet Zan in a spacesuit, Paul. I often found myself wondering what was real and what wasn't. But here it is!' I waved a hand at the screen. 'Independent confirmation. And if you can't believe *Rolling Stone*, who can you believe?'

'Zan himself?'

'Stay tuned for the next exciting episode – A Man, A Plan, A Canal, Panama. Or, I'm dreaming of a wide isthmus,' I said, quoting either Rocket J. Squirrel or Bullwinkle the Moose. 'And speaking of iconic cartoon characters, if I don't want to greet John Chandler while wearing PJs, I better get cracking.'

THIRTEEN

I may have been OK with Amtrak, but the thought of stepping on another Metro train at New Carrollton made my stomach heave. Even though it was raining cats and dogs, I let New Carrollton fade in my rear-view mirror and, with windshield wipers set to frantic, drove all the way into Washington, DC. I parked in the garage at Union Station, retrieved my umbrella from the trunk and hustled through the rain the few short blocks to the Lynx News headquarters building at New Jersey Avenue and C Street, NW.

At the information desk in the ultra-modern lobby, I shook out my umbrella, propped it up in the corner with several others to dry, and asked to see John Chandler.

'Do you have an appointment?'

'No, but tell him it's important. I have a story for him.'

'And your name is?'

I told her.

The receptionist looked me up and down, as if checking for explosives. I must have passed muster, because she picked up the phone and punched in a few numbers. Speaking softly, so that I could barely hear her, she said, 'There's a Hannah Ives here, asking to see Mr Chandler.' After a moment, she nodded, hung up, and said, 'Sign in here.'

After I showed her my driver's license and entered my name in her logbook, she gave me a visitor's badge and demonstrated how to clip it to my jacket. 'Someone will be right down.'

I was adjusting my badge when an elevator dinged and a fresh-faced young man sporting a layered do with fashionably shaggy bangs emerged, dressed in khakis, a pale blue tie and a white dress shirt with the sleeves rolled up. 'Hannah Ives?'

'Yes.' I shook his hand.

'I'm Jud Wilson. I work for Mr Chandler. Let me take you somewhere where we can talk.'

Jud and I rode the elevator up to the sixth floor where he led me on a circuitous route through a maze of eye-level, fabric-covered office cubicles, eventually escorting me into a small, glass-enclosed conference room. Scrawled in a rainbow of colored markers on a whiteboard mounted on the wall were odd notations connected by dotted lines, circles and arrows. Perhaps they'd been discussing football plays at an earlier meeting.

'Can I get you some coffee? Tea?'

When I declined, Jud indicated a chair at the head of the table. He sat down kitty-corner from me, folded his hands and leaned forward, preparing to do triage. Is this woman worthy to speak to the great John Chandler?

'So, you said you have a story for Mr Chandler.'

'I need to speak to him personally. Is he here?'

'Yes, he's here, but he's asked me to find out what you want.'

'As I said, it's a personal matter.'

'I'm Mr Chandler's PA. You can tell me.'

'No, I can't.' I laid my hands flat on the table. 'Look, if Mr Chandler's here, please find him and tell him this: Lilith Chaloux.'

Jud didn't blink. 'Chaloux.'

'Yes. Chaloux.'

'I'll be right back.' Jud left the room, closing the door carefully behind him.

Through the glass I watched as he crossed the office and disappeared down a hallway at the opposite end of the building. While I waited I studied the upholstery, the walls, the artwork, and tried to work out what the hieroglyphics on the whiteboard were supposed to mean. On the table was a business card holder made out of granite incised with the Lynx News logo. I picked up one of the cards. It was Jud's. I was tucking it into my pocket when the door opened.

John Chandler had taken the bait.

'That will be all, Jud. Close the door, would you?'

When Jud left, Chandler remained standing, arms hanging loose at his sides, looking like he'd stepped out of my television screen: dark suit, pale blue shirt, a patriotic red, white and blue striped tie. The commentator was clean-shaven, and his abundant white hair was combed straight back. A trace of make-up on his collar indicated that I might have interrupted a taping. *Good.*

'So, Mrs Ives. How can I help you?'

'I'm trying to locate a woman named Lilith Chaloux, and I think you can help me.'

'I don't see how. I'm not acquainted with anybody by that name.'

I stared at the man, not believing that he'd lie about knowing Lilith, his darling, his lover.

'I think you do.' I handed him a picture of Lilith that would melt the coldest heart. She sat on a middle step of a grand staircase, resting her elbows on her knees and cupping her chin with her hands, gazing at the photographer sideways through her lashes. She was dressed for a party in an off-the-shoulder black cocktail dress – its full skirt flounced out around her knees by an abundance of petticoats – and a simple strand of white pearls. She wore no other jewelry; she didn't need to. 'This is Lilith Chaloux.'

Chandler studied the picture with no obvious sign of emotion, but a telltale muscle twitched in his jaw. Still holding the picture, he eased himself into a chair. 'Sorry, she doesn't look familiar, although I meet a lot of people in my line of work.' He pushed the photo across the table in my direction. As he did so, I noticed that he wore a wedding band made of white, yellow and rose gold twisted into a rope, a ring so substantial that it practically screamed, 'I'm married! Hands off!' Maybe it was just a smokescreen, I mused. The thinner the band, the more faithful the husband – my personal theory, anyway, since Paul wore no wedding band at all.

I pulled a second photo out of the envelope, the photograph of the man I knew as Zan, surrounded by the Guatemalan children. 'Isn't that a picture of you, Mr Chandler?'

He grinned. 'Yes, that's me. I was in the Peace Corps in Guatemala, but I'm sure you know that already.'

'And you say you don't know anybody by the name of Lilith Chaloux.'

His smile might have disarmed a lesser woman, but I am immune to smiles from television commentators who are more expensively coifed than I. 'I'm afraid not.'

'Then, can you explain how this Polaroid of you got in among her letters? Love letters signed Zan. Short for Alexander?'

Chandler smiled indulgently. 'I see you've been reading my CV. Look, Mrs Ives, there are millions of men named Alexander in this world, starting with Alexander the Great back in 300-something BC. Those letters must be from some other Alexander.'

I shoved a photocopy of one of Lilith's letters across to him, the one Zan wrote from a hotel in Paris, the one signed

'God bless you, my darling, my lover, Z.' 'Is this your handwriting?'

His eyes hadn't left my face. 'It is not.'

'Maybe if you actually looked at it, you could give me a straight answer.'

The lobes of Chandler's ears turned red. He gave the letter a cursory once-over, shrugged, and shook his head.

'So, you're telling me that you never knew a woman named Lilith Chaloux, that you didn't have a ten-year relationship with her, and that somebody else, some other Alexander, wrote the fifty-some love letters that have come into my possession.'

'That's what I'm saying.'

'In that case, I don't think we have anything more to discuss.' I collected my things, stood up, and walked to the door.

Chandler followed. He twisted the knob, and held the door open for me. 'Sorry I couldn't be of more help.'

'Look, Mr Chandler. Perhaps I didn't make myself clear. My one and only goal is to return these letters to the woman they were written to. I don't care about her relationships, past, present or future, with you – excuse me, with Zan – or with anybody else. I don't even know if Lilith Chaloux is still alive.'

I thought I detected a spark, flicker, something in his eyes, but he waited me out.

'Well, goodbye.' I was halfway out the door with Chandler close behind me when I turned on my heel, meeting him face to face. 'You know, if I had loved somebody the way Zan loved Lilith . . . well, it's a complete mystery to me how you can live with yourself, Mr Chandler.

If I had clobbered him over the head with a medieval club, he couldn't have looked more stunned. After his eyebrows returned to their normal position directly over his eyes, Chandler said coolly, 'Jud will escort you back down to the lobby.' He held out his hand and seemed surprised when I didn't take it. 'Goodbye, Mrs Ives.'

Indeed, Jud was waiting. After we stepped into the elevator, just as the doors were closing, I asked the young man casually, 'How is Mr Chandler dealing with having a guy for a PA?'

Jud mashed his thumb down on the 'G' button. 'What do you mean?'

I shrugged. 'Sometimes women let themselves be taken advantage of. Pick up the dry cleaning. Buy a birthday gift for the wife. Darn my socks. Stuff like that.'

Jud laughed. 'You've been watching too many episodes of *Mad Men*, Mrs Ives. We've come a long way since the sixties.'

The elevator began its slow descent. 'I heard about your predecessor on the news, Jud. Scary stuff. Who would want Meredith Logan dead? Did she have a boyfriend?'

Jud shook his head. 'There was no one in her life. The job was all.'

'Anyone at work she was close to?'

'By "close to," you mean having an affair with?'

'The thought had entered my mind. John Chandler, for example. You.'

'Meredith was my friend and colleague. End of story. If you think that John murdered Meredith, you're crazier than I thought. They had a relationship, that part's true, but he was more like a professor to Meredith, or a mentor maybe.'

'So my hare-brained theory that Meredith issued an ultimatum – marry me or I'll tell your wife about our affair – doesn't hold water?'

'Leaky as a sieve.'

'On the other hand, what if Mrs Chandler suspected her husband was having an affair with Meredith and killed her to keep a scandal from ruining her husband's career?'

'You want my unvarnished opinion?' Jud asked as the elevator deposited us on the ground floor.

I nodded and stepped out into the lobby while Jud stayed behind in the elevator, thumb pressed on the button that would hold the doors open. 'Well, under that scenario, it wouldn't be so much a question of ruining her husband's career as embarrassing her and reflecting negatively on her social standing. But, no, I don't think that happened either. There was nothing going on between John and Meredith except work. And Mrs C. knew that.'

As the elevator doors closed over Jud's face, I waved goodbye. I returned the visitor's badge to the harried receptionist, and discovered that somebody had pinched my umbrella.

Muttering profanities under my breath, I pulled my jacket over my head and ran out into the pouring rain.

FOURTEEN

I drove home with the heat on full-blast. By the time I got to Annapolis my hair was dry, but my wool jacket smelled like wet dog. It would need a couple of trips to the dry cleaner before it could be restored to anything resembling its former glory.

A quick look in the hall mirror only confirmed what I suspected: I not only smelled like wet dog, I looked like a chew toy the dog had been gnawing on for a while.

Paul was in the basement office, grading papers. By the time he'd laid down his red pencil and come upstairs to the kitchen to join me in a glass of wine, I'd brushed the tangles out of my hair and fluffed it up at bit so I didn't feel like such a freak.

'What did you get up to today?' I asked as I handed him a glass of Chablis.

'Oh, nothing.' The man was positively twinkling.

'Liar!'

'A guy showed up today, asking for you.'

'Oh?' I grabbed a pretzel out of a bag I'd left open on the table and took a bite.

'He said he understood you had found a package on the Metro that belonged to him.'

I stopped in mid-nibble. 'He what?'

'I told him you weren't home.'

I pointed at the kitchen table with the pretzel. 'Sit.' When we were both sitting down, I asked, 'Do you think it was Skip?'

'No. He introduced himself as Jim Hoffner.'

'Hoffner, Hoffner. Why does that name sound familiar? Do we know any Hoffners?' I took a bite of pretzel, chased it with a gulp of wine. 'Please don't tell me that you gave him Lilith's box!'

Paul reached out and stroked my arm. 'Of course not. Mostly because he didn't look at all like the guy on the train as you described him to me. So, I told Hoffner, sorry, you weren't home, and that I didn't know where you'd put the package. Which is perfectly true.'

'Was he in a wheelchair? On crutches? Limping?'

'No, and I found that most peculiar, Watson. The way he sashayed down the steps was just a tad too spry for someone who less than a month ago had his lower body pinned under a couple of tons of twisted steel.'

'Can you describe the guy for me?'

'Better than that. I managed to snap a picture of him with my cell phone.'

'Clever boy! How did you do that?'

'Pure dumb luck. I'd just finished checking in with Emily when the doorbell rang, so I had the phone in my hand. When Hoffner left, I knew he'd have to turn one way or the other on the sidewalk, so when he headed up toward Maryland Avenue, I was able to get off a couple of shots through the living-room window.'

Paul slipped his iPhone out of the breast pocket of his shirt and thumbed the screen on. A few taps later, he turned the screen in my direction. There, in profile, was a guy I'd never laid eyes on before.

He was tall, at least six feet, big-boned, but not heavy. He kept his dark hair closely trimmed and was already working on a five o'clock shadow. 'What color were his eyes?' I asked my husband.

'You think I gaze deeply into the eyes of other men?'

'Paul!'

'They were brown.'

'Hmmm,' I mused. 'Brown hair, brown eyes, khaki pants and a brown jacket. I'll bet his shoes and socks are brown, too. What we have here is Mysterious Mocha Man.'

Using my thumb and forefinger, I flicked the image to enlarge it. Whoever this man was, he was not the man whose hand I had held on the doomed train. 'This guy is definitely *not* Skip.'

'I didn't think he was. The absence of a full-body cast was a bit of a clue.'

'But why would he claim to be the guy I helped on the train when he wasn't? Whoever he is, he'd have to know that *I'd* realize he wasn't Skip.'

'Ah yes,' Paul said. 'But once I told him you weren't home, the danger of being recognized was past. Maybe he thought I'd simply hand over the bag and he could leave, and you'd never be the wiser.'

'Maybe.' I studied the image again, flicked it until the subject's face filled the screen. Something clicked. 'I know why this guy looks vaguely familiar!' I turned the screen in Paul's direction, hooting in triumph. 'He's that guy on late-night TV.' I waggled my fingers and made mysterious woo-woo noises. 'Dark, rain-soaked highways and cars careening out of control. *Kee-runch!* Got a telephone? Got a lawyer!'

Paul slipped the phone out of my fingers. Illuminated by the light from the screen, I watched his eyes widen. 'By golly, I think you're right. Hoffner's one of those ambulance chasers.'

'Do you think he's working for Skip?' I wondered.

Paul turned his iPhone face down on the table. 'Could be, but why didn't he say so, then?'

'I don't know.' I lowered my head, resting my forehead against the tabletop. 'God, I'm tired.'

Paul got up from his chair and began to massage the tension out of my shoulders. 'Let's rustle up some dinner then, cowgirl, and talk about it in the morning.'

'Did the guy leave a card?' I mumbled as Paul worked his magic on the muscles in my neck.

'No, he said he'd call again. But I know how you can reach him, if you want.'

'How?'

'One-eight-hundred-GOTALAW. If you've got a telephone, Hannah, you've got a lawyer.

FIFTEEN

The next morning, around ten, I telephoned the Ellicott City offices of Hoffner, Smith and Gallagher – world headquarters of the Got a Telephone? Got a Lawyer! guys – and asked to speak to James Hoffner. A secretary took my number and promised she'd have him call me back.

While I waited, I poured a cup of coffee and flipped on the TV where I learned from CNN, to my horror, that the body of another young woman had just been discovered.

Earlier the previous morning, a young man walking his dog on the Mount Vernon Trail north of Reagan Airport near Gravelly Point had found Juliet Henderson's body behind the Porta-Potties. Like Meredith Logan, the twenty-four-year-old pharmacy technician had been strangled. Furthermore, the reporter said, another woman had been attacked a day earlier on a jogging trail in Rock Creek Park, but had beaten off her attacker using her aluminum water bottle. Police were hoping the Rock Creek victim could identify her assailant.

A police sketch of a 'person of interest' filled the screen. Clean-shaven, the suspect wore a ball cap pulled low over his forehead; a pair of dark glasses hid his eyes. He could have been anybody: the guy ahead of me in line at the gas station, the ticket taker at Orioles Park, even my nattily dressed son-in-law, Dante, when he was slumming.

Speculation was mounting that the three crimes were linked, the work of a serial killer.

The two murders and the attempted murder resurrected the media frenzy surrounding the Chandra Levy case. Levy, a twenty-four-year-old intern for California congressman Gary Condit, disappeared on May 1, 2001, while jogging in DC's Rock Creek Park. The young woman's body wasn't discovered until more than a year later. Now, as then, the public was demanding action, and the press was stirring the pot.

When Paul came home for lunch, I was still sprawled on

the sofa in front of the TV with the remote balanced on my chest. 'Another murder, Paul. It's really distressing. They're saying the girls had been clotheslined and dragged into the bushes. What the hell does that mean – clotheslined?'

'It's a wrestling move,' he explained. 'You come running at someone with your arm straight out at your side. If your opponent is running, too, you can knock them for a loop.'

I shivered. 'Ideal mugging technique for a jogging trail, then, isn't it?'

Paul wandered off to the kitchen. 'CNN reported that there was a spontaneous candlelight vigil for Meredith and the other victim on the steps of the Capitol last night.'

'I saw some video clips this morning,' I called after him. 'I wonder what Lynx News has to say. Meredith Logan was one of theirs, after all.' I aimed the remote and switched the channel.

On Lynx, John Chandler was reporting. Either his regular make-up person was on vacation, or something was getting to him. Meredith's murder? Me? Something had deepened the railroad tracks that ran across his forehead, the creases on either side of his nose, darkened the shadows under his eyes. As I watched him talk, I found myself trying his face on against the few pictures I had of Zan.

Recently, I'd been doing a lot of mental Photoshopping with men of a certain age. Dying their hair, styling it differently, moving their parting from the right to the left and vice versa. I'd drawn a full head of hair on James Carville, given Bill O'Riley eyeglasses and a beard, taken fifty pounds off Rush Limbaugh. Even Bill Clinton wasn't exempt. Clinton's hair was right, but I decided his nose was too big to be Zan's. You never know, though. The former president did get around.

Nothing was happening on the TV, so I decided to go high-tech. Carrying the few photographs I had of Zan, I trotted downstairs to Paul's office and powered up the scanner. While it was digesting the photographs of Zan, I went online to Google, selected Images, and downloaded several full-face publicity shots of John Chandler.

Finally, I imported the images into iPhoto and clicked on 'Faces,' bringing up Apple's face recognition software, an iLife application I'd never gotten around to using. I informed the software that the guy standing on the church steps was Zan, then sat back to watch as the software suggested matches.

A picture of Paul. Not Zan, I clicked.

A picture of Dante. Not Zan either.

A photo of me, mugging it up for Halloween. Definitely not Zan.

I turned the tables, telling the software that John Chandler was John and asking it to find more faces that looked like John. It suggested Paul (but not Dante), a stranger we'd photographed while hiking the Appalachian trail, and the assistant priest at St Katherine's Episcopal Church, but never once hit on Zan.

Google's Picasa gave me similar results, helpfully picking out faces in the background, like photographs on people's desks, and objects in the background – an unlaced tennis shoe? – and inquiring if they were Zan.

'What are you doing?' Paul asked, coming up behind me with a half-eaten apple in his hand.

'Face recognition software,' I said. 'The low-tech version, apparently.'

'Any luck?'

'No.'

'It always seems to work on TV,' Paul said, chewing thoughtfully. *'Chica, chica, chica, chica, ding!* A match! Pull that guy away from the blackjack table and kick him out of the casino!'

'The photos I have of Zan are too low-resolution to be of any practical use,' I complained. 'And the software seems to gag on facial hair or sunglasses. I wouldn't have been surprised if it picked out that picture I took of a buffalo in Yellowstone Park and asked, "Is this Zan?"'

Paul squeezed my shoulder. 'I'm fixing some sandwiches, do you want one?'

I turned off the computer and gathered up my things, feeling discouraged. 'You go ahead, hon. I'm not particularly hungry.'

'OK, but if you change your mind, I'll be in the kitchen.'

*   *   *

Back upstairs, I sulked in front of the television. Chandler was interviewing a woman who'd been Photoshopped to the max. She'd had so much plastic surgery that nothing moved when she talked except her mouth, not even her hair. I stared at the screen in morbid fascination, watching for something – anything – to shift on the smooth, flat expanse of her countenance. I failed, but was so caught up in the effort that I could only partially focus on what she had to say about self-defense tactics for women.

And Your Point Is? devoted the last twenty minutes to coverage of Meredith Logan's vigil, including Chandler's interview with Meredith's grieving parents via satellite from Lawrence, Kansas. Photographs of the slain woman slid on and off the screen, interspersed with quotes from her Facebook page, and clips from YouTube videos of Meredith in happier times, some of them clearly shot on the campus of Bryn Mawr. The dead woman was the same age as Emily and my daughter's friend. Just thinking about it made my stomach roil.

Chandler ended his program by announcing a survey. Did we think the DC police were handling the investigation properly? John Chandler wanted – no, *begged* – for my vote.

I flipped the television off in disgust. Would it help the unfortunate victims to know that, say, seventy-six percent of the people watching Lynx News that afternoon – the ones who managed to drag their fat, conservative asses out of their chairs long enough to dial an 800-number, that is – thought the DC police were incompetent?

'Sometimes I think they just make the news up,' I sputtered, when Paul rejoined me carrying his sandwich. 'They're so biased that they don't even try to be subtle about it.'

He sat down on the arm of the sofa nearest my feet. 'Why do you bother to watch, then, if it makes you so mad?'

I shrugged. 'To keep my blood pressure up?'

'That's my Hannah! Remember when Chandler was interviewing that conservative bishop from Pittsburgh, the one who made all the derogatory remarks about the Archbishop of Canterbury and that gay bishop, Gene Robinson?' Paul took a bite of his sandwich.

'Robert Duncan?'

'That's the guy.'

'I can't even stand to *look* at him. Those big round glasses. Fleshy face. Goofy grin. When Chandler deferred to him and kept calling him "Archbishop Bob," I nearly barfed. Duncan's been *deposed*, for Christ's sake.'

'Now Duncan's aligned himself with the Anglican Church in Kenya,' I continued. 'Will you kindly tell me what an Archbishop in Africa has in common with an Episcopal church in Plano, Texas?'

Paul licked mayonnaise off his fingers. 'I think you're being a little hard on Chandler, Hannah. He's fair enough, I think. At least he doesn't finish his guest's sentences for them, or goad them into yelling at one another like brawling drunks.'

'Oh, I agree. He's polite and Catholic to the core. Yes Father, no Father, let me kiss your ring, Father.'

'Since when do you have a problem with Catholics?'

'I don't! But Chandler's right up there with Pope Benedict on keeping the ban against allowing priests to marry. Mother Church better wake up, in my opinion, or pretty soon every Catholic priest in the United States will come from South America. Or, he'll be a disgruntled Anglican who left the Episcopal Church because he objected to either women and/ or gay and lesbian people in the priesthood. In that case, it's *OK* if you're already married. Pope Benedict said so.'

Paul opened his mouth to put in his two cents' worth, but was interrupted by the telephone. I raised an eyebrow. 'Maybe that's Hoffner!'

Paul answered, listened for a second, gave me a thumbs up, then handed the phone to me.

'Hannah Ives?' the caller said.

'Yes. James Hoffner, I presume.'

Hoffner cleared his throat. 'I represent a client who tells me that you have some papers that belong to him.'

'Who might that be?'

'I'm not at liberty to say.'

'Then, I'm afraid I'm not at liberty to tell you whether I have any papers that belong to your client or not.'

'Mrs Ives. These papers are treasured family items. Old letters and photographs. My client would like to have them back.'

'How do I know that these letters and photographs actually belong to your client?' I asked. 'How do I know he didn't find them on the street? For that matter, how do I know they aren't stolen?'

On the other end of the line, Hoffner sighed. 'Just as I said, we're talking about my client's family heirlooms here.'

'How is your client recovering from his injuries?' I asked, hoping to catch the attorney off guard.

'I'm not at liberty to say.'

'May I speak to your client?'

'Not at this time.'

'Does that mean he's not able to speak to me?'

'I'm not at liberty to say.'

'Look, Mr Hoffner. You tell Skip, or whatever his name is, that I'll be happy to return the papers, but it will have to be either to Skip himself, or to his certified representative.'

'I can assure you, Mrs Ives, that I have full power of attorney to represent my client in this matter.'

'Good. Mail me a copy of your power of attorney, then. You know where I live. And, in the meantime, you might ask your client why his attorney was trying to pass himself off as somebody he is not. When you called at my house, you told my husband that those papers were yours. We both know that they are not.'

'Your husband simply misunderstood me, I'm afraid. I said I was *representing* the owner.'

I listened as Hoffner dug the hole deeper. When he'd run out of lame excuses, I said, 'Look, call me when Skip is well enough to see visitors, and if he can convince me that he's the legal owner of that box of material, I'll be happy to arrange a meeting.' And I hung up on the jerk.

Paul rolled his eyes. 'Don't mess with Hannah when she's interrupted in the middle of homophobic bishop bashing.'

'Ah, yes. It can get ugly.'

SIXTEEN

When you need to take it down a notch, nothing tops walking a dog. Dogs take pleasure in such basic things: barking, chewing, digging and burying, endless games of SniffMe-SmellYou, wagging their tails off from the sheer excitement of being alive.

To make best use of dog therapy, however, it helps to have a dog, so sometimes we borrow Coco, our daughter's irrepressible labradoodle, and walk her in nearby Quiet Waters Park.

Paul and I had returned Coco to her owners – muddy-pawed but refreshed – and headed home, leaving our filthy running shoes outside the back door.

'Funny. I thought I locked the door,' Paul said as we let ourselves into the kitchen.

'I better get the pork chops out of the freezer, or we'll never eat tonight,' I commented as I laid my handbag on the kitchen table.

'Thaw them in the microwave.' Paul tossed the remark over his shoulder as he headed upstairs to shower and change. He'd been gone only a few seconds when I heard him bellow, 'Hannah! Come here!'

'What?' I dropped the pork chops on the kitchen counter and hurried to see what was bothering him.

Paul stood in the dining room, flailing his arms. Every drawer in the sideboard stood open, and my linen tablecloths and napkins – which had been ironed and neatly folded, a task I hate – were strewn all over the carpet.

'Shit, shit, shit!' I started toward the living room when Paul's arm shot out, holding me back. 'They may still be in the house,' he cautioned. 'Go back to the kitchen and call 9-1-1.'

The Annapolis Police must have been sitting in their squad car right outside our door, because they appeared in less than five minutes. While we waited anxiously in the kitchen, two officers checked the house upstairs and down. The burglars were, of course, long gone. A neatly cut hole near the latch in the kitchen window illustrated where they'd come in. They'd obviously let themselves out through the back door.

'Is anything missing?' the older of the two officers wanted to know.

'Nothing that I see in the dining room.' Together we wandered into the living room where the decorative pillows had been tossed aside and the sofa cushions upended, but thankfully nothing appeared to be missing, not even our expensive hi-def TV.

We have three bedrooms upstairs, and they'd all been tossed. Drawers yawning open. Mattresses hauled off the box springs. Bedding in untidy heaps.

'My jewelry!' I cried. I rushed to the dresser and opened the teakwood box that contained all my treasures. I pawed through the box and was relieved to find that everything appeared to be there, including the sterling silver sweetheart bracelet my late mother had given me on my sixteenth birthday. I clutched it to my chest, tears of relief hazing my vision.

My closet, however, was a mess. Clothes had been ripped from their hangers and tossed unceremoniously on the floor. Shoe boxes which I'd labeled and neatly arranged on the upper shelf now yawned open on the bedroom floor; wedges, flats and dressy heels lay strewn about in a jumble. It was all too much. I perched on the foot of the bed and began to weep.

By the time the police had finished their investigation, handed us a copy of their report and promised to check back with us, I'd gotten my act together. 'This is worse than when the FBI trashed the joint back in 2005,' I complained, picking up a heap of blouses, still on their hangers and returning them to the closet.

Paul stood, hands on hips, surveying the wreckage of our bedroom. 'Looks like a hurricane blew through. And we have some experience with hurricanes.'

'And equally fruitless,' I sniffed. 'Lilith's letters are locked in the trunk of my car.'

'Is that what they were looking for?' Paul gave me a look.

'What else?' I returned the little French chair that I'd found at an antique store in Galesville to its normal and upright position next to my dresser and sat down in it. 'But who'd go to all this trouble just for a bunch of old photos and love letters?'

'My guess? Your friend, Skip. Or his "legal representative."' Paul made quote marks in the air.

'If Skip survived the crash, and that's a very big if in my opinion, all he has to do is contact me, prove he has a right to these papers, and I'll happily arrange to give them back.'

'Do you think that Jim Hoffner is actually working for Skip, or for somebody else?'

I thought back to my conversation with the lawyer. 'He didn't say, did he? But Hoffner had to have gotten my contact information from the hospital, right? So why not come out and say that he's working on Skip Whatchamacallit's behalf?'

'Maybe the guy you know as Skip doesn't *want* you to know who he really is. Think about it, Hannah. You said he confessed to killing someone. Remember? If he survived, perhaps he's thinking better of his deathbed confession.' The lines deepened between my husband's brows. 'Shit, Hannah. You could be in danger!'

I stood up, waded through the piles of bedding, and gave my husband a hug. 'I'll be fine. I've told a lot of people about Skip, and I'll make sure that even more people know about him.'

Paul pressed his lips against the top of my head. 'Lucky you had the letters in the car, then. Why was that, Hannah?'

'I intended to photocopy some of the envelopes and a couple of the photographs. Just in case.'

'In case of what?'

I swept an arm. 'Exhibit A.'

'I wonder if they're still together?' Paul said after a moment of silence.

'Who? Lilith and Zan? A love like that? It would be nice to think so, wouldn't it? Anthony and Cleopatra, Troilus and Cressida, Romeo and Juliet, Heloise and Abelard . . .'

Paul made a 'T' with his hands. 'Time out! Didn't all of those relationships end badly?'

I felt my face redden. 'Guess you're right. And now that I think about it, Heloise's uncle had Abelard castrated.' I shivered. 'Bad example.'

'So what is Skip's relation to the letters?'

'At first, I figured that Lilith was his mother. Now, I'm not so sure. Zan mentions his daughters from time to time, but he never mentions a son. Perhaps Lilith married somebody else after her relationship with Zan ended. Maybe that's where Skip came from. I know one person who could clear this all up in a flash, though.'

'Who?'

'Lilith Chaloux. If only I can find her.'

'Miracles happen,' my husband said.

SEVENTEEN

Early the following afternoon I'd finished returning the house to its usual state of gracious clutter and was scrubbing spaghetti sauce off the inside of the microwave – lunch leftovers had gone volcanic – when the miracle happened.

The telephone rang. 'Hannah, this is Elspeth Simon. In New York.'

'Oh, yes. I'm so glad you called.'

'Claire was sorting through some old Christmas cards the other day and you'll never guess what she found!'

'A Christmas card from Lilith?' I guessed, my heart pounding.

'The next best thing. A postcard from the dear girl.'

'That's wonderful!'

'There's no return address on it, unfortunately, but there's a picture of a deer on the front.' Elspeth paused for a moment. 'I'm looking at it now. A Sika deer, it says. Never heard of Sika deer, have you?'

'Actually, I have. We have them here in Maryland. They're not native, of course. They originally came from Japan.'

'Well, this postcard came from Maryland, too. A place called the Blackwater National Wildlife Refuge.'

I sat down on a kitchen chair and tried to catch my breath. Lilith had moved to Maryland? How could I be so lucky? The Blackwater refuge was on Maryland's Eastern Shore, just south of Cambridge. I'd visited it often, sometimes taking the grandchildren along for wildlife drives, bird walks and the annual eagle festival. What would be the chances that Lilith was still there?

'Is there a date?'

'The postmark is faded, but it looks like it could be 1988.'

'What does Lilith say on the postcard?'

'I'll read it to you.' Elspeth gave a ladylike cough and began. '"Elspeth and Claire, Darlings." She always called us that – darlings. "You will be surprised to hear that your big city girl is loving country life. Today, while I was painting, a doe stuck her nose right through the open cottage door! Give Pedro a cuddle for me! Love" – then she writes "X O X O X" – and an "L."'

'Elspeth, could you do me a big favor? Could you fax me a copy of the postcard?'

'We don't have a fax machine, dear.'

Of course they wouldn't have a fax machine. The sisters had to be in their eighties. What was I thinking?

'But,' Elspeth continued, 'I'll be happy to scan it for you. What's your email address?'

I had to laugh. 'Elspeth, you are a gem.'

'That's what all my boyfriends tell me.'

Elspeth Simon was as good as her word. Two days later, an email arrived from TwoOldBiddies@nyc.rr.com, with two attachments, PDF versions of the front and back of Lilith's postcard. I printed them out, but they didn't tell me anything I hadn't already learned from talking to Elspeth Simon on the telephone.

All I knew now was that approximately twenty-two years ago, in 1988, a young woman, then in her middle thirties, had settled down in a cottage, most likely in Dorchester County, Maryland, intending to paint.

Even after the Chesapeake Bay Bridge had connected the western shore of the Chesapeake Bay to Kent Island and beyond to Delaware, Virginia and the Atlantic Ocean beaches, Dorchester County had remained rural. With the exception of a ghastly commercial stretch paralleling Route 50 that had seen the recent addition of the Hyatt Regency Chesapeake Bay Golf Resort, Spa and Marina – say that three times fast – bucolic rusticity still pretty much ruled the day.

I popped out to the car, found my Rand McNally and spread it open on the kitchen table. Cambridge – population 12,000 – was always a possibility, but the word cottage suggested a more pastoral setting, so I decided to start with the smaller communities and work my way up.

And I really wanted a partner in crime.

I picked up the phone and called my sister. 'Ruth, what are you doing today?'

Shouting over the roar of a vacuum cleaner, she said, 'Hutch and I are working on our routine for the Dancesport Festival at College Park in November, but he just called to say he's got a deposition to prepare, so I guess I'm free.'

'You're not working at the store?'

'Neelie's got the con at Mother Earth today.'

'Good! You don't want to spend the day cleaning house, do you?'

Ruth switched off the vac. 'So, what's up, Nancy Drew?' she wondered aloud.

'You know me too well. I have a good lead on Lilith Chaloux. There's evidence she may have settled down in Dorchester County and I'd like company while I go poke around over there.'

'Dorchester County's a big place, Hannah.'

'From a postcard Lilith sent to the Simon sisters, I think she might have bought a cottage in the vicinity of the Blackwater Preserve, near Cambridge.'

'Oh, well, that *really* narrows it down!'

'I know, but I'd like to give it a shot. Come with me, please. It's a gorgeous day. The worse thing that will happen is that we'll have a lovely drive, stop for a lunch somewhere, and swing by one of the farm stands on Route 50 to buy some of the last tomatoes of the season. Vine-ripened.'

'You drive a hard bargain, Hannah. I was teetering on the fence until you mentioned the tomatoes. I'll be over in about an hour.'

As we drove over the Chesapeake Bay Bridge, my sister and I discussed strategy.

'What do you plan to do if you find her?' Ruth wanted to know. She flipped down the mirror on the sun visor and began fluffing up her gray hair with her fingers.

'I've got her letters in the trunk. I plan to return them.'

'I hate to burst your balloon, Hannah, but my theory is that she's passed away.'

'What? Lilith is young, only fifty-eight.'

'If she's still alive,' Ruth argued, 'why is this Skip person carrying her letters around with him?'

'Well, if Lilith is Skip's mother, or aunt – related to her, anyway – perhaps she asked him to have them scanned, to preserve them for the family archives or something.'

'Would *you* ask Emily to help you scan love letters from Paul?'

I thought about the letters Paul had written when we were separated one summer – both the letters and the summer sizzled – and said, 'No way.'

'OK. So do we agree? If Lilith is still alive, Skip probably stole them.'

'That's my working theory, too. Especially since somebody broke into our house looking for them.'

Ruth gasped, offended. 'When? You didn't tell me that!'

After I shared the gory details, Ruth said, 'That creeps me out! You must feel so violated.'

'I do. We'd been putting off installing a security system, but this pushed us over the edge. A consultant's coming to talk to us about it this weekend.'

Ruth and Hutch had installed a security system in their Conduit Street home, so Ruth educated me on the finer points of ADT until we reached Kent Narrows, at which point she suddenly switched horses to ask, 'So, what's your plan, Hannah?'

I pointed to a six-by-nine manila envelope propped up on the console between us. 'I made copies of two of the photographs of Lilith. I plan to show them around and ask if anybody's seen her.'

Ruth hooked a thumb through the chest strap on her seatbelt, tugging it out a couple of inches so she could turn in the passenger seat to face me. 'And what street corner are you planning to stand on, pray tell?'

'Think about it, Ruth,' I said as I took the exit toward Cambridge at the 50/301 split. 'If Lilith is still living around here, she has to buy groceries somewhere. Send and receive mail. Get her car serviced.' I shrugged. 'It's worth a shot, anyway. And if that doesn't pan out, I'll ask at some of the local art galleries. Lilith was an artist, remember.'

'Well, frankly, I think it's a long shot, Hannah. I'm just along because you promised me lunch. And the tomatoes, of course. Where are we going for the aforementioned lunch, by the way?'

'Portside in Cambridge.'

'That place right on the water?'

'Yes.'

Ruth clapped her hands like a four-year-old. 'Goody, goody.'

An hour later, we crossed the bridge that took us over the Choptank River, turned right into Cambridge, and pulled into the parking lot at Portside. Soon, Ruth and I were sharing an order of the restaurant's award-winning hot crab dip, followed by fish and chips for me and spinach salad for Ruth.

On the off chance that Lilith might have dined at Portside, I showed her picture to the waitress when she came to refill our glasses with iced tea.

The waitress held the picture by the corner between a French-manicured thumb and forefinger, studied it briefly, then glanced back at me. 'You a private detective or something?'

'She's Nancy Drew,' said my sister.

The waitress grinned, displaying a full set of pearly whites.

'Get out!' She looked at the photo again. 'Wish I could help you, but I can't. Don't think I've ever seen this girl before, and I've worked here pretty much every day since the place opened.' She handed the photo back.

'Thanks anyway,' I said, tucking the photo into its envelope.

Ocean Gateway. Sunburst Highway. Route 50 to you and me. A strip of unrelenting concrete, bordered on both sides by gas stations, fast food restaurants, cut-rate motels, and big-box drug stores. From the CVS you could hit the Rite Aid with a well-aimed prescription bottle.

No surprise, then, that I decided to avoid Route 50 altogether and head out into the countryside the back way. I drove Ruth across the Market Street bridge, then took a slow loop through the historic colonial town before heading south on Race Street. We were driving through farmland in no time. Where Church Creek Road intersected with Golden Hill Road at the Church Creek community proper, I pulled into the parking lot in front of the tiny post office and stuck my nose in.

When the postmistress finished with a customer, I approached the counter, trotted out my high school reunion story, and showed her Lilith's picture. 'Her name is Lilith Chaloux, at least it was when I knew her.'

The postmistress shook her head. 'She doesn't keep a box here. If she did, I'd certainly know about it.' She handed the picture back. 'You might try Woolford.' She pointed west. 'Continue on that way. From this point on, it's Taylor's Island Road. Winds around a bit, but in about two miles you'll get to the Country Store. It's on the right. If your friend lives anywhere around there, that's where she'll do business.'

I thanked the woman and headed back to the car.

Five minutes later, Ruth and I pulled into the parking lot of the Woolford Country Store, a three-story, white-frame structure with dark chocolate trim. I recognized the post office by the American flag flying from a pole out front, otherwise I might have missed it. The single-story building was attached to one side of the store like an afterthought, which it prob-ably was.

While Ruth popped into the store to see if she could hook up with an Eskimo Pie, I ducked in to the post office.

The woman on duty behind the counter looked up from a form she was filling out and asked if she could help me.

'I'm trying to find this woman,' I said, handing her Lilith's picture.

The postmistress studied it for a moment, then said, 'She's older now, of course, but this looks a lot like Lilith Chaloux.' She pronounced the name Shall-locks. 'She's such a pretty girl, isn't she? Absolutely enchanting.'

My heart flip-flopped inside my chest. 'How long has Lilith lived here?'

'Oh, quite a while.' She handed the picture back across the counter. 'More than twenty years, I'd say. Isn't that right, Penny?'

The postmistress was addressing a woman standing at a chest-high table near the window, patiently peeling stamps out of a booklet and applying them with scientific exactness to the upper right-hand corner of a pile of bright orange envelopes. In the bad old days, her tongue would have been heavy with glue, and she wouldn't have been able to answer so quickly. 'Lilith? The artist? Oh, I say twenty years at least!'

'Can you tell me where I might find her?'

The postmistress frowned, but not in an unfriendly way. 'It would be against federal regulations for me to tell you any more than that, now wouldn't it?' She brightened. 'But you could write her a letter and I could slip it into her post office box. You'll need to stamp it, of course.'

'Well,' Penny interrupted, mashing her fist down on top of one of her stamps like a hammer. 'I certainly don't operate under federal government regulations. Why are you looking for Lilith? Do you mind telling me?'

'We went to the same high school, but we've lost track of one another. I'm trying to find her for our fortieth reunion.' With one eye still on the helpful postmistress, I added, 'I'd love to talk to her in person, of course. It's been too long.'

Penny pushed her stamped envelopes through the Outgoing Mail slot, then said, 'Lilith keeps pretty much to herself, always did, but when she comes to town, she's friendly enough. She lives off Deep Point Road, in a cottage that looks out over Fishing Creek. Woods all around. Very isolated. Haven't seen her recently, though.'

'Have you ever been to the cottage? Is it easy to find?'

Penny managed a crooked grin. 'It's up the road just a bit. Keep looking for Deep Point. It'll turn off to the right. You can't miss it. There's a green street sign. The cottage, now, it's on a dirt lane that turns off to the left between two fields. If you get to Deep Water Road, you've gone too far.' She whirled her index finger in the air. 'Just turn around and come back.'

'Good luck!' she said as I headed toward the door. 'I hope you find her.'

I smiled. 'If she's not at home, I'll just leave a note. Thank you both, so much.'

As I left the post office, Penny called after me, 'I hope your car has a good suspension system!'

I found Ruth still in the grocery, paying the cashier for two Eskimo Pies.

'I've found her!' I whispered in her ear.

'Oh my God! You are a witch!'

Because the day was still sunny, we decided to eat our ice cream on the front porch while I brought Ruth up to speed on what I'd learned. Eager to get underway, I wolfed down my ice cream so fast I got an excruciating case of sinus freeze. While squeezing the bridge of my nose between my thumb and fore-finger, I tossed the wrapper in the trash. I practically dragged Ruth, who was still licking ice cream off her fingers, from the porch by the intricate gold hoop dangling from her ear.

'Look for a dirt road between two fields,' I instructed my sister ten minutes later as we inched along Deep Point Road following the directions Penny had given me. 'It'll be on the left.'

After a short distance, Ruth's arm shot out across the dashboard. 'There!' she said, pointing.

I slowed to a crawl. Two ruts led off the road to our left. After approximately five hundred yards, they disappeared into the trees.

'Does *that* count as a road?' Ruth wondered.

I wasn't sure, so we drove a bit further. At Deep Water Road, I groaned, executed a three-point turn and headed back in the direction we'd just come, pulling to a stop at the rutted road we'd spotted earlier. 'I guess that's it.'

We turned right and bumped along for about half a mile, undergrowth brushing our undercarriage, the trees closing in, dark and dense, all around us. Eventually, the road opened into a clearing.

Perched on a low bank above the creek was an English country cottage built of stone, so English, in fact, that I suspected it had been standing there since 1750, built by one of our founding fathers. Two pairs of windows flanked a central door, all facing away from the water, which was another clue that the cottage hadn't been built in the twenty-first century, where water views sold at a premium. The road ended at a covered carport, but there was no car in the drive. 'I guess she's not home,' Ruth said. She looked as crestfallen as I felt. 'Do you suppose we should come back later?'

'Come on, Ruth,' I hissed. 'Moment of truth.'

As we approached the cottage, we could hear a conversation going on inside. 'She *is* home,' I said. 'Oh, ye of little faith.'

'Do you think Lilith has company?' Ruth wondered as we climbed the brick steps that led up to the front door. 'If so, where are the cars? Are we to assume that everybody *walked*? Not very likely.'

My sister and I paused on the narrow porch, listening, straining our ears. Men's voices in heated discussion.

I leaned to one side and peeked through one of the windows, but the curtains were drawn and no light shone through from the room inside. 'I think she has the TV on,' I said after a moment, feeling foolish. I tapped Ruth on the arm. 'Knock, silly.'

There was no answer.

'Maybe she can't hear you over the blare of the television.'

Ruth knocked again, harder this time, and as we stood on the doorstep gaping, the front door swung slowly open. 'Ooops,' she said.

I pushed against the door with the flat of my hand, but it wouldn't open more than a few inches. 'Something's blocking it from the inside,' I said, beginning to get worried.

'Let's try around back,' Ruth suggested, and headed off at a trot.

When I caught up with my sister, she was waiting for me by the back door. It stood wide open.

'She could be in trouble,' I reasoned. 'We should probably go in. Agreed?'

When Ruth nodded, I stepped inside.

Lilith's back door opened on to a narrow passageway which was piled nearly to the ceiling on both sides with cardboard boxes. Fearing an avalanche, we picked our way carefully through the tunnel, expecting it to lead to the kitchen.

It did.

One look at what lay ahead made me stop so suddenly that Ruth crashed into me from behind. 'Oh my God!' I said. 'How can anyone cook in this place?'

Like the hallway we'd just passed through, the kitchen was littered with boxes, some stacked, others leaning haphazardly against one another, their contents spilled, mingling with the contents of the box below. By the light of a single bulb in an overhead fixture designed for six, we could see that every surface – the kitchen counters, the stovetop – was littered with stuff with a capital 'S.' A mountain of newspapers, magazines and junk mail in the corner could have hidden a kitchen table, but it would have taken a forklift to tell.

I picked a pile of mail off the top of – what? – a toaster oven? – relieved to see that it was addressed to Lilith Chaloux. In 2006. We were definitely in the right house, I thought with relief, but where was Lilith?

I stepped carefully around a collection of Fiestaware mixing bowls – brand new – nested on the floor. I opened the oven. Inside I found hundreds of frozen food cartons – Lean Cuisine, Healthy Choice, Amy's Kitchen, Linda McCartney – washed, folded flat and stacked.

Ruth peered over my shoulder. 'What the hell is she saving those for?'

'I'm afraid Lilith's a hoarder, like those people on reality

TV.' I closed the oven door, wiped my hands on my jeans. 'How can people *live* like this?'

'Oh my God,' Ruth said, indicating some Styrofoam containers stacked six high that were filled with – she peeked into the one on top – unopened bags of Oreo cookies. Ruth held up a grocery store receipt. 'Can you believe it? These cookies were purchased on special in 1992.' She squinted at the receipt. 'Thirty packages of them.'

Lilith had kept a path clear between the refrigerator and the microwave, and from the microwave to the sink. Otherwise, it would have been impossible to move around the room.

I opened the refrigerator. Aside from a carton of eggs and a half gallon of milk two weeks past its sell-by date, all it contained were a dozen bottles of Veuve Clicquot Brut and ten 250g cans of Royal Beluga caviar.

That was a stumper.

I must be Alice, I thought, well and truly trapped on the other side of the looking glass.

At a signal from me, Ruth began to wade through the clutter toward the front of the house, stepping high. 'This is downright dangerous,' she complained, side-stepping an old typewriter table that was listing to starboard under the weight of a dot matrix computer printer and maybe a decade's worth of telephone books. 'Lilith could be in trouble.'

'Is anybody here?' Ruth yelled as she disappeared around the corner.

I hurried, bucking and weaving, to catch up. On the way, I popped into the living room and discovered why the front door refused to budge when we pushed on it. Over time, boxes from QVC and HSN had been stacked, still unopened, around the door. Plastic mailers from L.L. Bean and Lands' End had been piled on top, adding to the accumulation. At some point, the piles had collapsed, partially blocking the entrance.

To my right, under the window, a sofa and chair were heaped with unopened boxes from Amazon. And if you needed to reach the front door, like in an emergency, you'd have to first clear a path through the forest of light bulbs, toilet paper, paper towels, and batteries still in their plastic shopping bags from Target that were strewn over the carpet. Either that, or hire a guide.

I hurried as fast as I could after Ruth, kicking aside boxes of envelopes, paper clips and three-and-a-quarter-inch floppy disks as I went. I was surround by evidence of Lilith's aborted attempts to tame the chaos – Rubbermaid tubs in all shapes and sizes, nested Tupperware containers (still nested), space bags, desktop organizers – purchased with every good intention for $19.95 plus shipping and handling, from companies that advertised on late-night television that their amazing products were 'Not available in stores!'

I found my sister standing in front of the bathroom at the end of the cluttered hall, looking bewildered. Boxes loomed over her dangerously, like the walls of the Grand Canyon. She raised both arms. 'There's a bedroom on each side. Nobody's here,' she reported, 'but the TV is sure on.'

The television in the bedroom was cube-like and huge, a model so ancient that I expected it could receive *Howdy Doody*, *I Love Lucy* or *Bonanza* direct. On the screen, though, modern-day Lynx News social commentator Candace Kelly, every Titian hair perfectly contained, was nattering on about some girls who had been turned away from their homecoming dance because the school found their dresses unsuitable. 'Does everybody watch Lynx News?' I wondered.

'Why don't we turn it off?' Ruth suggested.

While Ruth floundered around the bedroom looking for the remote, I watched the crawl at the bottom of the screen where I learned that 'Hiccup girl' had been charged with murder and L'il Wayne was ready to party after his release from jail; pseudo-news that ran the gamut from 'What the hell?' to 'Who cares?'

'You'll need to send out a search party for the remote, I'm afraid.' Ruth waved an arm, taking in the piles of clothing draped over every available surface, including the bed, some still wearing their price tags. 'And good luck even reaching the TV. My bet? She leaves it on all the time.'

'Where the hell does she sleep?' I wondered, backing out into the hall and pushing open the door to the second bedroom. It, too, was chock-a-block with unopened boxes containing

God only knew what. If there was a bed in the room it would take Lewis and Clark, maybe Sacajawea too, to find it.

I bent over, out of habit, to pick up a pair of red leather gloves, still connected at the wrists by a plastic clip, that lay on the carpet at my feet. I held them in my hand for a moment, then tossed them over my shoulder. Even if Ruth and I became overcome by an irresistible urge to pick up, where on earth would we begin?

'Come on, Ruth. Let's get out of here.'

'Where does Lilith paint?' Ruth wondered aloud, as we ran the gauntlet, winding our way out of Lilith's pathetic cottage the way we had come.

'Unless she's given it up, she probably has a studio somewhere. Perhaps that's where she is now. The Simon sisters told me she kept a separate studio when she lived in New York.'

Once outside, I breathed deeply, expelling the dark and the dust. Face to the sun, I inhaled the fresh fall air in grateful gulps. To our left, a narrow path led off through the trees. Through the branches, just now beginning to shed their leaves, I could see the late-afternoon sun glittering on the waters of what my map had told me was a little cove off Fishing Creek. 'We're so close to finding her,' I said. 'I just hate to leave.'

'Hannah, for all we know, Lilith's away on vacation, sunning herself on a beach in the south of France. Who knows when she'll get back.'

'But the house is unlocked,' I reasoned.

Ruth snorted. 'Why lock it? Any self-respecting thief would take one look at that place, throw up his hands and high tail it out of there.' She grinned wickedly. 'Maybe that's Lilith secret plan to clear the place out!'

I laughed. 'You're right, of course. I'm going to leave a note. Ask her to call me.' I tore a sheet of paper out of the notebook I keep in the glove compartment to write down important things like the license plate numbers of cars that cut me off in traffic and the vehicle identification numbers of negligent trucks that spew out gravel and pockmark my windshield. On it I wrote: 'My name is Hannah Ives and I live in Annapolis. I have something that belongs to you. Please call me so that I can arrange to return it.'

I added my telephone number, stuffed the note into a Ziploc bag I had snitched from a box of one hundred on the floor of the kitchen, then tucked the note between the back door and the frame, closing the door securely over it.

'What now, Nancy Drew?'

'Now, we go home and wait.'

EIGHTEEN

Three days later, early on a Sunday morning, Lilith called. I was charmed by her voice, Lauren Bacall-esque, smooth, low and husky. 'I got your message,' she breathed. 'Can you tell what this is all about?'

'It's something best discussed in person,' I said. 'Is there a convenient time for me to drive over?'

'How did you find me?' she wanted to know.

'The Simon sisters in New York,' I said, shading the truth just a little.

'Oh, yes. Claire and Elspeth. They were very sweet to me. Are they well?'

'Very.'

'I don't suppose Pedro . . . well, no, he wouldn't still be alive, would he. It's been . . . well, more years than I care to admit.'

'Pedro's moved on to the Daisy Hill Puppy Farm in the sky, I'm afraid. They have a German shepherd named Bruno now.'

Lilith laughed out loud, a sound that bubbled out of her, overflowing like sparkling champagne. 'Who is walking whom, I wonder? Oh, I was so in love with those women.'

I'd never laid eyes on Lilith, but I was falling in love with her, too. 'When would be convenient for us to meet, Lilith? I'm fairly flexible.'

'I keep busy with my painting, but otherwise I have very

little on my schedule. Is tomorrow good for you? Around two?'

'That would be perfect,' I told her.

'You know where I live,' she said, 'but please meet me at my studio. If you carry on past the house about a hundred yards down a little path, you'll come to it. It's right on the water.'

No surprise that Lilith didn't want to meet me at the house. Where would we sit for our conversation? In the bathroom? Lilith on the toilet seat and me on the rim of the tub?

'Two o'clock tomorrow, then. Your studio,' I said. 'I'll be there,'

I hung up the phone and ran a little victory loop around the house, whooping like a rodeo cowboy.

I called Ruth at once, but she and Hutch had paid in advance for dance studio time and were locked into rehearsals. Paul was tied up teaching, and his sister, Connie, would be spending the afternoon waiting for the plumber to come repair her hot-water heater. My father, always game for adventure, was finishing up the last month of a year-long consulting job in Dubai. When the time came, I'd have to go alone.

What would I wear?

I opened my closet and reached reflexively for my favorite black and white paisley dress. My hand closed around the padded blue silk hanger where the dress normally lived. I pulled the hanger out of the closet. Empty.

Black and white and red all over.

My dress was ruined, I remembered with a pang, discarded, moldering in a landfill, soaked with somebody else's blood.

I pawed through the remaining garments, trying to find something else to wear. It was too hot for this one, too cold for that. Too long, too short, too small, too big. No, no, no, no! Tears began to stream down my cheeks.

I tossed a perfectly good A-line skirt on the floor, followed by a blouse, a pair of slacks. One dress, then another – no, no, no! I didn't stop, couldn't, until I collapsed in the middle of the heap, buried my face in a hand-painted sweatshirt and bawled until my eyelids swelled shut.

Paul found me there an hour later, dry-eyed and gasping,

the designer sweatshirt wrapped around my head. 'I couldn't find anything to wear,' I sobbed.

Paul fell to his knees, drew me into his arms, held my head gently against his chest, and rocked me like a baby. Next to the beating of his heart, I felt warm and secure.

'It's PTSD,' he said, stroking my cheek. He touched his lips to my ear and whispered, 'There are people who can help you with that, Hannah.'

'It's, it's . . .' I drew a shuddering breath. 'When I read in the paper about Tashawn Jackson's funeral, I wanted to go, I really did, even though I probably would have been the only white face in the church. I felt I owed it to him, Paul. But what would I say when his mother asked, "And who are you?" Do I say, "Your boy took my seat on that train. Now I'm alive and he's dead?"'

'Shhh, shhh,' my husband crooned, gently rocking.

'I could be dead, Paul, dead! I didn't live through the surgery and chemo just so I could die before my time on a stupid train! And then I thought, how selfish you are, Hannah. Tashawn had his whole life in front of him, and you're old. Old!' I looked up into Paul's face, touched his cheek, rough against my hand. 'It should have been me,' I whimpered. 'But, oh Paul, I'm so glad it wasn't me!'

'I thank God it wasn't you, too,' my husband said, stroking my hair.

I slept long and hard that night, awakening an hour after the coffee pot had started its automatic cycle.

Paul had already left for work, but while I slept, he'd thoughtfully picked up all the clothes I'd strewn about the room and hung them back in my closet.

In the end, for my visit with Lilith, I settled on a pair of slim black slacks and a lightweight blue sweater, paired with a matching set of aquamarine earrings. I took some time with my make-up. Why? I couldn't say. Perhaps I didn't want to feel frumpy next to a woman who, at least when young, had been a great beauty. Concealer to minimize the dark bags under my eyes. Eyebrows, eyeliner, lipstick and blush. A touch of twilight blue on the lids. If Paul had come into the bathroom that minute, he'd have thought I was cheating on him.

Lilith's Garfinkel's bag looked like it had been dragged through a hedge backwards, so before I left the house, I tucked it into a canvas tote.

I retraced the route to Woolford, parked behind Lilith's Toyota at the end of her drive, and was hauling the tote out of the back seat when Lilith appeared out of the woods, almost like an apparition. She was dressed in pipe-stem blue jeans and a tailored white shirt, unbuttoned, her shirt tails floating gently over a pale-pink scoop-necked tee. 'Hello,' she said. 'You must be Hannah.'

Although Lilith was thirty years older than the pictures I carried, I would have known her anywhere. We all should age so gracefully. Her dark hair was laced with threads of silver, but the graying had progressed so evenly that one could easily mistake it for highlighting. Skilful highlighting, too. A dye job you'd pay extra for. She had the same slight frame, and as she approached, she moved with elegant grace. I imagined her as a young girl, practicing that walk while balancing a dictionary on her head.

I held out my hand. 'I'm delighted to meet you, Lilith.'

Lilith's azure eyes strayed to the tote in my hand, then back to my face without betraying a single ill-mannered sign of curiosity. 'Before we get down to business,' she said, 'I'd like to show you my studio.'

After visiting Lilith's house, I was holding my breath, mentally bracing for the studio experience. I followed her down a straight, narrow path to a wooden A-frame structure a hundred yards or so from the creek. Imagine my surprise when she opened a door and led me into a spacious room that pulsed with light and color. White-white walls and pale oak floors seemed to go on forever. A chaise lounge was tucked into a corner by a wall of windows that framed the water view, a colorful crocheted afghan neatly draped over its arm. Next to the chaise, a camera was mounted on a tripod, its lens pointing outside, ready for the next shot.

On an easel in the center of the room stood Lilith's work in progress, a painting of a toy sailboat floating on water amid a sea of fall leaves. Clipped to the easel was a photograph of the same scene. 'You're still into photorealism, I see.'

With her eyes on the painting, she smiled. 'It's light that's always interested me, Hannah – how it's reflected, refracted, diffused and distorted by the water.'

Although the work was incomplete, I felt I could reach into the painting, swirl my hand through the leaves and come out wet. 'What's it called?'

She grinned. 'Sailboat Twenty-three.'

Finished canvases – still lifes and landscapes – were propped up against the wall to my right, and to my left was a tiny kitchenette with a hotplate, where a teakettle was just starting to scream.

'I'm making tea,' she told me. 'Lady Grey. Would you like some?'

'Yes, thank you. That would be lovely.'

When the tea was ready, she carried the tray outside to a table on a round concrete patio. From the patio, a leaf-strewn lawn sloped gently down to the creek where, at the end of a short dock, a motorboat was tied. Closer to shore, a kayak bobbed.

'Milk and sugar?'

I shook my head. 'Do you get out on the water often?' I asked as Lilith stirred milk and sugar into her tea.

'Every day I can. I find paddling a kayak very relaxing. Nature's chorus sings all around you in a kayak. A motorboat drowns it out. I keep the motorboat in case of emergency, of course.'

'I know what you mean about motors,' I agreed. 'My husband and I sail, but only on other people's boats.' We sipped in silence for a while, listening to the susurrus of the wind in the trees.

'You mentioned you had something that belongs to me,' Lilith said at last.

I pulled the Garfinkel's bag out of my canvas tote and set it on the table between us.

Lilith's eyes widened in genuine surprise. She laid a hand lightly on the bag. 'Where on earth did you get this?'

'I'm afraid it comes with some bad news.' I told Lilith about the Metro crash, about the gravely injured man I'd comforted. 'He told me his name was Skip.'

Lilith exhaled slowly, then looked away, swiping sudden tears away with the back of her hand. 'That's what they called him in school, because he was always cutting class.'

'Your son?'

Still staring out over the water, Lilith nodded. 'His given name is Nicholas. Nicholas Ryan Aupry.'

Aupry. Where had I heard that name before? Was Nicholas actually Aupry's son?

'I'm so sorry,' I said. 'I wish I could tell you what happened to your son, but when I asked the hospital for information I didn't know his name, so naturally they refused to tell me anything.'

While I waited for Lilith to comment, my mind raced, paging through the names of the seven train crash victims. None had been named Nicholas Aupry. I was positive of that.

Lilith set her cup down carefully, centering it on the saucer. She smiled knowingly. As if reading my mind, she said, 'He's not dead, I'm sure of that.'

My heart did a somersault. 'So, you've been in touch?'

'No. But, if Nick had died of his injuries, somebody would have contacted me. I'm his only next of kin.'

'I don't mean to pry,' I said, fully intending to, 'but why did Skip – excuse me, Nick – have your letters with him?'

'I didn't even know they were missing. I haven't seen them since Nicholas . . .' Her voice trailed off.

Small wonder, I thought to myself. If the box of letters had been in Lilith's cottage . . . well, you could park a construction dumpster in the driveway and spend a week hauling stuff out of Lilith's cottage and no one would notice a bit of improvement.

Yet her studio was impeccable. Clearly, this place was her refuge.

'So Nick stole your letters?' I asked.

She nodded, her face twisted with anguish. 'Apparently.'

'Why?'

'I imagine he's trying to track down his father.'

Something wasn't making sense. There had been no mention of a child in the letters. No mention of anyone named Aupry. Yet, if clues to Skip's paternity lay in those letters, then his father had to be Zan.

'Zan?' I asked.

She raised one elegant eyebrow.

'Sorry,' I said. 'When I couldn't track Skip down, I had to look through the letters for clues in order to find you.' After a moment, I said, 'I hope I'm not being too nosy, but is Nick's father named Alexander Aupry?'

Lilith smiled enigmatically. 'No.'

'Why didn't Skip take his father's name, then?'

I was hoping she'd let her lover's name slip and I could catch John Chandler in a lie, but she simply looked pained and said, 'Things were different back then, Hannah. An unmarried woman. An unexpected pregnancy.'

Suddenly, Lilith smiled. 'Unexpected, but definitely not unwanted. Nick was my gift from Zan, and Zan . . .' She shrugged. 'Well, Zan was no longer part of my life. So . . .' She took a deep breath and let it out slowly. 'We, that is my family and I, decided it would be best if Nick were raised by my mother's brother in Switzerland. Nick always knew I was his mother, but . . . well, for many reasons, it was easier if he took his uncle's name.'

That's where I'd heard the name before – in the report of the Air France crash that took the lives of Lilith's parents: Lucille Aupry. Aupry was Lilith's mother's maiden name.

I wondered what Lilith meant by 'family.' By my reckoning, her parents had been dead for almost twenty years by the time Nick was born. Who did the troubled young woman turn to for advice? Her aunt? Her grandmother?

Lilith sat quietly, gnawing on a thumbnail as if trying to decide how much to tell me. Finally, she looked up. 'When Nick got old enough to ask about his father, I lied. I told him I didn't know who his father was. Before Nick was born, I lived in New York City, as you know, working as an artist. I was part of the "New York scene."' She drew quote marks in the air with her fingers. 'Painting all day, clubbing every night. Sex, drugs, rock and roll. Some nights I never went to bed at all. I'm not proud of that, mind you. I'm just telling it like it was.

'Do you remember Andy Warhol's show, *Fifteen Minutes*? On MTV?' she continued.

I stifled a groan. I suppose there must have been a time when MTV actually aired music videos rather than littering the television landscape with mindless prank and reality shows like *Jackass* and *Jersey Shore* respectively, but I was never a dim-witted twelve-to-eighteen-year-old, so I never fit in with their demographics. 'On MTV? I must have missed it.'

'I appeared in Warhol's first episode, along with Jerry Hall and Dweezel and Moon Zappa.' Lilith grinned. 'That was in 1986.

'I don't know what came over me, but I told Nick that he was the result of a one-night stand. Honestly, you'd think I could come up with something better than that, even when stoned.

'The last time Nick came to visit, we had an argument about . . . well, never mind. I left him alone in the house, to stew in his own juice, and went out by myself to the movies in Cambridge. Nicholas doesn't deal very well with chaos. That's probably when he found . . .'

Lilith slid the package off the table and placed it in her lap, cradling it against her breast like the precious object it was. 'Nicholas looks a lot like his father when his father was the same age,' she said. 'Sometimes when I look at my son . . . well, my heart aches.'

'And Zan is . . . who?'

Lilith chuckled. 'If I wouldn't tell Nick, my own son, why would I tell you, Hannah?'

I felt my face redden. 'Sorry.'

'No need to be.' She drained her cup and set it down carefully on the saucer. 'It's something that happened a long time ago. No need to dredge it up. Both Zan and I live other lives now.

'One thing that puzzles me, though, Hannah. If Nicholas is still alive, most likely recovering from his injuries somewhere, why didn't he contact you? You said you left word at the hospital telling him that you had his package.'

I decided there'd be no harm in telling Lilith about the sleazy lawyer who'd come knocking at my door. 'I believe your son is working through an attorney. I think there's a very good reason he's doing that. He doesn't want me to know who he is.'

Lilith blinked. 'Why on earth?'

'Back on the train, when Skip thought he was dying?' I paused, trying to recall Skip's exact words. 'He confessed to a killing.'

'Nick? You have to be joking.'

'I'm afraid not. He didn't tell me any more than that, but I held his hand and we prayed together. Whatever happened afterwards, I like to think that prayer gave him peace of mind.'

Lilith reached out and squeezed my hand. 'Thank you for that, Hannah. Not everyone would have been so caring, especially under the circumstances. My God, it must have seemed like a war zone.'

The horrors of that day seemed another world away from Lilith's quiet garden, where the sun dappled the autumn leaves and decorated the water with shimmering light. 'What troubles me is this,' I said after a moment. 'If Skip asked me to pray with him about his role in a killing, maybe he doesn't *want* to be found.' A chilling thought entered my head. 'Do you think Skip tracked down and murdered his father?'

Lilith smiled. 'No, no. Zan is very much alive.'

Hearing that, I felt a great sense of relief. 'You still see him, then?'

'Alas, no. We haven't been together since 1987.' Again, she stared off into the trees as if a memory were painted there. 'We spent a magical New Year's Eve in Seville.'

'If Skip is twenty-three . . .' I counted backwards and came to the obvious conclusion. 'Zan doesn't know about Skip, does he?'

'No. I never told him.'

'Why not?

'Hannah, Zan was Roman Catholic. He had a wife and two young daughters. I just couldn't.' She pressed a hand to her mouth, took a deep breath. 'We'd already gone our separate ways when . . . well, when I found out that Nicholas was on the way.'

'But surely, if Zan had known—' I began.

Lilith raised a hand, halting me in mid-sentence. 'Zan and I were soulmates. Separating from him was the hardest thing I ever had to do. It nearly killed me. It nearly killed us both. But after we'd made the decision to part, the last thing in the world I wanted was for Zan to come back to me purely out of a sense of obligation.'

I nodded, encouraging her to go on.

'I wasn't much of a mother, I'm afraid. More tea?'

As she tipped the teapot and refilled our cups, she continued. 'Money wasn't an issue, so Nick went to boarding schools, here and abroad. He got a great education, that's true. Graduated with honors from Stanford. He's just started working at the Johns Hopkins Applied Physics Lab on some project involving thought-controlled prosthetic limbs. I can't begin to understand it.'

'What did he hope to find among your letters?'

'Proof of his father's identify, I guess.' Then she told me something I already knew. 'But there's no evidence of that in Zan's letters. As I said, he didn't know.'

'But wouldn't DNA testing establish that Zan is his father?'

'Of course. But Nick would have to locate his father first.'

'And get him to submit to the test,' I added.

Lilith nodded in agreement, then said, 'As I said, I didn't even know Nick had taken Zan's letters. I keep them in . . .' She waved a hand. 'Under my bed.'

'What do you suppose he wants from his father?'

'Acknowledgement would be my guess.' She stared off into the trees where two crows were engaged in a noisy squabble over prime position on a limb. 'As I said, Nick's last visit ended badly. I've tried calling him on his cell to smooth things over. I've left messages, but he's not calling me back. I thought maybe the lab sent him away on business. I didn't know about the accident, of course.'

'I lost my cell phone in the crash. I suspect that Nick did, too. And if he's still in the hospital . . .'

'I love my son, Hannah, but he's never been a very likable

boy. He's willful. Selfish. It ate him up inside that he didn't have a dad like the other boys.' She folded her hands on the table in front of her and leaned forward. 'How will I find Nick if he doesn't want to be found?'

'Now that I know Nick's real name, I think I can help you with that. My brother-in-law is a policeman. They have their ways!'

Lilith's face brightened. 'Thank you! You'll let me know?'

'Of course.' Since I seemed to be in Lilith's good graces, I decided to risk pushing my luck. 'Can I ask you a personal question?'

'What's that?'

'You told me Zan was married. Does Zan's wife know about your relationship?'

Lilith stared deep into her cup, swirling the liquid around as if reading her answer in the tea leaves. Without looking up, she said, 'Honestly? I don't know.'

'Whose idea was it to break off the affair?'

'Believe it or not, it was mine. "I looked for no marriage bond, no marriage portion. The name of wife may seem more sacred or more binding, but sweeter for me will always be the word friend."'

It was obvious that she was quoting, but I didn't recognize the source. 'Sorry?'

Lilith sighed wistfully. 'Heloise to Abelard. Zan was fond of quoting Barrett-Browning. I think it rather annoyed him that the poetry I borrowed was far more Catholic and philosophical in nature.' She swept her arm in a theatrical arc. '"She is all States, and all Princes, I. Nothing else is. Shine here to us, and thou art everywhere; This bed thy centre is, these walls, thy sphere." John Donne,' she quickly added, in case I didn't recognize the poet.

I hadn't.

Lilith looked so somber that I burst out laughing. 'Give me a moment and I might be able to recite Part One of *The Rime of the Ancient Mariner*, but I think I'll spare you.'

'Zan could have confessed to his wife after we separated, of course,' Lilith continued after a moment. 'As I said, he was a devout Roman Catholic – we both were – but repentant wasn't the word I'd use to describe us. There's only so many times you can go into a confessional and ask forgiveness for the sin of adultery before the Good Lord sees fit to slap you down.'

'Ten years,' I muttered softly.

'Exactly. And Zan and I embraced that particular sin every chance we got, as you probably surmised from reading Zan's letters.'

My face grew hot. A voyeur, I'd been caught in the act.

Lilith's smiled sympathetically. 'You know how I signed *my* letters to Zan? No, of course you don't. "My only love." I still love him. Always will.'

The lyrics of a hauntingly beautiful duet sung by Placido Domingo and Maureen McGovern began running through my head, a song that never fails to make me cry when it pops up on my iPod shuffle, and was doing its best to unhinge me now: *a love that comes but once and never comes again, a love until the end of time.*

Lilith began chewing on her thumbnail again, worrying it so hard that I feared it might bleed. 'Heloise dealt with her separation from Abelard by becoming a nun, you know, but the cloistered life simply wasn't my style.'

It seemed to me that Lilith's life of virtual seclusion in Woolford-Freakin'-Nowhere on Maryland's eastern shore had a lot more in common with convent life than, say, a high-rise condo in Ocean City, but didn't say so. Instead, I asked about something that had been puzzling me. 'If Nick was brought up in Switzerland, Lilith, how come he doesn't speak with an accent?'

Nick's mother grinned. 'Four years at Phillips Andover can knock an accent out of any kid, especially one struggling to fit in.'

'And you?' I asked.

'Me? I'm a Noo Yawka. That's how I tawk.'

I laughed. 'No you don't.'

'A bit surprising I don't, actually, since I studied art at NYU.' Lilith set her teacup down on the table. 'My mother was American. They tell me I sound like her.' She grimaced. 'It troubles me sometimes that I can't remember her voice.'

'I understand completely. Like you, I lost my mother way too soon.' I swallowed the lump in my throat, then quickly changed the subject. I shared news of my visit with the Simon sisters and their irrepressible dog, Bruno, with Lilith and by the time we finished our tea, she was smiling again. It seemed like a good time to go, so I stood up. 'I'll contact my brother-in-law and get back to you as soon as I know something.'

'Thank you, Hannah.' Lilith accompanied me back to my car. 'I'll keep trying to reach Nick, too. Perhaps the lab knows where he is. I think it's time for a little mother-to-son chat.'

I climbed into my car and closed the door behind me. As I turned the key in the ignition, Lilith tapped on my window, so I powered it down. 'Thank you for returning my letters,' she said, blinking rapidly, fighting back tears.

I patted her hand where it rested on the window frame. 'Back home where they belong.'

NINETEEN

It's a hundred times easier to find a missing accident victim when you know the fellow's name, even if you work for the Chesapeake County police department. Armed with the name Nicholas Ryan Aupry, we'd invited ourselves to dinner at the Ives family farm where Dennis (according to Connie) was enjoying a rare Tuesday afternoon off.

'Paul, my man!' Dennis greeted us warmly as we hiked up the drive. 'Come to meet the cows?'

'Cows? What cows?' I wanted to know.

'Dexters. Smaller than your average cow. Dual-purpose animals, really. Good for milk or beef.'

'The cows and I vote for milk!' I called after the boys as they wandered out to the back forty to converse with the livestock.

Carrying the lasagne I'd brought as an offering, I followed

Connie into the kitchen. 'Three-hundred-fifty degrees for about an hour,' I instructed as she slid the casserole dish into the oven. 'How go the gourds?'

For some time, Connie had been earning a modest income constructing figures out of ornamental gourds she grew in her garden. 'Come see for yourself,' she said, and led me down the narrow hallway to her workshop where pots of paints and brushes waited, lined up in orderly rows on her workbench. The smell of oil paint and shellac permeated the air, warring with the aroma of cinnamon and cloves from several dozen pomander balls dangling from a clothesline strung across one end of the room. This season's batch of gourds had a Christmas theme – Santa Claus, the elves, his reindeer, and Mrs Santa, too.

I fingered the price tag on Rudolph's ear – $65 – and thought, damn, I'm in the wrong business. Dasher and Dancer were similarly priced. Add Prancer and Vixen and the rest of the team, plus Santa and his sleigh and an assortment of elves, and you'd have a major investment in folk art. 'I can afford Comet,' I said, fingering the fifty-dollar price tag on the whimsical reindeer, 'but it'd be a shame to break up the set.'

Connie selected an elf and dabbed a spot of pink on each of his cheeks. 'Sorry, Han, the whole family's spoken for. They're going to Homestead Gardens for the holidays,' she said, naming an upscale garden center south of Annapolis whose Christmas light display rivaled that of Rockefeller Center. 'We're part of the decorations.'

Mrs Santa had been assembled from more than a dozen gourds. I moved in to examine her more closely. 'How do you do it, Connie?' I asked, admiring the way a sleeve had been constructed out of a slice of dried squash.

Connie passed me a gourd that looked like an apple with warts. 'Her sleeve's from one of these. It's called a bule,' she explained. 'And I made her skirt from a hollowed out crown of thorns.'

'Next to you, I have zero talent,' I whined.

'Do, too. You knit,' she said, pointing at my new sweater with the business end of her paintbrush.

'That's not talent, it's mechanical. You follow a pattern. Knit, purl.' I set Mrs Santa back down on the worktable next to her chubby hubby. 'How do you keep all those pieces from falling apart?'

'I am the Hot Glue Gun Queen of the Western World,' Connie claimed, brandishing her brush like a scepter.

Back in the living room, over cocktails, everybody seemed to be tiptoeing around the Metro crash, so I brought it up myself at the dining table over the barley vegetable soup. 'You remember that guy I met on the Metro, named Skip?'

Connie's soup spoon paused in mid-air. '"Met" isn't the word I'd choose, Hannah. You held the guy's hand and prayed with him while he died. God, I admire your composure. I'd have freaked under the same circumstances.'

'I did. Freak, that is. But, I'm beginning to think he didn't die.'

'No kidding!'

'Using those letters I showed you, I was finally able to track down his mother. She tells me his name is Nicholas Ryan Aupry.'

I passed the basket of rolls to my brother-in-law. 'I know I'm always asking you for favors, Dennis, but do you think you can find out where they've taken him? It's not for me,' I added quickly. 'It's for his mother.'

Dennis dabbed at his mouth with his napkin. 'Excuse me, I'll be right back.' He disappeared into the kitchen where, after a few seconds, I could hear him talking on the phone. Two minutes later, he was back. 'Stay tuned,' he said, and returned to his soup.

By the time we had finished the lasagne and were helping ourselves to seconds of gingerbread with warm applesauce topping, I had my answer.

Dennis's cell phone buzzed. He took the call in the living room, then returned to the dining table with good news. 'They took Aupry to P.G. in critical condition, but once he was stabilized, they transferred him to Kernan up in Baltimore.'

'What's Kernan?' Connie asked.

'It's the biggest rehabilitation hospital in Maryland,' Dennis explained. 'They specialize in trauma of all kinds. Brain, spinal cord, multiple fractures, you name it.'

'His condition?'

'Upgraded to serious, but they expect him to survive.'

'Thank you, Dennis.' Relief washed over me in waves.

He saluted me with a spoon. 'No problem. So, Hannah,' he asked before attacking his dessert once again, 'what do you plan to do now?'

'Telephone his mother, of course. That's step number one.'

'Why hasn't that happened already?' Dennis wondered.

'I suspect he didn't *want* his mother to know.' I said. 'They weren't on the best of terms.'

'What's step number two?' Connie wondered.

'I'm going to buy some flowers and a Wishes-for-a-Speedy-Recovery balloon and pay Mr Aupry a visit.'

'Hannah thinks she's found evidence that John Chandler is Aupry's biological father.' Paul tipped his chair back from the table and laced his hands across his chest.

'Chandler? The *And Your Point Is?* Chandler?' Connie whooped.

'It's true,' I said. 'I'm absolutely convinced of it. But I went to see him the other day, and Chandler's not owning up to it.'

Dennis scowled. 'Why should he? Chandler is your enigmatic Zan? Preposterous!'

'The information's out there, Dennis. I found it on the Internet. And it's persuasive.'

Paul held his wine glass out for a refill and Dennis obliged. 'Nicholas Aupry had access to the same basic information you did, Hannah – his mother's letters and the Internet. I wonder if he's reached the same conclusion as you have about Zan?'

'Only one way to find out, I guess. When I pay a call on the patient, I'll grill him. But Aupry didn't hold the trump card like I did.'

'Trump card? What trump card?' Connie wanted to know.

'Elspeth and Claire Simon.' I stole a quick look at my husband. 'And the clue of the squiggles.'

I left it to Paul to explain about *čárkas* and *háčeks* and went off to the kitchen to telephone Lilith with the good news and brew up another pot of decaf.

Whenever I get within ten miles of Baltimore, I have to drop in on my little sister, or when she finds out, I never hear the end of it. Georgina, the baby of our family, lived with her husband and four kids in the Roland Park section of the city.

When I called to say I was stopping by, Georgina told me that the twins were at soccer practice with their dad, a successful CPA, but that 'the girls' were at home.

When I let myself in through the kitchen door, I found my niece Julie, now eleven going on thirty, perched on a stool at the kitchen counter playing a game on the family computer. 'Where's your mom?' I asked, peering at the screen over Julie's shoulder.

'Doing laundry in the basement.' She manipulated the mouse, and a panel of miniature chairs appeared on the screen, each with a price tag attached. Julie clicked, then dragged an ornate chair into a house she was building on the screen.

'What are you playing?'

'The Sims.' She tapped the screen with a chubby index finger. 'Look, Aunt Hannah, that's you and that's Uncle Paul.'

On the screen, the avatar known as Paul seemed to be preparing a meal in a vast Jacobean-style kitchen, while Hannah swam laps in a backyard swimming pool. Julie clicked her mouse a few times and the swim ladder disappeared from the pool. 'If I do *that*,' Julie grinned impishly, 'Hannah will drown! She'll turn into a tombstone in the back yard!'

'Oh, I hope not!'

'Just kidding.' Julie giggled, clicked the mouse a few times and restored the ladder.

As I watched, Hannah used the ladder to climb out of the pool. She turned around three times like Diana Prince transforming into Wonder Woman, and emerged wearing a gray business suit. 'Off to work, now!' Julie ordered as Hannah rode off in a car. Back in the virtual kitchen, Paul was washing his dirty dishes.

'I've made houses for everybody,' Julie told me. 'Aunt

Ruth has a store in Pleasantville, too.' She looked up, wide-eyed. 'Wanna play?'

'Sweetie, a game like that would eat my brain right up. Although it would be nice if your Uncle Paul did the dishes like that.'

Georgina suddenly materialized from the basement carrying a wicker basket heaped with clean laundry. 'Have you done your homework, Miss?'

Julie looked ceiling-ward, rolled her eyes elaborately, and flounced off to her room. Obviously not.

On the computer screen, Paul and Hannah's life seemed to go on. Hannah returned from work and took a shower. Paul watched TV. Eventually he headed for the exercise equipment Julie had installed for him in the family room and Hannah picked up the telephone to order some pizza. Maybe I should build a cottage and move a Sim named Lilith Chaloux into it; construct a house nearby for John and Dorothea Chandler; add a condo for Skip then click 'Play,' stand back and wait to see what happens.

'How's everyone?' I asked Georgina as I helped her fold a king-sized sheet into a compact, origami-like package.

'Hunky dory. And I'm volunteering as a tour guide at Evergreen House, so that keeps me out of trouble.'

Evergreen House was a Baltimore gem, a magnificent nine-teenth-century Gilded Age mansion formerly owned by John Garrett, a B&O railroad tycoon. Its exterior, Georgina told me, had been the inspiration for the Haunted Mansion at Disneyland. She oohed and ahhed over the library, the theater and the twenty-three-carat gold-plated bathroom, then segued into the current exhibit called 'Cheers! The Culture of Drink in Early Maryland,' which must have reminded her of the upcoming holidays because she suddenly switched gears and asked, 'You're coming to us for Thanksgiving, right?'

'Well, duh.' I put the towel I had folded on top of the pile.

'Good. Which reminds me, why are you here today? When you called, you didn't say.'

'I'm going to visit somebody in the hospital. At Kernan.'

She snapped the wrinkles out of an undershirt, folded it into neat thirds. 'Anybody I know?'

'No. It's the guy I was sitting next to when the Metro train crashed.'

Georgina's head shot up. 'Wow! You found him, then!'

'Dennis did,' I said, giving my brother-in-law full marks.

'It's certainly an advantage having a cop in the family, that's what I always say.' Georgina stacked the folded laundry in the basket, picked the basket up, and balanced it on one hip. 'I'm glad the guy made it. How's he doing, anyway?'

'As soon as I find out, I'll let you know.'

From Georgina's, it was a quick six-mile drive to the sprawling, multi-acre Kernan Hospital campus just off Windsor Mill Road. I parked in the visitors' lot.

I hadn't been kidding about the flowers and balloons. Before I left Annapolis, I'd popped into the Giant near I97 and made what I thought was a suitable selection – an arrangement called Autumn Daze, and a Mylar 'Get Well' balloon in a cheerful yellow. I hauled them out of my trunk, locked, then strolled up the sidewalk past a flagpole and into the main entrance of the hospital, with the balloon bobbing gaily overhead.

'I'm here to visit Nick Aupry,' I told the volunteer at the information desk. 'I'm his Aunt Hannah, from Iowa. I just got off the plane, and hoo-boy! I don't know why I bother to fly. I could have *walked* here faster than that. I was supposed to be here yesterday,' I rattled on. 'And Delta Airlines? Don't get me started! You know what they say?' I paused for breath. 'They say Delta means Don't Expect Luggage to Arrive!' I chuckled. 'Isn't that good?'

The woman behind the counter smiled indulgently. 'I'm sure he'll be glad to see you. He hasn't had very many visitors since they transferred him up here from trauma.'

'We're a small family, all spread out. Go where the jobs are, you know! I just found out about Nick's accident! Can you believe it?'

The woman handed me a visitor's pass. 'He's in 129B. Just down the hallway there, and take the first left.'

I found the man I knew as Skip in a private room, lying flat on his back with a brace like a halo encircling his head.

From the halo, four long metal rods extended, screwing the device directly into his skull. Other metal bars stretched from the halo down to a stabilizing shoulder brace.

The TV was tuned to the Discovery Channel where MythBusters appeared to be exploring the dangers of taking a shower during a thunderstorm.

I walked into his line of sight. 'Hello, Skip. Remember me?'

Skip closed his eyes for a long second, then opened them again, and blinked as if trying to focus. 'The lady on the train.'

'That's right. Hannah Ives. I came to see how you're doing.' I still held the flowers in one hand and the balloon in the other.

Skip's hand rose slightly, then fell back on to the covers. 'As you see.'

'That looks like a medieval torture device,' I said, indicating the head brace.

'It is.'

'I'm very glad you survived the crash,' I told him as I set my autumn bouquet on the windowsill next to another similar arrangement. 'These are pretty,' I told him, touching a yellow chrysanthemum.

'They're from my mother.'

'Ah. Well, now you have a matched pair!' Keeping my back to the window, I added, 'You're incredibly lucky, you know. When you passed out on me . . . well, I thought you had, you know . . .'

'Died?'

'Yeah.'

'Only the good die young,' he said.

The TV remote lay next to his hand. He patted his way over to it, fumbled for a moment, then switched off the set.

'What's wrong with you, if you don't mind my asking. Your legs . . . ?'

'I have a C5 contusion,' he said. 'The legs are the least of my worries.' He whacked his right leg with the remote. 'Smashed, but healing.'

'What's a C5 contusion?''

'A spinal injury. To begin with, I was pretty much paralyzed from the chest down. I've come a long way since then.'

'Kernan is as good as it gets, I understand.'

'So they tell me.'

I pointed to the halo. 'How long do you have to wear that contraption strapped to your head? Is it really *screwed* into the bone? My God.'

'Dr Frankenstein's finest invention. It might come off in a week or two, they tell me, but I'll still have to wear a neck brace of some sort.'

'Can you walk?'

'That remains to be seen.' Beneath the blanket, he wiggled his toes. 'They're coming back, slowly, but they are coming back.'

'Do you remember the crash?' I watched his face closely. With his head completely immobile, the eyes said it all. They stared back at me vacantly.

'I spend my days just lying here, trying to remember, but it's all a blank. I remember the heat. God, it was hot! I remember sitting next to you on the train, lusting after your iPhone. Asking about the weather. After that, nothing, until I woke up here.'

'Ah. Probably just as well. It was pretty horrific.'

'So they tell me.'

'I was attending a charity luncheon that day, Skip. I'm curious. What were you doing in DC?'

Skip closed his eyes as if the answer to my question was written on the insides of his eyelids. 'I was doing genealogical research at the Library of Congress.'

'In the Adams Building?' I asked, feeling a little mean about trying to trip such a sick man up.

'No. The Genealogy Library is in the Thomas Jefferson Building. The one with the dome.'

'Oh, you're right.' And he was, too. I'd visited the Genealogy Library on several occasions.

An aide slipped into the room to top up Skip's water pitcher with fresh ice. After he'd gone, I said breezily, 'Say, Skip. A guy named James Hoffner came to see me the other day.'

'Hoffner, yes. He's my attorney.'

'Oh.' What else could I say? *Who is that asshole you hired?*

'You probably don't remember, but I was carrying a bag on the train. A ratty old one from Julius Garfinkels.'

'I remember it well,' I told him. 'We chatted briefly about the store. Do you remember that?'

Skip nodded. 'Hoffner's supposed to be helping me get it back. It's got family stuff in it.'

'I know. There was a mix-up at the hospital and they gave the bag to me by mistake.'

Skip's eyes widened in what seemed like genuine surprise. I made a mental note to check if he'd majored in theater at Stanford. 'Great! Do you have it with you?'

'No, but relax! Don't worry about it. I was able to locate your mother, and I returned the bag to her. It's perfectly safe.'

If Skip was alarmed by this news, he didn't show it. 'It's her birthday coming up,' he rushed to explain. 'I was having some old photographs restored as a surprise. Re-colored. Matted and put in a nice frame. You know.'

'Sure,' I said, catching him in the fib almost at once. I'd seen his mother's passport, but he didn't know that. Lilith's birthday was on April 4th, some six months away. Unless Skip was a guy who really planned ahead, his birthday surprise story was pretty fishy.

'I had to look at a couple of letters,' I confessed. 'You know, to track the owner down.' I imagined Skip, left alone in his mother's appalling house, tossing clothes and shoes and unopened boxes around the cluttered house in disgust, frustration and rage. I pictured him finding the bag, opening the shirt box, going through it with growing shock and surprise.

'Who is Zan, do you know?' I asked.

'My mother's old boyfriend.'

'Do you know his full name?'

'What's it to you?'

I shrugged, but probably not very convincingly. 'Just curious. I guess I thought Zan was your dad. Is he?'

Skip stared past me at the dark and silent TV. 'I don't have a father. I was conceived spontaneously by the process of parthenogenesis,' he said bitterly.

'My dad's still alive,' I said conversationally. 'But I lost my mother a long time ago.' I reached out and laid my hand very gently on the blanket covering his good leg. 'Take care of your mother, Skip. She needs you.'

'She doesn't need *anybody*,' he snarled.

'We all need somebody, Skip. Do you have a wife?'

He snorted.

'A girlfriend?'

'She decided that Maryland was a foreign country, and that leaving the beaches of sunny California would be worse then living naked among the Tlingit in Alaska. So, fuck her.'

'Well, OK then!' I had to laugh. 'So, tell me how you really feel.'

'Do you remember praying with me?' I asked after a moment of silence.

Skip's eyes flicked to the right, in the general direction of the bedside table where a rosary hung from the knob of the drawer. 'Sorry, I don't,' he said.

I pointed. 'Would you like me to hand you the rosary?'

When he said yes, I gently unhooked it from the knob and held it up. I fingered the rosary, running the cool, smooth black beads between my fingers before dangling the crucifix over his open palm. I let it fall, and his hand closed over it. Skip's eyelids drooped. He breathed in deeply, held his breath for a moment, then let it out slowly.

'I *am* tiring you,' I said. 'I better be going.'

Skip's eyes flew open. 'I'm sorry. How are *you*?' he asked, which I appreciated, even as an afterthought.

I raised my arm, still encased in the brace. 'Broken arm. Almost completely healed.'

'Good, good.'

'Would you like me to visit again?' I asked.

'Yes, please. The cable channels are fascinating, but I honestly think King Tut has given up all his secrets. The *Titanic*, too, you know?' His eyes closed, his chest rose and fell, slowly, rhythmically.

I was tiptoeing toward the door when somebody in the hall outside bellowed, 'Nick, buddy,' and barged into the room. When the man saw me, he stopped dead, as if his shoes had suddenly hit a patch of superglue.

'Well, well, well. This must be your mother.'

'Shhh,' I warned, tapping an index finger against my lips like the proverbial librarian, although I'd never seen a real librarian actually do that. 'He's asleep. Can we talk in the hall?'

'And you are?' I asked as I pulled the door shut behind me.

'Jim Hoffner, Ms Chaloux. I'm working for Nick.' He held out his hand.

I didn't think much of Hoffner's investigative skills if he mistook me for the elfin Lilith Chaloux. 'Sorry, my name is Hannah Ives. We've spoken on the phone.'

Hoffner's hand retracted as if I'd zapped him with a gag hand buzzer.

'And I believe you have visited my home on a *couple* of occasions.' I sent icy shards in his direction. After what he'd had done to my house, I wanted to slap the jerk silly, but, for the moment, I was enjoying making the worm squirm. 'I believe you may have left something behind the last time you were there.'

'Oh?'

'Your fingerprints.'

'I don't have the slightest idea what you're talking about Mrs Ives.' His face grew red beneath a tan that owed more to a tanning bed in a strip mall somewhere, than it did to a week spent lounging on a Florida beach.

'Your goons, then. I should send you the cleaning bill. Do you know how hard it is to get fingerprint powder off wallpaper?'

'I . . .' he began.

I raised a warning finger. 'Just stay away from me, Mr Hoffner. Concentrate on squeezing whatever you can out of the Washington Metropolitan Area Transit Authority, take your thirty, forty percent, whatever, and stay out of my life.

'I have nothing to interest you now,' I announced airily. 'I just stopped by to tell Nicholas that I was able to locate his mother and return the box of letters you were so interested in getting your hands on directly to her. So . . .' I rubbed my palms together. 'They're back home where they belong. All's well that ends well, don't you agree?'

I left Hoffner sputtering in my wake.

Out in the parking lot I passed a green Ford pickup. The state of Maryland allows seven characters on a vanity plate and James Hoffner had managed to use them all: GOTALAW.

I stopped, peered through the window into the cab. Tossed carelessly on the front seat was a New York Yankees baseball cap. A pair of sunglasses with ice-blue lenses dangled by one earpiece from the sun visor. My heart flopped. Had Hoffner followed me to New York City? Had he been the guy watching me from the corner of 5th Avenue and 11th Street the day I found the Simon sisters?

TWENTY

T hursday dawned bright and clear but too damn cold to walk a dog. Too cold to do anything, in my opinion, except slip into a bathtub full of bubbles and try to soak off the oily feeling I got after my confrontation with James Hoffner.

I'd been almost fully immersed, a hot washcloth neatly folded and pressed over my eyelids, when Paul knocked on the door. 'Would madam care for coffee?'

I raised a corner of the washcloth and peeked out. 'Madam would. Very much.'

Paul pushed the door open with one foot and eased into the bathroom, a mug of coffee in each hand. He handed one to me, then lowered the toilet seat lid and sat down on its chenille cover. 'You really shouldn't have provoked the man, Hannah.'

'Who? Hoffner?'

'Who else have you been provoking lately?'

I slid the washcloth completely off my eyes so I could glare at my husband. 'But he needed provoking. Especially after what he did to our house. And I think he followed me when I went up to New York City, too. The creep.'

'You can't prove that he did either of those things.'

'That's why he needed provoking.'

'To what end?'

I slithered down in the tub until bubbles covered everything but my head. 'The way he smiled, like he was smarter than me. Made my blood boil! He shouldn't be allowed to think that he can get away with spying, with trashing other people's houses, even if he has it done by some goons *in absentia*.'

Using my toes, I turned the tap so that more hot water would trickle into the tub. 'Help me sort something out.'

Paul leaned back against the toilet tank, extended his long legs and crossed them at the ankles. 'I have a feeling this is going to take some time, so let me get comfortable,' he grinned.

'I've been working on a timeline,' I said, 'and some things just aren't fitting in. The Metro crash was on Tuesday afternoon, September seventh.'

'"A date that will live in infamy,"' Paul quoted.

I wrung the washcloth out and placed it over my eyes again. 'And when did Meredith Logan go missing?'

'I don't know. We didn't hear about Meredith until much later, from Emily. I'm assuming that you know the answer to this question.'

'I do. Meredith disappeared on Tuesday, September seventh, around lunchtime.'

'And you believe there's a connection?'

If my eyes hadn't been hidden under a washcloth, I would have rolled them. 'What do you think Nicholas Ryan Aupry, aka Skip, was doing on September seventh before he stepped on to a Metro train and sat down next to me?'

'I don't know. What?'

'He told me he was doing genealogical research at the Library of Congress, in the Thomas Jefferson building, just four or five blocks away from the Lynx News building.' I raised a single finger. 'Opportunity.'

'OK, but what's his motive?'

'Like me, he'd figured out that John Chandler was his father and he wanted to confront him. Meredith Logan simply got in the way and, I don't know, maybe something snapped.'

'You did say that he'd confessed to a murder when he thought he was dying.'

'Exactly! Yet when I saw Skip in the hospital yesterday afternoon, he claimed he didn't remember praying with me. But when he said it, his eyes shot right over to the rosary on his bedside table, so I'm convinced he *did* remember it happening. And if he remembers praying, he also has to have remembered that he confessed to a killing.'

'He could have been speaking figuratively, Hannah. What were his actual words?'

'"I think I killed somebody."'

'He *thinks* he killed somebody? How can one be ambivalent about that? Either you killed somebody or you didn't. It's not like Skip pushed Meredith off the edge of a cliff then left her lying on the rocks below, not knowing whether she was alive or dead. Meredith's death was very hands-on. She was strangled.'

'Motive and opportunity,' I said. 'Skip's number one on my suspect list.'

'Your theory should be easy enough to prove one way or the other. Don't you have to sign in at the Library of Congress? Wouldn't he have to apply for a Reader Identification Card? And there are security cameras all over the joint, as I recall.'

Underneath my washcloth, I nodded, agreeing. 'Security is really tight. Airport-like. Last time I was there . . .' I raised a corner of the washcloth and fixed an eye on my husband, '. . . I was doing research for good old Whitworth and Sullivan, damn them.'

I repositioned the washcloth over my eyes and lay back. 'Security guards paw through your packages, handbags, backpacks, you name it, coming and going, and you have to pass through metal detectors and theft detection systems, too.'

Paul balanced his mug on his left thigh. 'So, let's say, for point of argument, that Skip lied about being at the Thomas Jefferson building. He wouldn't show up on their surveillance tapes at all. And if he was doing research at the Jefferson building, as he claimed, the tapes would show when he came and when he left, wouldn't they?'

'They would,' I agreed. 'But I'll bet the police are not looking at Library of Congress surveillance tapes because nobody knows what you and I do, that Skip confessed to a murder, that he was in the neighborhood at the time, and that he may have a family connection with the boss of the murder victim.'

'And you're going to point this out to them, right?'

I whipped the washcloth off my eyes and tucked it into the soap dish. 'I don't know *what* to do! I wish I knew somebody with access to those security tapes.'

'The long-suffering police lieutenant Dennis Rutherford?'

I sighed. 'There may be twenty-one police jurisdictions in the Washington, DC area, but, alas, Chesapeake County is not one of them.'

'Aren't you forgetting something, Hannah?'

'What?'

'The press has been speculating that Meredith's death was the work of a serial killer. How about that other victim, the girl they found near Reagan Airport? And the woman who was attacked in Rock Creek Park? They can't *all* have been Skip's doing. He could have murdered Meredith, I'll give you that, but you and I both know that he was teetering between life and death in intensive care when the other two girls were attacked.'

I extended my arm. 'Hand me a towel, Professor, and stop being so damned reasonable.'

Paul stood, grabbed a towel off the rack next to the sink, and when I climbed out of the tub, he wrapped me snugly in it. 'I feel like a taco,' I said.

'You don't look like a taco.' He kissed the top of my head.

'Who knows almost as much about what the police are up to as the police do themselves?' I asked my husband a few minutes later as I was struggling to pull my jeans on over damp legs.

'Police scanner hobbyists?'

I hadn't thought about that one. '*Zzzzt!* No, the correct answer is the media.'

'And so?'

'I think it's time I paid another visit to Lynx News, don't you?'

TWENTY-ONE

I found Jud Wilson's card where I had left it: in the pocket of the jacket I was wearing on the day I first met John Chandler at Lynx News. Hoping he was as first-to-come-and-last-to-leave as Meredith Logan, his predecessor, I telephoned Jud at eight o'clock on Monday morning. He wasn't available to take my call, so I left a message reminding him who I was and asking to see him.

When my telephone rang about ten minutes later, I was up to my elbows in soap bubbles, washing out a cashmere sweater in the kitchen sink.

It was Jud, sounding out of breath. 'Sorry I didn't get back to you sooner, Mrs Ives, but it's been pretty hectic here this morning. How can I help you?'

'The first thing you can do,' I said lightly, 'is start calling me Hannah.'

'Sure. How can I help you then, Hannah? John Chandler told me he'd settled everything with you on your last visit. Is this something new?'

'It is. And it's not Mr Chandler I want to see, it's you.'

'Why me?'

I thought about appealing to his ego. Such a bright young man! What a promising career! Do I have a scoop for you! But he *was* a bright young man with a built-in, finely tuned bullshit-o-meter, so I decided to tell him the truth. 'This is about Meredith Logan,' I said. 'Did you know Meredith well, Jud?'

'I did. She was going to be moving up to production – echoing rolls and cuts, locking up, a bit of talent wrangling. I was going to take over her duties on the office side of things, so I had been shadowing her off and on.'

After his speech, Jud was quiet so long that I thought I'd lost the connection. 'Jud? You there?'

'Sorry. I was just thinking that if I had been shadowing her on the day she disappeared, she might still be alive.'

'That's not your fault, Jud. You couldn't watch over Meredith twenty-four seven.'

'I called in sick that day,' he confessed.

'You can't help being sick.'

'But I wasn't. Sick, that is. Monday was the last day of Abbey Road on the River, the Beatles Tribute Festival. I took a water taxi over to National Harbor with some friends because the band "All You Need is Love" was performing the entire "White Album" that night. Later, we ended up at a bar in Georgetown and, oh man, I don't remember coming home, but I must have because I woke up around ten in my own bed with a headache so evil I thought my eyeballs were going to explode.'

'I've been sick like that before.'

'But I'll bet nobody died because of it. God, I feel so guilty!'

'I'm feeling guilty about Meredith, too,' I confessed. 'I'm afraid I've been sitting on some information that might point the police in the direction of her killer, and I'm hoping you'll be able to help me.'

'You? But you don't even know Meredith.' A note of suspicion had crept into his voice. 'Or do you?'

'When I knew Meredith, she was Meredith Thompson, a student at Bryn Mawr College, and she was my daughter Emily's best friend.'

'Jesus! You're Emily's mother? Emily Ives?'

It took a moment for this to sink in. 'You know my daughter?'

'Know her? I dated your daughter, Mrs Ives. Emily Ives. Hannah Ives. I never made the connection. I feel like an idiot.' While I gaped like a beached fish, grateful that Jud couldn't see me, he continued. 'I thought we had a good thing going, too, until Emily met Dan.'

Dan. Daniel. Last name Shemansky. My son-in-law's given name until he took it into his head that he wanted to be called 'Dante.' Just Dante, one name, like Cher or Madonna or Elvis.

'You must have gone to Haverford, then,' I said.

'Right. Emily was my lab partner in Environmental

Geology. I met Meredith in German 101. We were all pretty tight.'

A long-ago phone call popped into my head. Emily had needed a science credit so she'd registered for Environmental Geology at nearby Haverford College, not because Bryn Mawr didn't have a course that would satisfy the requirement, but because the geology class was scheduled before lunch, and the vegetarian food options at Haverford – particularly the lentil casserole – were way better, in Emily's opinion, than those at Bryn Mawr.

'So, can you meet me somewhere where we can talk, Jud?'

'After what happened to Meredith? Do you think I'm nuts?'

The thought that anyone would suspect me of murdering Meredith, or anyone else for that matter, left me temporarily speechless.

'I'm sorry, Jud. I remember how close the two of you were.'

'She got me this job, Mrs Ives. I'd been working as a paralegal for a major law firm and not enjoying it much at all. I'd always wanted to break into broadcasting and it was Meredith who gave me that opportunity.'

'I see what you mean,' I said after a moment. 'Let me come to the Lynx offices again, then. I'll buy you a cup of coffee.'

'We have plenty of coffee in the office, but it's pretty horrible. Pick me up a soy latte at Union Station and you'll be my friend for life.'

'Consider it done,' I said.

'We can talk, but, soy latte or not, I can't make any promises, Mrs Ives,' I could tell there was no way he was going to call me Hannah now.

So I told Jud what I knew about Skip, aka Nicholas Ryan Aupry, and what I wanted him to do.

'I'll call you back as soon as I have anything,' Jud promised.

Nearly a week went by and I was beginning to think that Jud Wilson had blown me off. Then late one afternoon, when

I was down in the basement wrestling with a load of laundry, he called.

'It wasn't easy, Mrs Ives, but I think we've managed to get copies of the Library of Congress security tapes for the date that you asked me about. I don't know what Nicholas Aupry looks like, of course, so when do you think you can come in and go over the tapes with me?'

Without even bothering to check my calendar, I said, 'Tomorrow?'

'Great. Shall we say ten o'clock? Come to the reception desk and ask for me. I'll escort you up to the viewing room.'

The following day, I presented myself bang on time carrying a soy latte from Starbucks. Jud was waiting for me in the lobby, as promised.

'How did you manage to get your hands on those tapes?' I asked as we rode the elevator up to the fifth floor.

He waggled his eyebrows and twirled an imaginary mustache. 'Ve haf our vays.'

He looked so comical, I had to laugh. 'You aren't going to tell me, are you?'

Jud grinned. 'If I told you, I'd have to kill you.'

I raised a hand. 'Understand completely!'

The elevator dinged and the door slid open. Jud waited for me to step out ahead of him, then escorted me to a double glass door at one end of the elevator lobby where he punched some numbers into an electronic keypad. The door buzzed, clicked and he pushed it open.

Jud led me to a windowless, soundproofed room crammed with electronic equipment. A large, flat-screen television dominated one end. Smaller screens stacked in fours bracketed the larger one and seemed to be carrying feeds from all the major networks. The room pulsed with flickering Technicolor, like a department store Christmas display on meth.

'I can't believe you were actually able to lay your hands on these tapes,' I told Jud as he pointed a remote at a DVD player and cued up the disk he'd just slid in. 'I'm really impressed.'

'Thanks, but you're overestimating my clout, Mrs Ives. 'I'm about as low on the totem pole as you can get at Lynx News. This is way above my pay grade. It took someone with a lot more pull than I have to make the arrangements. I'm expecting he'll join us.'

'Is it possible to get information like this through the Freedom of Information Act?'

Jud shook his head. 'Security tapes are, in general, exempt from FOIA. I think you can understand why.'

'Dear US Government Infidels. Please send me tapes of your security procedures. Signed, Osama bin Laden.'

Jud chuckled. 'Something like that.'

On the large screen, a uniformed guard observed as a brief-case passed through an X-ray machine. 'This is the Thomas Jefferson checkpoint, around eight thirty when the library opened,' Jud explained. 'Do you know when Aupry is supposed to have checked in?'

'No, I don't. I'm assuming morning, just as I'm assuming he came to the Thomas Jefferson building because he told me he was researching some family papers and that's where the Genealogy Research Room is.'

Jud speeded up the video and I watched as the time stamp crept up from eight thirty to nine o'clock to ten. At ten fifteen, I caught a glimpse of a familiar face. 'There! That's him. That's Nicholas Aupry!'

Jud slowed the video down, reversed, replayed. I watched as Nicholas Ryan Aupry passed through the library security checkpoint carrying nothing but a notebook.

'Are you sure this is Tuesday, September seventh?' I asked. 'Aupry should have been carrying a distinctive shopping bag, one with Julius Garfinkel written on the side.'

Jud aimed a laser pointer at the screen, highlighting the date, 2010/09/07 with a wavering red dot. 'What was in the bag, do you know?'

'Family letters and photographs. The same ones I came to talk to John Chandler about the other day.'

Jud shot me a quizzical glance, but when I didn't elaborate, he returned his attention to the large monitor.

We continued watching until the tape ended just after five

thirty when the last researcher left the building. Nicholas Aupry wasn't among them.

Jud furrowed his brow. 'So, who is this guy? Houdini? Or did he just spend the night in the building?'

'Have you ever done research at the Library of Congress?' I asked.

'Not yet. Lynx News has an extensive library right here in the building, with desktop access to an incredible number of online databases. I've never felt the need to go anywhere else.'

'What you probably don't realize is the three main Library of Congress buildings are connected by underground tunnels. You can walk from the Jefferson Building under Second Street to the Adams Building, and from Adams underneath Independence Avenue to Madison, all without going outside.'

I pulled an old Annapolis Symphony concert program out of my handbag, turned to the back, and sketched the three buildings in the blank space between 'We Wish to Thank Our Sponsors' and 'Upcoming Concerts.' 'There's even a tunnel that leads from the Madison Building to the Cannon House Office building,' I added as I roughed it in, 'although you have to be staff to use that one. Tunnels are great when it's raining, like it was the last time I was here. Can you believe some creep stole my umbrella out of your lobby?'

'My apologies on behalf of Lynx News,' Jud said with a crooked grin. 'So, let me get this straight. Aupry can check in at the Thomas Jefferson checkpoint, but he doesn't have to stay in that building. Once he has his pass, he can move around pretty freely, building to building.'

'That's right. He might want to get something to eat, for example, and the main cafeteria is up on the sixth floor of the Madison Building. That's the big white building on Independence Avenue, the newest one.'

When I worked for Whitworth and Sullivan I often had occasion to come to the Library of Congress to attend programs or do research, and I'd usually ride the Metro to get there. 'I'm pretty sure Aupry boarded the Metro at Capitol South, so it's likely that he used the D Street exit on the south-west corner of the Madison Building. That would put him out at First, right across the street from the Metro escalators. Do you have the security footage from Madison?'

Jud aimed the remote and brought up a menu. 'Yes, here it is. September seventh, Madison, D Street. What time do you think we should start?'

'Can you fast-forward to three o'clock?'

Before Jud could aim the remote, the door to the viewing room opened and John Chandler walked in looking like he'd just stepped off the golf course. He wore a green Polo shirt, chinos and Sperry Topsiders without socks. A pair of Oakley's were shoved back on his head. Chandler gave us a two-finger salute. 'Jud, Mrs Ives. Sorry I'm late. Hope I'm not missing anything.'

I gaped at the man like a mouth-breathing idiot. You can change your name and your hairstyle, I thought, shift your allegiance to other designer brands, your face can even age, but your taste in fashion is a dead giveaway, Mr Alexander Svíčkář.

'I'm sorry,' I said, when I'd recovered my power of speech. 'I wasn't expecting you, Mr Chandler.'

The tips of Jud's ears turned red. 'I guess I should have been more specific. John's the heavyweight who arranged for these tapes.'

Chandler selected the chair next to me and sat down, stretching his legs out straight in front of him, looking casual, relaxed, ready to move on to the fourteenth tee. 'So, where are we?'

'When Jud invited me here, Mr Chandler, I expected to find that Nicholas Aupry, the man I knew as Skip, had lied when he told me he was doing research at the Library of Congress on the day Meredith Logan was murdered. These tapes seem to prove otherwise. He definitely came in, now we're trying to determine when he went out.'

Chandler tented his fingers and tapped them against his lower lip. 'And what's Aupry's connection to Meredith?'

I stole a quick glance at Jud. 'Didn't Jud tell you?'

'Jud briefed me, of course, otherwise I wouldn't have called in all my IOUs to lay hands on these tapes, but I'd really like to hear it from you.'

So I explained about Skip and the Metro crash, his deathbed confession, and how I came into the possession of a certain Julius Garfinkel shopping bag full of letters and photos.

'And your theory is? Humor me. I'm a reporter. I like to get things straight.'

'Sometime before September seventh of this year, Skip, who I now know is Nick, stole some love letters from his mother's home. I figure Nick reads the letters, does the math, and realizes, based on his birthday, that he has to be Zan's son, conceived on or about New Year's Eve 1986. He has no idea who Zan is, but naturally he wants to find out. He's just moved to Baltimore, doesn't know anybody, and he doesn't want to use his mother's high-profile attorneys because they might tell her what her son is up to, so he hooks up with a fly-by-night he saw advertising on late-night television.'

'Always a good plan,' Chandler said. 'Like thinking you'll get better service by picking up bimbos in bars rather than paying for high-end call girls.'

'The Tiger Woods effect,' Jud cut in.

Chandler rolled his eyes, then said, not unkindly, 'Wilson, do shut up!'

'So, Nick meets with this lawyer, a guy named James Hoffner by the way, shows him the letters and photos, and Hoffner, to his credit, actually figures out who Zan is. He tells Nick, who decides to pay a call on the guy Hoffner tells him is his father to check it out for himself.'

'Like you did.'

'*Exactly* like I did. My research led me to the same conclusion, Mr Chandler.' I glanced from Chandler to Jud and back again, silently requesting Chandler's permission to go on.

Face solemn, Chandler raised a hand like the Pope issuing a blessing.

I took a deep breath. 'That conclusion is that you are the Zan who wrote those letters.'

Chandler remained silent. I could almost hear the wheels going around. *I can neither confirm or deny . . .*

Meanwhile, Jud seemed to have stopped breathing. He sat frozen in his chair, mouth at half-mast.

'But whether you are Zan or not doesn't really matter,' I

hastened to add. 'What matters is what Nick *believed*. He believed you might be his father, and so he called Lynx News and tried to get an appointment to see you.'

'And Meredith Logan answered the phone.'

'Right. Just like Jud did when *I* called, coming down to meet me when I showed up at Lynx asking to see you, pretty much on the same errand.'

'And Nicholas murdered Meredith because?'

'I don't know. Maybe she wouldn't let him in to see you, he got angry, frustrated. He lashed out, lost control.'

'So, how is this theory of hers holding up?' Chandler asked, addressing this question to Jud.

Jud aimed the remote. 'Nick came into the library, that's certain. Now, as I said, we're trying to find out when and where he left it.'

Chandler flapped a hand. 'Carry on.'

For the next ten minutes we watched library employees come and go through the D Street entrance at herky-jerky silent film speed. Finally, Nick showed up. When I shouted, 'There he is!' Jud paused the image, then clicked forward slowly, frame by frame.

'That's definitely Nick,' I said, leaning forward. 'And this time he *is* carrying a shopping bag. Can you make the image larger?'

Jud twiddled a dial and zoomed in on the bag. As the image came into focus I could clearly read: Julius Garfinkel & Co.

'That's the bag,' I said, staring meaningfully at Chandler. 'That's the one Nick had when he sat next to me on the Metro.'

Next to me, Chandler stirred. 'Pan over a bit, Jud, then zoom in on his face.'

Jud did as he was asked.

Chandler grunted, sighed. 'So, let me get this straight. On the morning of September seventh around ten o'clock, a guy named Nick Aupry goes to the Library of Congress. Security cameras show him checking in at the Thomas Jefferson building, but he is not carrying anything but a notebook. Yet, when he left at three thirty – from the

Madison building – he's carrying a distinctive bag. How do you think that happened?'

I opened my mouth to speak, but Jud beat me to it. 'Either he left the building during the day, or he didn't. If he left, say to have lunch, he could have picked the bag up then and brought it back in with him. On the other hand, if he didn't leave the library complex at all between ten o'clock and three thirty, somebody must have given it to him.'

I raised my hand. 'Permission to speak?'

Chandler smiled, nodded, so I continued. 'My working theory is that Nick left the library, met Meredith, they got in an argument, he strangled her, fled, and got back to the library in time to catch the Metro.'

'If he left and came back, it'd be on one of the tapes,' Jud reasoned.

Chandler pointed at Jud. 'Put our people on it.'

'Do you think Meredith had the package of letters?' I asked. 'That Nick took it from her after her killed her?'

Chandler shook his head. 'We've been over that footage a hundred times. When Meredith left our building, the only thing she carried was her handbag.'

'But if the tapes show that Nick didn't leave the library all day,' I pointed out, 'then he couldn't have killed Meredith. Somebody else did.'

'Exactly.'

'So, either someone on the library staff gave him that bag, or somebody brought the bag in from outside the library,' Chandler speculated. 'Jud, have them check the videos for that, too.'

'That could take hours,' I said. 'Days. Do I get to hang around?'

Jud smiled. 'We've got Mugspot.'

I smiled at the name. 'Facial recognition software?'

He nodded. 'I'll check with our experts, but if it can be programmed to look for a certain face, maybe they can tell it to look for a face that's square and has Julius Garfinkel written across its forehead.'

Chandler stood. 'Get on it, Jud, and call me when you have something.'

Jud snapped to attention. 'Right away, Mr Chandler.'

After Jud left carrying the disks, Chandler turned to me. 'I'm grateful that you came to us first with this information, Mrs Ives. Meredith was dedicated to her job, perhaps too dedicated. If you're right, she died in an effort, however misguided, to protect me, to keep someone from tarnishing my reputation. I'm having a tough time dealing with that.'

It didn't escape my attention that Chandler, smooth-tongued and unflappable, had never admitted to being Zan. He held out his hand. 'We'll be in touch, you can be certain of that.'

'What are you going to do with the information?' I asked as he accompanied me down the hall.

He hesitated in front of an oversized painting of the Washington Monument, a fitting backdrop, I thought, for a television journalist. Pain lined his face, as if he were about to report on a plane crash, or the death of a president. All he needed was a microphone. 'We'll check out the videos, all of them. If Aupry looks like our guy, we contact the police. That goes for Hoffner, too.'

Into the awkward silence that followed, I said, 'And then?'

Chandler seemed to be studying his reflection in his shoes. Without raising his head, he said. 'Then? Then we break the story.'

The answer came sooner than I expected. I was still in Union Station, down in the crowded food court, polishing off my creamy chicken at Pasta T'Go-Go when Jud texted my cell phone.

'Got it. C U soon?'

'In 10,' I texted back.

Fifteen minutes later, Jud and I were back in the screening room sitting in front of the large television screen.

'The suspense is killing me,' I said, as Jud cued up the video. 'Can't you give me a hint?'

Jud smiled enigmatically, aimed, and pressed play.

As I watched, library patrons came and went, waddling through the checkpoint at high speed like cartoon penguins. 'There!' Jud said, freezing the frame on the Garfinkel's bag as it made its way slowly along the conveyor belt and disappeared into the X-ray machine.

I squinted at the faces passing through the checkpoint, but the images were grainy. 'Who brought it there?'

'I'm hoping you can tell me.' Jud diddled with the controls, the camera pulled back, panned, and refocused as somebody picked up the bag at the end of the line. Jud zoomed in on the man's face.

It was James Hoffner.

'My God,' I said. 'That's definitely Aupry's lawyer.'

Jud grinned, fast-forwarding – five, ten, fifteen minutes. 'And here's our bad boy again,' he said, freezing the action. 'At two fifteen, leaving the way he came. And this time, he's not carrying the bag.'

I didn't know that there was a telephone in the room until it warbled like an ill-tempered turkey. Scowling in annoyance at the interruption, Jud punched the speaker button. 'Yes?'

'Have you seen John?' a woman's voice inquired.

'He's taping right now.' Jud checked his watch. 'Should be finished in about ten minutes.'

'Thanks, Jud.'

'Who was that?' I asked after the woman hung up.

'Doro. Dorothea Chandler. Mrs John C. She who must be obeyed.'

'I take it you don't get along.'

Jud shrugged. 'She's OK, but it drives me crazy how she's always popping in, fussing about one thing or another. The latest bee in the Missus's bonnet is her Christmas fundraiser. They're having an auction, and she's twisting John's arm to sign on as auctioneer. John told me he'd rather have a root canal, but short of starting a war in a third world country so he can jet over there to cover it, I think he's going once, going twice, doomed!'

'Where is this event taking place?'

'At her club.'

'Which one?' I asked, although, from Chandler's bio on Wikipedia, I thought I already knew the answer to that.

'The Women's Democratic League.'

'I'd like to meet her,' I said.

At my comment, Jud rolled his eyes in a you'll-be-sorry way.

'Seriously,' I said. Even though recent developments seemed to be pointing the finger of blame for Meredith's murder squarely at James Hoffner, Dorothea Chandler, the wronged wife, wasn't entirely off the hook, at least not in my mind.

Much later, at home, I looked up the Women's Democratic League on the Internet, clicked on the pull-down menu labeled 'Events.' As luck would have it, a Talk & Tea was scheduled for the following day, featuring Susan Woythaler, a woman who'd been active in the women's rights movement since the early years, a mover and shaker at the 1977 National Conference of Women in Houston, where she'd appeared on the dais with such pioneers as Gloria Steinem and Betty Friedan. I made a few phone calls, setting everything else on my calendar – a mani-pedi and lunch with a friend – aside, and hastily made plans to attend.

TWENTY-TWO

Pat Nixon had her 'good cloth Republican coat,' but what did a good lady Democrat wear to a Talk & Tea these days? Using Hillary Clinton and Tipper Gore as my imaginary fashion consultants, I pawed through my closet, finally settling on a periwinkle-blue pants suit that hadn't seen daylight since Bush defeated Kerry and a white silk, scoop-necked blouse. I fastened a single strand of pearls around my neck, and added matching ear studs. Standing in front of the full-length mirror in a pair of classic black Ferragamo pumps, I nodded in approval. I looked so Democratic that I'd even vote for myself.

I drove into the District and spent a good twenty minutes cruising the neighborhoods around Dupont Circle searching for a parking space. In spite of the exorbitant hourly rates, I was seriously considering Plan B – one of the hotel parking garages in the vicinity – when an SUV pulled out of a space adjacent to a driveway on Newport Place. I slipped into the spot, pulling as close as I dared to the car in front of me, and climbed out. From the sidewalk, I squinted at my rear bumper, calculated how far it extended into driveway territory and decided that a scant two inches didn't put me at risk for a ticket. Satisfied, and praying that the meter minder didn't carry a ruler in his or her pocket, I locked my doors and walked the three blocks to the Women's Democratic League, located in an imposing red-brick mansion near the corner of 22nd and O Streets, NW, not far from Washington DC's famed Embassy Row.

Built at the turn of the last century for a former Supreme Court justice whose taste ran to high Victorian, the mansion welcomed visitors into a spacious lobby which would have been as dark as the inside of a coffin had it not been for the light streaming in from a clerestory window on the landing of a grand, central staircase. The staircase itself was a work of art, constructed of dark oak. Poseidon and his twin, complete with tridents, formed the newel posts, and the spindles that supported the banisters were carved naiads, dancing up the stairway in orderly fashion like Radio City Rockettes.

A bronze plaque on the wall to my left indicated the 'Cloak Room' where I should hang my coat, and a poster on an easel near a massive Jacobean sideboard directed me to 'Talk & Tea: Susan Woythaler, VP of Women Now! speaks on the Changing Face of Feminism. 10 a.m.'

Following the arrow on the poster, I found myself in a small anteroom where two women who looked enough alike to be mother and daughter sat behind a long table covered with a white cloth, tending to a spreadsheet and an alphabetical array of name tags. I straightened my spine, smiled broadly and approached the table. 'Hi. I'm new to the area and just heard about the tea today. Is it too late to sign up?'

The older woman wore a hot-pink suit. Clipped to its lapel was a Lucite nametag that told me that her name was Jeannette Williams. 'Of course not,' she smiled back. 'Welcome!'

'How much is a ticket?' I asked, resting my handbag on the table.

'It's twenty dollars for members and twenty-five for non-members.'

'Well, I guess it's worth it to hear what Susan Woythaler has to say!'

'And there's tea before and after, of course.'

'Of course.' I pried open my handbag and forked over three tens.

'We hope you'll like what you see and hear today, and that you'll decide to join,' the second woman, the one holding the spreadsheet, said. She handed me a pre-printed, three-by-five index card. 'If you'll fill out that card, we'll put you on our mailing list.'

'There's the holiday party coming up in December, of course, and in three weeks, we'll have our annual fashion show.' Jeannette passed me a brochure along with my five dollars in change. 'There's an application form on the back.'

I didn't think I could deal with another fashion show so close on the heels of the one that very nearly became the last one I'd ever attend on this side of the Pearly Gates, but I didn't tell her that.

Jeannette pushed a paper name tag in my direction and handed me a felt-tip marking pen. 'If you have any questions, please don't hesitate to ask.'

I uncapped the pen, bent over the table and before I could stop myself printed 'Lilith Chaloux' on the name tag in big, black letters. 'I'm sure I will,' I said, stripping the backing off the tag and patting it, adhesive side down, to my lapel. Under my hand, I could feel my heart pumping like a jackhammer.

'Feel free to look around, Lilith,' Jeannette said after consulting my name tag. 'Refreshments are just through there, in the ballroom.'

'Thank you.' I waved the index card, then tucked it into my handbag. 'I'll return this to you later, if that's all right.'

Inside the former ballroom, which was set up with rows of folding chairs in preparation for Susan Woythaler's lecture, I accepted a cup of coffee from a uniformed server manning an elaborate bronze samovar, stirred in some cream and sugar, then wandered around the downstairs rooms of the mansion, checking out the décor.

The brochure explained that the mansion had been donated to the club in 1961 by the granddaughter of the original owner, and that it was decorated with 'period pieces.' There seemed to be a war going on among the pieces, and it would have been hard for me to say which period was winning. A Federal dining-room table warred with a Duncan Phyfe buffet, which was flanked on either side by some fine Chippendale dining chairs. In a sitting room, Georgian end tables provided arm-side support for Arts and Crafts reclining loungers that were illuminated by standing lamps with Tiffany shades. In another corner of the same room, two women sat chatting on an Art Nouveau loveseat.

If the furnishings had anything at all in common, it was size. Enormous. A Victorian fainting couch in a sunny, chintz-decorated glassed-in porch was so large that I felt like the Incredible Shrinking Woman when I sat down on it to chat for a few minutes with a dynamic young woman named Helen Sue Loftiss, who was bubbling over with information about the club's upcoming holiday arts and craft fair.

Eventually, Helen Sue's presence was required elsewhere and I was left alone with visions of handcrafted sugar plums dancing in my head.

Attracted by gas logs twinkling in the grate, I wandered back into the dining room to inspect the massive marble fire-place mantel and surround, sumptuously decorated for the Thanksgiving holiday with fat, sage-colored candles and wicker cornucopia, overflowing with festive fruit and vegetables. Reflected in the gilt mirror over the mantel was one of the room's enormous chandeliers, dripping with crystals. Identical chandeliers illuminated the ballroom. In almost every room, dark wood paneling extended all around up to shoulder height.

As I wandered from room to room, I looked around ner-vously, expecting to run into Dorothea Chandler at any moment. Did she know about her husband's extramarital affair with Lilith Chaloux? When she saw my name tag, would she recognize the name? More importantly, would she take one look at my face and know that I was definitely not

Lilith Chaloux? And if so, would she freak? I smiled to myself. If she did, this might turn out to be the most exciting Talk & Tea the Women's Democratic League had ever seen.

I thought I might recognize Dorothea from the images I'd turned up on the Internet, but after twenty minutes of cruising the mansion, smiling casually, avoiding direct eye contact, and checking other women's name tags as subtly as possible, I hadn't run into her. It was getting close to the time scheduled for the lecture to start, and I was beginning to fear that Dorothea had bagged the meeting.

In my travels, I'd noticed that club officers wore Lucite badges like those of the two women at the registration table, so when the next officer crossed my bow, I flagged her down. 'Hi. I'm looking for Dorothea Chandler. Have you seen her?'

'You just passed her. Over by the coffee urn. In the blue suit.'

I turned, overcome by a sudden craving for a fourth cup of coffee. I waited in line behind Dorothea, standing so close that I was practically breathing down the woman's neck. When she turned, there was no way she could miss me.

'Oh!' A bit of coffee sloshed into her saucer.

'I'm so sorry!' I apologized. 'I zigged when I should have zagged.'

Dorothea smiled. 'No problem.' She glanced at my name tag and added smoothly, 'Lilith.'

Her hazel eyes never wavered. She didn't blink. Either she'd never heard of Lilith Chaloux or she was a damn fine actress.

Dorothea Chandler was built like an athlete, solid, straight up-and-down, like a tree. Her dark hair had been cut in a shaggy bob, the tips of her bangs fringed with copper, as if they'd been dipped in paint, a style Emily would describe as 'upmarket punk.'

I held out my hand. 'I'm new here, Dorothea.'

'Please, call me Doro. Everybody does.' She took my hand, and I noticed that she wore a wedding band identical to her husband's, although smaller: a twisted rope of white, yellow and rose gold.

She smiled in a friendly way. 'Where are you from, Lilith?'

'Upstate New York,' I told her.

'What brings you to DC? Husband? A job?'

'Both,' I improvised. 'Divorced the former and looking for the latter.'

'Sorry about the divorce,' Doro said.

'I'm not. S.O.B. had been cheating on me for years. His mistress . . .' I flapped my hand. 'Sorry. T.M.I.'

Doro stared at me, quietly sipping her coffee. If I expected her to open up about her personal life to a total stranger while standing between the egg-salad sandwiches and the petit fours, I was mistaken.

'What do you do, Lilith?'

I had to think fast. 'I'm a nutritionist.' Before she could start helping me network, I added, 'I have three interviews lined up, so I'm pretty hopeful. And you?' I asked, raising an eyebrow.

'Volunteer work, mostly.'

'Ah.' There was an awkward silence while I tried to think of something to say. 'So, you don't work outside the home?'

'Not since before the children were born,' she said. 'We have two grown daughters.'

'I wish . . . I wanted . . .' My voice broke rather convincingly. I wasn't very good at producing tears on demand, so I thought about the sad-eyed, abused and abandoned animals I saw on the Animal Planet channel when Animal Cops came on, and flapped my hand apologetically.

'I'm so sorry. Is there anything I can do?'

I shook my head and scrabbled in my purse for a tissue.

'How long had you been married?' she asked.

'Fifteen years. You?'

'Almost thirty-five years.'

'Has your husband ever . . . you know?'

Her gaze was cool. 'Not to my knowledge.'

'You're lucky. Bob's mistress was his choir director. He was a minister, for Christ's sake, a man of God. Pardon me while I laugh. Morality isn't just a concept, it's supposed to be his business.'

I dabbed at the corners of my eyes. 'The only good thing about the situation is that I'll never again have to sit through one of Bob's excruciating sermons.'

For some reason, this cracked Doro up.

As I joined in the laugh fest, I wondered if she ever watched her husband's broadcasts and, if so, what she thought about them. Did they ever discuss his programs? At dinnertime, did she offer advice about his choice of wardrobe? Pump him for gossip? Inquire about what his guests were really like? What if she went home tonight and told John over steak and potatoes about the troubled woman she met today, poor Lilith Chaloux, whose husband was cheating on her big time. Would Chandler spew wine all over the tablecloth? Choke on his steak?

Doro smiled sympathetically. 'In the early years of our marriage, we moved around a lot. I know how hard it is to be the new kid on the block.'

I nodded, sniffling for effect and feeling like a bit of a shit. I had been fully prepared to dislike Doro for depriving Lilith, who I liked a lot, of the love of her life. Disliking Doro would have been a lot easier if she weren't being so nice.

At a summons from one of her well-coifed minions, who had been hovering nearby like a bodyguard, Doro breezed away in a cloud of Shalini perfume – a gorgeous mélange of bitter orange, coriander and ylang ylang with undertones of sandalwood and vanilla. I'd been squirted with eau de Shalini at Bergdorf Goodman the previous summer and loved it, but when the saleslady told me it cost $900 for a two-ounce bottle, I knew I had to pass. Doro could afford luxuries like that. I wondered what would happen if something threatened that cash flow and suddenly she was reduced to buying Chantilly at WalMart like the rest of us?

Back in the ballroom for a coffee refill (my fifth!), I saw Doro at a distance, standing near the podium conferring with an attractive dark-haired woman wearing black slacks and a lavender brocade jacket, who I took to be our speaker *du jour*.

'Lilith?' somebody said.

I turned. It was Jeannette Williams, chugging toward me like a woman on a mission, holding a white carnation in one hand and a large, pearl-headed corsage pin in the other. 'We like to present our newcomers with a little something special,' she said as she pinned the flower to my lapel.

'Thank you.' I cringed inwardly, knowing it would mark me as Someone You Must Talk To and Make Feel Welcome, when all I wanted to do was fade into the woodwork.

The effect was almost immediate. Like moths to a flame, club members fluttered over.

'Jeannette! Please introduce us!'

'Ah! I saw you talking to Helen Sue earlier and thought you might be new!'

'Lilith. What an unusual name. Is it French?'

I was the quarterback in the middle of the huddle, except everyone else was calling the plays.

'No, yes, not French, but Biblical . . .'

Whirr, click, click, click. I turned my head and found myself face to face with a photographer as she aimed her Nikon D80 and its periscope-like flash attachment in our direction. My heart flip-flopped.

Whirr, click, click, click. At the first flash, the women with me slapped on their perma-grins, sucked it in, posed prettily, while I was caught, wide-eyed, temporarily blinded, like a deer in the headlights. The photographer had a sidekick, I noticed, a buzz-cut reporter with a notebook, steadily advancing. 'Excuse me,' I managed to blurt out, panic seizing my vocal cords. 'I think I'd better visit the powder room before the lecture begins.' Ducking, I hurried off before the reporter could sidle up to us, ask for our names and how to spell them.

I could see it all. A spread in the *Washington Post* Style Section: Pictured left to right, Lilith Chaloux and . . . and . . . oh shit, those women knew 'my' name!

I was doomed.

Several minutes later, I found refuge in the powder room. I plopped myself down in one of a pair of Louis XVI, striped silk-covered dining chairs in front of an enormous gilt mirror, foxed with age, where I was taking deep, steadying breaths. When the door to the powder room creaked open behind me, I knew it couldn't be the reporter – unless the guy got off on crashing ladies' restrooms in search of a story – so I ignored the newcomer and began rummaging through the dribs and drabs at the bottom of my handbag, an expedition to lay hands on the tube of lipstick and the stub of an eyeliner pencil I knew was in there somewhere, so I could repair the damage done to my make-up by my crocodile tears.

'Who the *hell* are you, anyway?'

I nearly jumped out of my pantyhose. I looked up and into the mirror. Dorothea Chandler stood directly behind me. She wasn't wearing her happy face.

'I beg your pardon?' In the mirror, my eyes looked enormous, innocent, even to me.

'Is this some kind of sick joke? Just what are you playing at?'

I simply stared at Doro's reflection, letting it do all the talking.

'I don't know who you are, but you are *not* Lilith Chaloux.'

I opened my mouth to claim that she must be mistaken, she must be thinking about some other Lilith Chaloux, but I knew from my searches of the Internet that the Lilith Chaloux of this world were thin on the ground. I was well and truly busted.

'I owe you an explanation,' I said, swiveling around to face her, rearranging my features into the reasonable facsimile of an apologetic smile. 'Aliens occasionally take over my body, I'm afraid. I came here today because I wanted to talk to you. I should have just introduced myself and asked you right out, rather than playing at silly games.'

Her green eyes narrowed. 'Asked me what?'

'If you knew about Lilith Chaloux.'

'My husband's mistress? Of course I know about her. But all that ended more than twenty-five years ago.'

'I realize that, but—'

Doro raised both hands, palms out, cutting me off. 'Then what are you on about? Do you know who my husband is?'

Even though she managed to make it sound like a threat, I smiled, nodded. 'John Chandler. Lynx News.'

'John confessed ages ago,' Doro said, folding her arms across the shelf of her bosom. 'I forgave him. We moved on.'

We glared at each other without speaking for several long moments, like gun molls in a spaghetti western; a Mexican stand-off that would only be resolved by diplomacy, surrender or a pre-emptive strike. I tried to put myself in Doro's patent leather pumps. What would I do if some crazy bitch came up to me at a social event and informed me that Paul had fathered a child by another woman? Would I have 'moved on' quite so gracefully? And if Doro didn't know about Nicholas, I decided I wasn't the person to rock her world with the bad news.

I was the first to blink, rejecting the pre-emptive strike scenario and choosing diplomacy, not normally one of my strong suits. 'I'm working on my PhD in Political Science at Georgetown,' I lied smoothly. 'I was researching Jimmy Carter's Peanut Brigade for my thesis when I stumbled across a folder containing some old correspondence between a woman named Lilith Chaloux and your husband, back when he was still calling himself Zan. I was able to track Lilith down for an interview – that's when I learned about their affair – but your husband was always too busy to see me. I thought I might be able to get to him through you.'

Doro raised an eyebrow. 'You're a fool if you think I have any say-so where my husband's calendar is concerned.'

'I tried that route, too, but Jud Wilson certainly earns his salary, doesn't he?' I tipped an imaginary hat. 'Great gate-keeper.' I sighed, looked away, pensive. 'Maybe if I had been able to talk to Meredith Logan it would have been a different story.' When Doro didn't react, I swooped in for the kill. 'My daughter was a classmate of your husband's production assistant, Meredith Logan. I knew her, too, although not as well.'

'John had always been discreet,' Doro mused, sounding distracted. 'I appreciate discreet. One of the seven virtues, in my opinion. Meredith understood that, too.' There was cold, hard steel in her gaze, a warning, perhaps: I expect you to be discreet, too, or maybe I'll shoot you.

She who must be obeyed.

'How did you know I'm not Lilith?' I asked, genuinely curious.

'I found a photo in John's wallet. I admit that you – rather, *she* – could have changed, but . . .' Doro looked me up and down, smirked. 'But not that much.' Like a sudden rain-storm, Doro's face turned cloudy, dark with fury. 'Look, whoever the hell you *really* are, I'm asking you to stay out of my life.'

'My name is—'

She held up her hand, cutting me off in mid-sentence. 'Shut it! I don't want to know your name because I'm quite sure I'll never see you again.'

'I . . .'

'Isn't that right?' Doro glared. She must have had practice at issuing threats. I bet she ran though housekeepers like Congress ran through money.

Thoroughly cowed, I nodded.

'I see we understand one another.' Doro executed a neat about-face, nearly yanked the powder-room door off its hinges and stalked out, leaving me alone, still clutching a tube of NARS lipgloss in a too-pink shade called Easy Lover that a saleswoman at Nordstrom had once talked me into. I had painted the color on my lips and dropped the tube back into my handbag when I heard a toilet flush.

I froze, hardly breathing, waiting to see who it was who had overheard my argument with Dorothea Chandler.

The door to the stall eased open. A woman emerged. She wore the blue and white uniform of one of the kitchen staff. A Bluetooth wireless cell phone was clamped to her ear. 'I told you and told you, Mama, don't you go listening to that woman. She's so full of shit she could fertilize the whole state of Maryland,' the woman said as she twisted the taps and began washing her hands.

I realized I was still holding my breath when I let it out. I'd caught one of the workers sneaking off to make a personal phone call, that was all.

Sometimes, I thought, it's better to be lucky than smart.

I'd read Woythaler's book, I'd seen her on Oprah, and I wanted like crazy to stay, but Dorothea Chandler had rapped my knuckles, hard, planted her size-eight Cole Haans firmly against my butt and pretty much booted me out. As I skulked out of the powder room, however, I caught sight of Doro at the podium, leaning into the microphone, calling the members to order, preparing to introduce the speaker. 'Ladies, ladies. Take your seats, please.'

Sensing that the coast was clear, I slipped into a chair at the back of the ballroom and was just settling in when that damn reporter spotted me. As he homed in, I shot out of my chair, made a U-turn and headed for the cloakroom where I'd left my coat. Five minutes later, I was back on Newport Place, peeling a parking ticket off the windshield of my car. Sixty damn dollars fine.

Eight-five dollars down the tubes, and I never got to hear what Susan Woythaler had to say.

TWENTY-THREE

I waited patiently for a story about Aupry and Hoffner to break.

In-between meal prep and laundry and watching my grandkids, I logged so many hours watching Lynx News that Paul cheerfully concluded that I must have gone over to the dark side and joined the Tea Party Patriots. As if.

I checked the *Washington Post* daily, Style section, too. After a week went by with no story about Susan Woythaler's appearance at the Women's Democratic League, illustrated by a photograph featuring me masquerading as Lilith Chaloux, I began to relax.

Chandler was keeping a low profile. A full-page promo for his upcoming four-part series *Stand by Your Man?* appeared in prime real estate on the inside back cover of *TV Guide* and promos for the show were running 24/7 on all the major networks.

I couldn't wait to tell Paul. 'Seems our boy is going to be interviewing political wives who've been dumped by their husbands.' I did an arm pump. 'Or vice versa.' Chandler was hitting all the biggies – Elizabeth Edwards, Jenny Sanford, Silda Spitzer, even Dina McGreevey who had stood on the dais wearing a sky-blue suit and a stoic perma-grin, while her husband, then governor of New Jersey, confessed to a long-time affair with another guy.

I telephoned Jud Wilson and left a message, but when he didn't call me back, I took it as a sign that John Chandler was still covering his ass.

Until my brother-in-law gave me a call. 'Hannah, this is Dennis. Just thought I'd give you a head's up.'

'On what?' I'd been washing a wool sweater in the kitchen sink. I reached for a towel.

'We've just arrested a suspect in the jogging trail attacks.'

'We? Does that mean *you*?'

'The guy attacked another woman on Bayside Trail near Pearson's Corner early this morning. But he definitely picked the wrong victim this time. She's a former army helicopter pilot. She saw him coming, ducked, turned the tables on the sonofabitch big time. Broke the guy's collarbone in two places.'

'Good! I hope it hurts. Who is the creep, anyway? Can you say?'

'It'll be all over the news shortly. As soon as he gets out of the ER, he'll be our guest in the Chesapeake County lock-up. I'm not sure where he'll be heading eventually. Everybody wants a piece of this guy. DC, Maryland, Virginia. The murders took place in the District and in Virginia, so I imagine they'll have first crack at him.'

'Go for Virginia,' I urged. 'They still have the death penalty in Virginia. DC doesn't.'

'Hard-hearted Hannah, the hanging judge.'

'Damn right. Meredith Logan deserved to live a long, happy life, and this creep deprived her of it. Some criminals commit crimes so heinous that they forfeit their right to live, Dennis. I truly believe that.' After a moment of silence, I added. 'Has the guy confessed?'

'It's early days yet, Hannah.'

'Do this right, Dennis. Please. Make sure your people don't mess up.'

'Since I know you and Emily are close to this, I'll let the implied criticism slide.'

'Sorry. I didn't mean to sound snarky. So I guess Nicholas Aupry is off the hook?'

'Maybe.'

'How about Hoffner?'

'We'll see.'

But . . .' I began. Something was niggling at me. The Jogging Trail Murders, the press was calling them. But, unlike the other girls, Meredith Logan hadn't been attacked anywhere near a jogging trail.

'Hannah, the only "but" I need from you is this – butt out. Let the police do their jobs.'

'Dennis . . .'

'Hannah, you have to trust me on this.'

Leaving the sweater to soak in the sink, I tuned the television to Lynx News where a reporter I didn't recognize was conducting an Up Close and Personal with a baseball player who had blown the whistle on steroid use in the major leagues, a program timed to the release of his tell-all book on the subject. I switched to CNN in time to catch a 'Breaking News' bulletin.

'Jogging Trail Killer Apprehended,' a sidebar announced, superimposed over a shot of a reporter standing outside the Chesapeake County hospital emergency room, holding a microphone. 'An unemployed computer programmer has been arrested in connection with the murders of two women on metropolitan area jogging trails and is implicated in attacks upon two others,' she began. Her image was replaced by the police sketch of the suspect that had been widely distributed since the assault on the woman in Rock Creek Park. The reporter seemed primed to go on, but suddenly there was a flurry of activity. She turned and viewers got to watch while plainclothes police officers appeared in the background, escorting a man whose arm was in a blue sling, his head covered with a jacket. As cameramen from all the major networks scuttled to follow, a police officer mashed his hand down on the top of the prisoner's head, stuffed him into the back seat of a black and white patrol car, and sped away.

The reporter had nothing new to add, so I telephoned Emily on her cell. She picked up on the first ring. 'Hey, Mom. What's up?'

'Your uncle called, and I just saw a report on the television. They think they've got the guy who killed Meredith.'

On Emily's end of the line there was a gasp, then silence as the news sunk in. 'Thank God,' she said at last.

'It's on CNN right now,' I told my daughter. 'All the channels will have it soon. Are you anywhere near a TV?'

'I'm at the spa, and heading toward the conference room right now. I want to see this guy.' I heard a door open, then close, then the sound of a television springing to life. 'Actually, I want to murder him with my bare hands, dismember him bit by bit, drop the pieces in—'

I cut in. 'Can I watch?'

'Sorry, Mom. I got carried away. You must be relieved that it wasn't that fellow you met on the Metro who did it.'

'I'm sad that anybody did it. But yes, I'm relieved that it wasn't Nick, and that they finally nailed the bastard.'

With the Jogging Trail Murders suspect locked away in my brother-in-law's detention center, the nation's capital was breathing a huge sigh of relief. So was I, until a DC homicide detective paid me a call.

'I'm Detective Terry Hughes,' he said from my doorstep, presenting his shield for my inspection, 'and this is Corporal Sherry Miller.'

Holding the door open, I gawped, rendered temporarily speechless.

Hughes was big, black, broad-shouldered and beautiful, with eyelashes that curled over his amber eyes and shaded them like awnings.

His partner, in contrast, was petite and as pale as Hughes was dark. Freckles splashed across her nose, and her white-blonde hair was tied back in a pony tail at the nape of her neck.

'We're investigating the murder of Meredith Logan,' Hughes explained, 'and I understand you might be able to help us.'

'I really didn't know Meredith very well, detective,' I said. 'Why don't we sit in the living room. Can I get you something to drink? Coffee? Tea?'

They declined.

After we were seated comfortably, I continued. 'Meredith was my daughter's friend. They were classmates at Bryn Mawr College up in Pennsylvania, but that was some time ago.'

'We'll want to talk to your daughter, too, of course. How can we get in touch with her?' Detective Hughes asked.

I gave him Emily's address and phone number, watching with fascination as Sherry Miller wrote it down in a minuscule notebook, using neat capitals letters.

'I'm confused, Detective Hughes. I thought the police had arrested a man for Meredith's murder. That Jogging Trail guy.'

Sherry Miller glanced quickly at Hughes, but Hughes sent a withering glance in her direction and whatever she'd been about to say died on her lips. 'We're interested in what you might be able to tell us about a shopping bag that has shown up on some security tapes at the Library of Congress.' Hughes reached into the leather portfolio he'd been carrying and handed me a picture, a close-up of Lilith's Garfinkel's bag. 'Can you tell us anything about it?'

'What would you like to know?'

'What's in it, for a start.'

'Letters and photos. At least that's what was in it when I had it.'

'When was that?' he asked.

I told him about the Metro crash, described how I had met Skip, and explained the mix-up at the hospital.

'What date would that be – the crash, I mean?'

I opened my mouth to say that I couldn't believe he wouldn't know the answer to that. For weeks, there had been nothing else in the papers or on TV. But, I paused, counted to three and told him anyway. 'September the seventh.'

'Do you know where the bag is now?' he asked.

'No. I mean, yes. I returned it to its owner.'

'Who is?'

'A woman named Lilith Chaloux. She lives on the Eastern Shore in Woolford, a few miles outside of Cambridge.'

'When you had the bag, at any time was it out of your possession?' he asked.

'Absolutely not.'

Corporal Miller glanced up from her notes and spoke for the first time. Her voice was clear and light, almost like a child's. 'What kind of letters and photographs were they, Mrs Ives?'

'Personal ones.'

'Can you elaborate on that?' she asked, one eyebrow arched suspiciously as if she expected me to say 'porn.'

'I don't feel it's my place to go into a lot of detail. For that, it's best you ask Lilith Chaloux yourself. But I don't think she'd mind if I told you they were love letters.'

'What is Ms Chaloux's connection to Meredith Logan?'

'None, as far as I know. Ms Chaloux lives out in the country by herself, in a cottage on the water. She paints. I don't think she socializes very much.'

Hughes reached into his portfolio and withdrew another picture. 'Who is this man?'

I was sure he knew the answer to this question, too. 'His name is Skip – I mean Nicholas Aupry. He was riding the Metro with me when it crashed. It was his bag.'

'And this?' Another picture came sliding across the coffee table my way.

The minute I laid eyes on it, I gave myself a silent high five. John Chandler had made good on his promise. The surveillance tapes that Jud Wilson had shared with me were now in police possession. The picture showed James Hoffner in profile, just after he dropped the Garfinkel's bag off on the conveyor belt that would take it through the X-ray machine at the Library of Congress. 'That is a sleazy lawyer named James Hoffner.'

Sherry grinned, then quickly recovered, dropping her voice almost an octave to ask, 'Why is Mr Hoffner carrying the Garfinkel's bag in this picture?'

'He's Nicholas Aupry's attorney.'

I handed the picture back. 'Look, why are you asking me these questions? Shouldn't you be asking Mr Aupry and Mr Hoffman?'

'We've talked to Mr Hoffman,' Miller volunteered. 'And you've just confirmed what he told us.'

'How about Nicholas Aupry?' I asked. 'What did he have to say?'

Detective Hughes slid all three photos into his portfolio and snapped it shut. 'Unfortunately, we haven't been able to locate Mr Aupry. We're hoping you could help us with that, too.'

My jaw dropped. 'What do you mean you can't locate him? He's at Kernan Hospital up in Baltimore. As you probably know, he was gravely injured in the accident. He's in rehab.'

Hughes exchanged glances with his partner. 'Was. Mr Aupry was discharged from Kernan two days ago.'

I sat silent for a moment, stunned. 'Have you talked to his mother? Checked where he works? His mother told me he's got some sort of research position at the Johns Hopkins Applied Physics Lab in Laurel.'

'We haven't talked to her yet, but we will.'

Corporal Sherry Miller folded her notebook, but before she could stuff it into her pocket, she asked, 'Is there anything else you think we need to know?'

James Hoffner is a lying, murdering son of a bitch? But I bit my tongue. 'I'm not sure whether it's related or not, but we had a break-in several weeks ago.'

Hughes glanced quickly at Miller – *be sure to write that down* – then back at me. 'Did you report it to the police?'

I nodded. 'Nothing seems to have been taken, though. Whoever it was could have been looking for the letters. Hard to say. The police dusted for prints.' I shrugged.

'We'll check with them.' Hughes stood and extended his hand. 'Thank you, Mrs Ives. You've been very helpful.'

'Promise me you will find the person who did this to Meredith,' I said as I shook his hand. 'She was a lovely young woman.'

'We're working flat out on that, Mrs Ives.' Corporal Miller started toward the door, paused and turned. 'You can be sure of that.'

'Detective Hughes?' I asked as I opened the door to see them out. 'Have you ever played football for the Redskins?'

His laugh started somewhere deep in his chest and rumbled

out of his mouth like a runaway locomotive. 'I get that a lot.'

Not long after Hughes and Miller left, something struck me like a knife though the heart. The picture Hughes showed me of Nicholas Aupry. It wasn't taken at the Library of Congress at all. In that picture, Nick was waiting near a reception desk, and hanging on the wall behind him was the distinctive red, white and blue logo of the Lynx News Network.

TWENTY-FOUR

I telephoned Lilith right away.

'Hannah, how good to hear from you.'

I didn't shilly-shally around. 'Lilith, is Nick with you?'

'No, he isn't. Why do you ask?'

If I mentioned the police it might alarm her, so I said, 'I just called Kernan and they say he's been discharged! I found that so hard to believe that I made them check the patient inventory again. How can he have gone home so soon? The last time I saw him he was flat on his back with stainless steel rods screwed into his skull.'

Lilith spoke lightly. 'He made a lot of progress since the last time you visited, Hannah. When I was there last week, he had a brace on his leg, but was using a walker.'

'Do you have a cell phone number for him. I'm assuming he got a new one?'

'Nick gave it to me, Hannah. It's around here somewhere.'

Great, I thought. They'll uncover it in the next century when they dig down to the Mesozoic level. 'Do you know where he went? I'd like to send him a card,' I said, making it up as I went along.

'I don't know his mailing address. He'd just started at Hopkins before the accident and hadn't found a place to live yet, so he was living in a motel while a realtor helped him find a condo. The lab's been incredibly understanding.

They're holding the job for him until he gets back on his feet. Wait a minute!' I heard papers rustling. 'I knew it was here somewhere. Before the accident, Nick was staying at a Night and Day Suites, near Laurel.

'Where on earth have they discharged him to, Hannah? I wish he'd told me!' she rattled on, almost without taking a breath. 'But then, we haven't been close for years. I'm trying, I really am, but after all the baggage that we both bring into the relationship, it's unrealistic to expect changes overnight.' Lilith paused for air, then asked, 'Do you want me to go to Kernan and see what I can find out?'

'No, no, I'll be happy to do it. I'm a hundred miles closer than you are, Lilith. Try to relax. I'll let you know when I find out anything.'

'Thanks, Hannah.' Her voice faltered. 'You're the first real friend I've had in . . . well, just thanks.'

After that unsolicited endorsement, I got a little misty-eyed, too.

Two minutes after saying goodbye to Lilith, I telephoned Kernan Hospital and asked to speak to Nicholas Aupry.

'I'm sorry, he's no longer a patient here,' the operator informed me.

'Oh my gosh! I'm his aunt, and I was planning to send him this big box of chocolates, his favorites, dark chocolate with caramel. I can't believe he left the hospital without telling me. Can you tell me his forwarding address?'

I figured the woman wouldn't be a pushover, and I was right. 'Sorry, dear. Even if I had it, which I don't, I couldn't give it out to you. Patient confidentiality. I'm sure you understand.'

I lowered my voice, spoke softly and slowly, adding a snuffly sniffle in the middle of the sentence for effect. 'Sure. I understand. I understand completely. I've tried him on his cell, too, but he doesn't pick up. Frankly, I'm worried. Nick isn't in the best of shape.'

The woman on the other end of the line brightened, her next words sounding positively chipper. 'You shouldn't worry about that for a minute. Your nephew is listed as an outpatient now. He's due here for physical therapy at three thirty this afternoon. Why don't you come and wait for him here?'

I clucked my tongue. 'You are *kidding* me! I go away for a couple of days . . . Men! They never tell you anything, do they? He probably thinks he can manage all by himself, but you know what that means. Living on Hungry Jack frozen entrées delivered by Pea Pod or something. I am going to make him the biggest lasagne . . .' And I hung up.

I left Annapolis in plenty of time to arrive at Kernan in order to waylay Nick when he appeared for therapy. I sat in a waiting-room chair for a while, thumbing through copies of *People* magazine, then I paced. Thirty minutes, forty, an hour went by. Still no Nick.

The volunteer watch changed at four o'clock, and I was elated when the same woman who had been on duty the first time I visited the hospital strolled out from a staff area and took a seat behind the desk. I waited until she got settled, then approached her. 'Hi. Remember me?' I flapped my hand in an 'aw shucks' way and laughed. 'Oh, of course you don't. You see *hundreds* of people every day. I'm Nicholas Aupry's aunt. He was supposed to come in for his physical therapy session today.' I tapped the face on my watch. 'But he's over an hour late! Did he call or anything? I'm kinda worried.'

'Sorry, honey. We don't have that kind of information.'

In spite of how I felt about Hoffner, over the past several months he had been the closest thing Nick had to a friend and confidant. Grinding my teeth with distaste, I dialed 1-800-GOTALAW, but it rang once and went over to voicemail, making me wonder if the man had any partners at all. Where the heck was Smith? Where was Gallagher? Where was the receptionist, for that matter? The same smarmy syrupy voice that made my skin crawl came on the line. 'Got a phone? Got a Lawyer! This is James Hoffner and I'm not available to take your call right now. But your call is important to me, so stay on the line and leave your message at the beep. And remember: Got a phone? Got a Lawyer!'

'This is Hannah Ives,' I told his machine. 'You've got my number. Call me.'

* * *

Following the directions of the volunteer behind the desk, I found a vending machine and bought a Coke, popped the cap and carried it out to my car where I could think. What would I do at this point if I were the delectable Detective Hughes? I'd start where Nick last lived, I told myself; at the Night and Day Suites near Laurel.

Laurel is only about twenty-five miles from northwest Baltimore, but I got snarled in rush-hour traffic on the Baltimore–Washington Parkway, arriving at the Night and Day Suites behind a group of seven businessmen who'd just been deposited in the lobby by a Blue Shuttle van from BWI. I stood in line at eighth position as they began checking in one by one with a registration desk staffer.

Three people had received their key cards and headed for the elevators before it occurred to me to find a house phone. I located one near the rack of tourist brochures – The Baltimore Aquarium! The National Zoo! Luray Caverns! – dialed '0' and asked the harried receptionist to put me through to Nicholas Aupry.

'Can you hold, please?'

After a long silence in which I watched the receptionist hand over a key card to the next person in line, she came back on the line. 'Sorry, but we have no guests by that name.'

So I got back in a line which had grown by another two hotel guests in my absence. One step forward, Hannah, and two steps back.

When I finally made it to the desk, the receptionist, a mouse of a girl, smiled in a way that transformed her face, as if the sun had come out from behind a cloud. She wore a brass name tag that said 'Julie. Racine, Wisc.'

'Checking in?'

I rested both hands on the counter, spread my fingers. 'No, thanks, Julie. I'm trying to get some information. My nephew was staying here a couple of months ago, Nicholas Aupry, but he was badly injured in that terrible Metro crash.'

Julie's eyes narrowed suspiciously. 'Didn't you just call and ask about him?'

Ooops! I shifted gears. 'Yes, I did. It was such a long line and I thought . . . well, I have your full attention now!'

'I do remember your nephew,' Julie said with a sad little smile that made it all the way up to her eyes. 'I'd just started working here then. How's he doing?'

'It was touch and go for a while, but he's finally out of the woods. Nick's still in the hospital, but we hope he'll be released to rehab before long. That's why I'm here, actually. I can't believe Nick didn't think about the luggage he left behind here until just yesterday! He's asked me to come pick it up for him. Do you have it in storage somewhere?'

'That's really not my department,' Julie from Racine told me. 'Hold on a minute.' She picked up the phone, spoke a few words to someone who appeared almost immediately from a cubbyhole of a room behind the reception desk. Rick – from San Diego – shook my hand, told me how sorry he was to hear about my nephew's accident and then got right down to the nitty gritty. 'Sorry, you made the trip for nothing, but we already sent your nephew's luggage on.'

I made a production of rolling my eyes. 'Oh, for heaven's sake! I *told* Nick I'm coming to take care of it! What was he thinking? Did it go to my apartment on Cathedral Street in Baltimore?

Rick's brow wrinkled in concentration. 'No, I distinctly remember sending it to a Night and Day Suites up in Baltimore.'

'The one near Kernan Hospital?'

He pointed a finger like a gun. 'That's the one.'

I pressed my hands together in silent applause. 'That's great. So it'll already be there when he checks in. Thanks so much.' I turned to leave, then spun around. 'But just wait until I get my hands on that boy! I made a trip all the way down here from Baltimore for nothing! I'll kill him.' Clapped my hand over my mouth. 'Whoops! My bad.'

I left Laurel, driving north on Route 29, then made my way east along I70 until it intersected with I695, the Baltimore beltway.

I found the Night and Day Suites, distinctive yellow awning and all, on Whitehead Court, where it had an unobstructed view of the elevated cloverleaf formed by the intersection of several interstate highways, a complicated, multilevel structure that resembled the movie set for Star Wars *Attack of the*

Clones. Someone had cared enough to plant bright red flowers in planters on either side of the entrance to the motel, in an attempt to brighten up the view in an otherwise depressing neighborhood.

I took the steps one at a time – counting six – and wondered where the handicapped entrance was. In his present condition, Nick could certainly never handle the stairs.

For that reason, I had assumed Nick would be living in one of the handicapped rooms I'd seen advertised when I checked out the Night and Day Suites on the Internet. From the parking lot in Laurel, I'd tried to call ahead to let Nick know I was coming, but when I dialed the number suggested by my iPhone, I was patched through to the hotel's 800 number. 'No, I don't want reservations,' I insisted. 'I want to talk to somebody actually *at* the Night and Day Suites in Baltimore.' Apparently this request was too difficult for the operator to handle, so after three disconnects I hung up.

Inside the hotel, manning the desk, was the same receptionist, I swear, who had helped me out in Laurel. Or her twin sister, maybe. Lonnie was from Geneva, New York, had a smile as big as Christmas, and, when I walked in, was charming a couple who were checking in with a dog. I wondered if Julie from Racine and Lonnie from Geneva had attended the same school of hotel management, earning 'A's in Hospitality 101. I waved breezily as I passed by and marched straight to the house phone, where I dialed '0' and asked for Nicholas Aupry.

The phone rang. And rang, and rang, and rang. I was about to hang up when Nick answered, sounding out of breath and out of sorts.

'What?'

'Nick, this is Hannah Ives.'

'God! Just a minute while I catch my breath.' Even over the sound of the television playing at one hundred decibels in his room, I could hear him panting. Finally he said, 'I'm back.' Followed quickly by, 'How did you find me?'

'It sounds like you didn't want to be found, Nick.'

'It's not that, really. It's just that I don't like people making a fuss over me.'

I thought that was a lot of malarkey, but . . . well, you

catch more flies with honey, or so they say. 'OK, I promise not to make a fuss. I just wanted a report on how you're doing. Your mother does, too.'

Nick snorted. 'Mother! That figures.'

'Lilith didn't know that you had been discharged from the hospital.'

'I didn't tell her.'

The last thing I needed was to be sucked into another family's internecine squabbles. I'd blundered through enough family crises of my own, thank you very much. When Emily eloped with a college dropout named Dante, for example, the man who was now the successful owner of Spa Paradiso and the father of my three unbelievably beautiful and talented grandchildren.

'I stopped by Kernan to visit you,' I said, shading the truth just a tad, 'and they sounded concerned that you'd missed rehab today.'

'Yeah, well, that was unavoidable, I'm afraid.'

His voice sounded distant, distracted. Whatever Nick was watching on television must have been far more interesting than I.

'Look, I'm talking to you from a phone in the lobby. How about meeting me down here for a cup of coffee or something?'

'Sorry, I can't.'

'Can I bring something up to you, then?'

On Nick's end of the line, an ad for Little Blue Pills blared. While Nick considered my offer, I listened to a sultry-voiced female boldly hinting at what those little blue miracles could do for 'a certain portion of a man's anatomy.'

'What would you like?' I quickly added, trying to tempt him. 'There's an Indian restaurant down here. Menu looks good. Oh, damn, they don't open until five thirty.'

'I'd kill for a glass of wine,' Nick said at last.

'Gotcha. Red or white?'

'White. I'm in 121, just past the elevators.'

Even though the restaurant wasn't open, I put on my most wheedling smile and persuaded a waiter to stop rolling silverware up in linen napkins long enough to sell me two glasses of wine. Carrying the wine, a glass in each hand, I made my way carefully down the hall and knocked on the door of 121 with the toe of my shoe.

It took Nick a while to open up, and when he did, I saw why. A brace supported his left leg and he leaned heavily on a brass-handled cane. He wore jeans and a Grateful Dead T-shirt. A pair of square, frameless eyeglasses I'd never seen before sat crookedly on his nose.

'Gosh, were you napping? Did I wake you up?' I had to smile. Nick had a case of classic bedhead. I resisted the urge to lick my palm, reach out and smooth down the boy's unruly cowlick.

Assisted by his cane, Nick hobbled over to a chair near a little round table and sat down heavily. I waited by the door, still holding the wine, sipping mine. Once he was settled, I handed him a glass and joined him at the table.

Although the room was more spacious than a normal motel room, presumably to allow for the passage of a wheelchair, it still seemed cramped. It was also one of the most patriotic motel rooms I'd ever seen, right out of a 1776 fantasy: pseudo-colonial white oak furniture, a red, white and blue striped quilted bedspread and matching blue, star-spangled curtains. I felt like saluting.

On the wall, over the king-sized bed, was a print of the United States Capitol building in winter, with skaters gliding over the ice on a pond that didn't exist.

I could see now that the television was tuned to Lynx News. One of their big name neo-cons, even more conservative than John Chandler, if that was possible, was on a tear about illegal immigrants, yelling at some hapless woman on the other side of the split screen, 'What don't you understand about the word "illegal?"'

'Bet she's glad to be in LA and not actually sitting next to the jerk in Washington,' I commented.

Nick dredged up a smile. He picked up the remote and switched off the commentator in mid-harangue.

'You're recovering amazingly well,' I said when my eardrums had recovered. 'Quite frankly, I'm surprised. But the young heal fast, they say.'

'They do good work at Kernan. And I haven't always been a cooperative patient.'

'Who would be with metal rods screwed into their head?' I sipped my wine. 'So, how come you missed your physical therapy appointment today? You don't have to tell me if you don't want to.'

'Goddam Hoffner. I can't drive yet, as you probably noticed. Son of a bitch ran off and left me stranded.'

'Why didn't you have the hotel call you a cab or something?'

Nick waved the idea away. 'By then, I was already late, so I said screw it. I called the hospital and let them know, so it's no biggie.'

'When's Hoffner coming back?' I asked.

Nick snorted. 'Probably never. I think I fired him.'

Well, I thought, as I gazed into the pale gold depths of my wine glass, that was the best news I'd heard in a month of Sundays.

'Was Hoffner the person driving you back and forth to therapy?' I asked. 'If he was, I'd guess firing him would be a problem.'

'Trust me. It's not a problem. I'll be making other arrangements in the morning.'

'Anything I can do to help?'

'No, thanks, Hannah. The rest of me may be a mess, but my dialing finger isn't broken. Yet.'

Nick studied me over the rim of his wine glass which was beaded with condensation. I watched his face carefully as I shared with him the next bit of news. 'The DC police are looking for you.'

Nick sputtered, choked as he aspirated his wine. He pounded his chest with the flat of his hand, coughing, trying to clear his lungs. 'What did you say?'

'It has something to do with the investigation into the murder of Meredith Logan.'

Nick set his wine glass down on the table casually, too casually. 'Who?'

'Meredith Logan. The PA at Lynx News who went missing.'

Nick's eyes narrowed. 'What could I possibly know about that?

I waited him out, slowly sipping.

'I don't even know her,' he added, twirling his wine glass, making wet circles on the table.

'She was John Chandler's production assistant.'

'So?' He was indifferent, or wanted me to think so.

'Honestly, Nick, if I know you're lying through your teeth, don't you think the DC police will know it, too?'

While Nick gawped at me, I pressed on. 'You told me you were doing research at the Library of Congress on the day of the crash. But guess what? You were caught on the security cameras in the lobby of Lynx News. The detectives showed me your picture.'

Nick screwed up his face, as if I'd just asked him to solve a particularly difficult equation. 'I was only at Lynx News once, on the Friday before . . . well, before I met you.'

'Why did you go there, Nick?'

Nick chortled. 'Don't play dumb with me, Hannah. You know very well why I paid a visit to Lynx News. I wanted to see John Chandler.'

'Your father.'

And the truth came out, in one breathless burst. 'Yes, my hotshot father who's too famous to see anybody unless they make an appointment first! That woman, Meredith whatever, she came down to meet to me, but said I couldn't talk to Chandler. She told me he was taping a show, but I didn't believe her. Then she asked how she could help. I didn't know how best to get the great man's attention, so I gave her a photocopy of one of Zan's letters to Mother.'

Nick had been leaning forward in his chair as he delivered his speech, but when it was done, he collapsed, melting into the upholstery.

'What did Meredith say when you gave her the letter?'

'She asked who Lilith was, so I told her. She kept me standing in the lobby while she stared at the letter, people coming and going, swerving around us, and I'm feeling like a fricking salesman or something. After a bit, she told me she'd see to it that Mr Chandler got the letter, took my contact information, said Mr Chandler would be in touch, blah blah blah. Of course, he never called. Big surprise.'

Nick blinked rapidly, and I thought he might be fighting back tears. 'I swear to you, Hannah! That's the first and only time I saw that woman. Until you told me just now, I didn't even know she was dead!'

Actually, I could believe that. By the time Nick was out of the woods, the story had left the headlines.

'Murdered? Jesus. That's terrible!' he said.

I finished my wine and set the glass down. 'What will you tell the police when they show up?'

'Just what I told you.'

'And what if they say maybe you telephoned Meredith, asked her to come out and meet you on that day?'

Nick made a fist and pounded it lightly on the table. 'No, no, no, no! That simply didn't happen! I was totally at the Library of Congress. Somebody will remember seeing me there.'

He opened his mouth, took a breath and I thought he was winding up to tell me something else, but he slammed his lips shut instead.

'At least we agree on one thing, you and I, Skip.' I raised my empty glass. 'John Chandler is your father, isn't he?'

Nick simply nodded, not looking directly at me, but at the ridges and swirls on the textured wall, still absent-mindedly twirling his wine glass.

'What a pair!' I said, referring to Zan and Lilith. 'He's denying and your mother's not telling, but facts is facts is facts.'

'Amen!' Nick said, hoisting his glass. He raised it to his lips and emptied the remaining wine in one gulp, then slammed the glass down on the table. If there'd been a fireplace in the room, no doubt he would have dashed the glass against the hearth and shouted *Prost!*

But Nick was in no mood for celebrating. 'Do you know what it's like to be rejected? No father, an absentee mother, and a fossil of an uncle who squeezed every nickel until the buffalo pooped? Spending every Christmas with the families of friends because my mother was living . . .' He whipped his glasses off and massaged his eyes. 'Well, I'm not going there.'

I could only imagine. I came from a close-knit military family that moved, together, all over the world. Even when our father was deployed, we stayed in touch with cassette-tape recordings sent back and forth through the mail. It hadn't seemed important when we lost the tapes in one of our many moves, but I would give anything to hear my late mother say 'I love you' again.

At that moment, Nick looked so lost and vulnerable that my own motherly instinct kicked in, big time. I pictured Lilith's house as I had last seen it. Thanksgiving dinner hadn't been prepared in that kitchen for a very long time, perhaps not since the early pilgrims.

'Do me a favor, will you, Nick?'

'What's that?'

'Let me take you to dinner downstairs. It's an Indian restaurant. I've looked at the menu, and I think there's a chicken vindaloo with my name on it.' Holding my wine glass, I popped up from my chair and whisked his empty glass off the table. 'Let me rinse these out.'

In the bathroom, I ran hot water into the glasses, swirled it around, then dumped it out, shaking off the excess drops over the sink. As I reached for a towel on the rack behind the toilet, I noticed scraps of paper on the floor. Neatnick that I am, I bent down for a closer look.

Each piece was a ragged one-half inch square. I scooped up a handful and examined them closely. 'Waiting for' was written on one scrap; 'I dream' on another; 'Venice we' on a third. I recognized the handwriting. It was Zan's.

The scraps were from a photocopy, not an original letter, I noticed with relief. When I checked the trash can, I found thousands more bits which, had they been put together, would chronicle Zan's love for a beautiful young woman named Lilith. Leaving our wine glasses sitting on the edge of the sink, I picked up the trash bin and took it out to Nick. 'What's this?' I asked, practically waving the bin under his nose.

Nick smiled ruefully. 'That's what Hoffner and I had our little disagreement about.'

'Photocopies of your mother's letters?'

'Yeah. Before the crash, he had the originals, but I felt uncomfortable about that, so he made copies. For security, he said. He gave me back the originals. That's why I was carrying them that day.'

'I'm puzzled. Why did Hoffner want the photocopies? They're not his letters.'

'Well, I hired him to find my father, so I guess he figured he needed copies of the letters in order to do his job.'

I shook the basket. It rustled like a cheerleader's pompom on homecoming night. 'Why did you tear the photocopies up? I'm assuming this is your work.'

He shrugged. 'I don't need them. I know who my father is, and that's all I wanted to know. Whether he'll ever get around to acknowledging me or not doesn't change that fact.'

'You said there was a disagreement between you and Hoffner.'

'Hoffner was pissed. He had some hare-brained idea that Chandler . . . Well, never mind.'

'Please, Nick. Go ahead. I'm interested.'

Nick seemed to be gathering himself together. With the business end of his cane, he repositioned his footstool. Then, using both hands, he lifted his braced leg and rested it on top of the stool. That done, he leaned back, looking considerably more relaxed than when I first entered the room.

'This is how it went down,' he began. 'Hoffner showed up to take me to physical therapy. He noticed that I'd taken the photocopies out of his briefcase and torn them to bits. He totally flipped out. Swore like a trucker – fuck this, screw that – then walked out, slamming the door behind him.

'Want to know the truth?' he continued.

Of course I did.

'Hoffner ordered me to chill out. Said there was more money in bleeding Chandler than there was in the measly amount we might get out of the Metro settlement. He was planning to blackmail my father. Hoffner wouldn't call it that, of course. He was always running on about manning up, taking responsibility for one's youthful mistakes. That's a good one! And this is my favorite: making it up to me financially, all those years of struggle without a father. Yada yada yada.' Nick laughed out loud. 'Hoffner's a big-time bullshitter, once he gets going. Anyway, I told Hoffner that I didn't need to be compensated for being deprived of a father in my formative years. I wrote Hoffner a check for what I owed him, and told him to fuck off, so he did.'

'Where is Hoffner now?' I asked, growing increasingly uneasy.

'Do I look like somebody who gives a shit?'

Nick rose to his feet with difficulty, supporting himself on the cane, his hand clutching the brass knob, knuckles white, his arm trembling. 'Come on, Hannah. Now that I'm up, didn't you mention something about chicken tikka?'

'Vindaloo.'

'Whatever. Grab those wine glasses and let's roll!'

TWENTY-FIVE

The vindaloo was still burning its way though my small intestine when I got home around eight.

Paul uncurled from his spot on the sofa and rose to meet me. 'So, I graded exams today. How was your day?'

I gave him a peck on the cheek, then dragged him down on the sofa to sit next to me. 'It's all coming together now, Paul. It was Hoffner who had Zan's letters. Although I can't prove it, I think he called Meredith, arranged to meet her somewhere, told her he wanted money to keep his mouth shut about Chandler's love child, something went wrong and she died. Hoffner panicked and gave the letters back to Nick at the Library of Congress, figuring if he didn't get caught with the letters, no problem.

'Now I find out from Nick that he'd made photocopies of some of the letters. Hoffner had a fit when Nicholas destroyed them. Why?'

'That's easy, Hannah. Because he still needs them, that's why.'

'The only thing that makes sense is that Hoffner planned, or even still plans, to blackmail Chandler. Nick even suggested that in a not so subtle way.'

I was playing with a loose thread on Paul's ragged sweater, the one he kept rescuing from the Goodwill bag, when something occurred to me. 'I'm going to call Jud Wilson.'

'Hannah, it's too late.'

'Right,' I agreed. 'And I don't have his cell. I guess it can wait until tomorrow.'

Paul's arm snaked around me. 'Come here.' He kissed me and said, 'You taste like curry.'

'Vindaloo,' I said. 'Extra spicy.'

'Ooh, hot kisses.'

'You should experience it from my side.'

The next morning, I called Jud, left a message saying it was important I talk to him. In five minutes, he returned the call.

'Jud, did that guy on the LC tape, James Hoffner, ever show up at Lynx News?'

'Not that I'm aware of. Why?'

'Is there any way to reach Chandler, other than through you?'

'Sure. If you have his private number. Or his cell.'

'What if you didn't have his private number? How would one reach him?'

'Dunno. Wait until he left the building and corner him, maybe. Or . . .'

'Or, what?'

'Go through his wife.'

'Where's Dorothea today, do you know?'

'Mrs C. is always out and about. Sometimes hard to pin her down. Right now she's flitting around town trying to wheedle donations out of businesses for a vintage hat party and jewelry sale that'll take place next spring.'

'Do you have Doro's cell?' I asked, starting to panic.

'Nope. I can give you the home phone, though.'

'Jud, I'm going to try to track Doro down, but I really, really need to talk to John. It's important. Can you put me through?'

'Sorry, Hannah. Would if I could, but he's out of the office today. Off the radar.'

'Damn it. Where?'

'I don't have a clue. When he called this morning, he said he had some sort of family emergency.'

'Did he say what?'

'He rarely does.'

'Do me a favor. Call his cell and leave a message. Tell him James Hoffner is on the loose and he's in a bad mood.'

'Sure.' Jud took a deep breath, puffed it out into the receiver. 'You think *Hoffner* killed Meredith?

'Of course. Don't you?

TWENTY-SIX

I was having a gorgeous, rejuvenating early-morning soak in a tub of lavender bubbles. I had just tipped a mug of coffee to my lips when my iPhone rang, vibrating like an electric shaver on the edge of the sink. I set the mug down on the bathmat and fumbled for the phone.

'Hannah, it's Lilith Chaloux.'

'Lilith, how are you?'

'I was wondering if you are free today. I need some moral support.'

'Why?'

'That man, James Hoffner, keeps calling and bothering me. Nick must have given him my number, damn it.'

'Hoffner's a creep, but what can we do?' Quite likely, he was a blackmailer and a murderer, too, but what good would it do to share my suspicions with Lilith? It could only alarm her further.

'He says he has a proposition to discuss with me. I don't want to discuss anything with him, but he says it will be to my advantage. He's coming over today. Wouldn't take no for an answer.'

'Why don't you simply leave, Lilith? Go shopping at

the Queenstown Outlets for the day? I'll be happy to join you.'

'That will only delay the inevitable. He doesn't give up easily.'

Lilith had hit the nail on the head. I pictured Hoffner in his green pickup truck, engine idling, waiting at the intersection of Taylors Island and Deep Point, watching for Lilith's Toyota to appear in his rear-view mirror. 'Do you want me to call the police? Say he's harassing you?'

Lilith drew a quick breath. 'It's not harassment yet. Besides, I'm just getting back on good terms with my son, and I don't want any setbacks in that department. Hoffner seems to have Nicholas's ear, so, as much as I dislike the man, I don't want to alienate him.' She paused for a moment, the air on her end of the line filled with the babble of a television. 'I've never approved of the people Nicholas likes to hang out with and I don't suppose I will start to approve of them now.'

'It'll probably please you to hear, then, that Nicholas has fired the creep.'

'The first sign of common sense I've seen in the boy.'

Realizing my bath was going to be cut short, I pulled the plug. There was no way I'd leave Lilith alone with Jim Hoffner, at least not intentionally. With the phone anchored to my ear, I stood and fumbled for a towel. 'It'll take me about and hour to get there, maybe an hour and fifteen.'

'Oh, thank you, Hannah!'

'My fee is high, Lilith. You might just have to paint me a picture some day.'

'Hannah, I would be delighted!'

I drove as fast as the speed limit allowed – and at times a bit faster – making it to Lilith's cottage outside Woolford in a little over an hour. Her Toyota was in the drive. I pulled up behind it, pocketed my iPhone which had been recharging in the console, and climbed out.

The sun slanted through the trees, but a bit of early-morning chill still clung to the air. I regretted running out of the house so quickly that I'd forgotten to put a fleece on over my T-shirt and jeans.

Lilith had told me she'd be in her studio, so I jogged through the woods in that direction, but when I stuck my head into the studio and called out, she wasn't there. She wasn't on the patio either, or sitting on the dock near the water.

Lilith had telephoned from her house. I knew that because I had heard the television. Surely she didn't intend for me to meet her there! But if her car was in the drive, I reasoned, she had to be around somewhere.

I jogged back to the house and let myself in through the kitchen door. 'Lilith! Are you here?'

There was no answer.

I listened to the silence, made even odder by the fact that I couldn't hear the television. 'Lilith?'

Following the path Lilith had made through the disaster that was her kitchen, with one eye constantly on where I was placing my feet, I stepped carefully into the central hallway, calling her name. She wasn't in the shambles of her living room, or anywhere in the wreck of the hall.

The door to the bathroom was closed. Fearing Lilith had taken a tumble in the tub, I knocked, pushed it open, but she wasn't in the bathroom, either. 'Lilith!'

While wending my way out of the bathroom, I was distracted by a noise. Was somebody calling my name? I high-stepped cautiously over a pile of folded towels, but didn't see – until it was way too late – the Charmin UltraSoft 2-Ply Jumbo Pack just on the other side. My foot came down on the Charmin, slipped out from under me, and suddenly I was flying head-first across the narrow hallway. My forehead came to a sudden stop against the doorframe of what might have been, in a previous life, a linen closet, knocking me silly.

'Damn, damn, damn!' I shook my head, trying to dissipate the stars that were doing colorful loop-de-loops behind my eyeballs. With my fingers, I explored the knot on my forehead, already beginning to swell.

Feeling stupid, I struggled to my feet, leaning against the wall for support. I imagined my obituary: Hannah Ives, late of Annapolis, died in a tragic accident when she tripped over a twelve-pack of toilet paper. How embarrassing. Paul would never forgive me.

'Lilith!'

This time, I thought I heard a reply. The door to the guest bedroom stood ajar, but Lilith wasn't in among the ruins. Still massaging the bump on my head, I staggered over to the master-bedroom door and pushed on it hard, but it refused to open. 'Lilith!' I called.

'I'm in here!' Her voice, normally soft, was now only a whisper.

'I've been looking for you everywhere!' I rattled the doorknob, turned it, pushed, but the door still wouldn't budge.

'I was searching for the TV remote, so I started moving boxes and suddenly everything fell in on me.' Lilith was in tears.

Oh dear, the domino effect. Having been in Lilith's bedroom, it wasn't hard to imagine. Borrowing a move I'd seen on a dozen cop shows, I stepped back, then rammed the door with my shoulder, but only succeeded in creating a one-inch gap. I put my lips to the opening and called out, 'Are you hurt?'

'I think my ankle's broken,' she wailed. 'Oh, God, it hurts!'

'I can't get the door open, Lilith! What's blocking it on your side?'

'Stupid, stupid, stupid! I'm so embarrassed, Hannah!'

'Lilith, don't worry about that now. Can you crawl over to the door?'

A whimper. 'No.'

'OK. I'm going to call for help. Hang in there.'

I reached into the pocket of my jeans to retrieve my iPhone, but it wasn't there. I patted all my pockets, front and back. No luck. I leaned against the doorframe, momentarily confused. I distinctly remembered slipping the phone into the right back pocket of my jeans when I got out of my car. Where the hell had it gone?

The toilet paper, Hannah! Your daredevil dive across hall, like one of the Flying Wallendas, but without a net.

Shit!

I staggered down the hallway to the bathroom, sank to my

knees and began pawing through the piles of debris that littered the area. My phone hadn't landed in the Tupperware container of toothbrushes, dental floss and mint-flavored floss picks. It hadn't slipped under a tipsy stack of *Architectural Digests* going back to 1978. It wasn't nestled among the jumble of brand new towels and washcloths, still wearing their price tags, now strewn across the beige shag carpet.

I collapsed against the wall in dismay. I had been traveling at high velocity when I took that header, and so had my iPhone. It could have ended up anywhere among all the rubbish.

'I've lost my cell phone, Lilith. Do you have yours?'

'It's on the dresser, but I can't reach it from here. My ankle's pinned.'

Great.

At that point my choices were two. Leave Lilith and drive out to look for help, or stick around and try to rescue her myself. I decided to stay.

'All right, don't panic. Are you near the door?'

'No, I'm over by the television. My ankle's *under* the television!'

'OK, stay put. I'm going to get this door open if it's the last thing I do.'

I stepped back and studied the situation. Lilith's bedroom door opened in, so the hinges were on her side of the door. So much for Plan A: hammering out the hinge pins and simply removing the damn door.

On to Plan B. It took me a few minutes to move a heap of mail-order catalogs aside – Harry & David's Fruit of the Month Club! 1994! – clearing a spot in the hallway where I could sit down. I took a deep breath, braced my back against the wall, placed the bottom of both feet against the door and pushed, hard, so hard that my legs began to tremble. The door rewarded me by moving a scant two inches.

I got down on my hands and knees and slid my hand inside the room, feeling around carefully for the obstruction, expecting something big, a chair for example, but the first thing I touched was a shoebox, then a book, then a pillow, then something square and flat that could have been a picture frame. Keeping my hand through the crack, I stood, feeling my way slowly up, higher and higher, obstruction after obstruction.

'Tell me what I'm working against, Lilith!'

'Shoeboxes, blankets, sheets and a bookcase, I'm afraid.'

'Keep your head down!' I wrapped my hand around something soft near the top of the pile and threw it as hard as I could toward the far corner of the room.

One object down and how many thousands to go?

I sent another object flying, then another. After every ten tosses, I shoved on the door. At the end of five minutes it had moved another half inch, no more.

Breathing hard, I rested my throbbing forehead against the door in frustration. There had to be another way. 'Lilith! Do you think I can get in through the bedroom window?'

'Oh, Hannah, I'm sorry. The previous owners nailed the windows shut. And I never got around to, to . . .'

'Never mind. Just keep your head down.'

After a bit more work, the gap in the door had widened enough so that I could start pulling smaller items – shoes, handbags, cross-stitch embroidery kits – out into the hall with me. I was working on a decorative pillow which gave up the fight with a soft sucking sound, when somebody called out, 'Anybody home?'

I recognized the voice at once. Jim Hoffner, making his promised appearance. As much as I despised the man, I didn't take the time to engage in any confrontational banter. 'Hoffner! I need help. Lilith's trapped inside her bedroom and the door is jammed. I can't find my cell phone. Can you call 9-1-1?'

'Sorry.'

I stood up, pillow in hand. I stared at Hoffner as he weaved down the hallway in my direction, his yellow windbreaker shining like a beacon in the dark. I took his 'sorry' to mean he didn't have his phone.

'OK, but you're a strong guy. Help me break this door down, will you?'

Hoffner simply glared. 'Where are Chandler's love letters?'

'What's going on out there?' From her bedroom prison, Lilith sounded like a little girl lost.

I ignored Lilith and answered Hoffner instead. 'How the
hell am I supposed to know? I returned the letters to Lilith.
You can ask her that question yourself, *after* we get her out
of there.'

Hoffner's eyes narrowed dangerously. When he raised a
hand, I flinched. I pointed at my eye. 'I'm already working
on a hell of a shiner, Hoffner. You planning on giving me a
matched pair?'

Hoffner kicked a pile of wicker baskets out of his way and
strong-armed past me. He began pounding on Lilith's
bedroom door. 'Where the hell did you put those letters?'

Her answer was simple. 'In a safety deposit box.'

'Where?'

'They're mine, Mr Hoffner,' she shouted. 'Why should I
tell you?'

'Fuck!' Hoffner spun on his heel and careened down the
hall, scattering Lilith's things in his wake. Instead of leaving
by way of the kitchen, though, he hung a right into the living
room where I could hear him crashing about in frustration,
swearing, giving every profanity in his vast vocabulary an
airing before giving up and leaving via the back door, the
way he had come.

No way Hoffner could make the mess in the living room
any bigger than it already was, so I ignored his rampage and
focused on the bedroom door. 'I think he's gone,' I told Lilith
after a while.

The gap between the door and its frame was now about
twelve inches. I tried to squeeze my body through sideways,
sucking and tucking and regretting, when it didn't work, that
I'd eaten three pancakes for breakfast.

Push, grab, toss.

Push, grab, pull.

I stopped work for a moment to catch my breath, inhaled
deeply, smelled smoke. A neighbor burning early fall leaves,
I thought, or cranking up the wood stove to ward off the
morning's chill.

'Hannah? Are you still there?'

'I'm still here.'

Just for the sake of variety, not because I thought it would work, I leaned against the bedroom door and tried shoving it with my back instead of my shoulder. Suddenly, something on the other side gave up the fight, the door yawned open another two inches and I was able to ease myself through.

I found myself standing knee-deep in a jumble of boxes and loose clothing. The bookshelf I'd been working against lay askew, its top butted against the footboard of the bed.

'Lilith? Where are you?'

From around a lopsided aluminum rack hung with plastic-covered dry cleaning, a tiny hand waved like a flag of surrender. 'Over here.'

I found Lilith, wearing pink silk pajamas, lying on her side between the bed and the window. It was immediately obvious what had happened. The elderly television stand – a K-Mart blue light special, unless I missed my guess – had collapsed, sending a DVD player, a cascade of DVDs and the television itself forward, pinning her legs.

I waded closer, slipping and sliding over plastic storage containers that shifted dangerously under my feet. The television was an ancient, wedge-shaped model, housing a giant cathode ray tube. It was still connected to the DVD player by old-style audio and video cables, snarled and tangled like a platter of colorful spaghetti. I kicked clothing aside until I was standing on solid floor, bent my knees, wrapped my arms around the massive set and tried to raise it. 'Ooof!' I said, defeated. 'Damn thing weighs a ton.'

Bracing my back against the footboard of the bed, I shoved the television up and aside with my feet, freeing Lilith at long last.

'Oh, thank you, thank you!' Lilith breathed. She dragged herself into a sitting position.

I kneeled down to check my friend for damage. Both her shins were scraped and bleeding, her left ankle purple and beginning to swell. I touched the ankle gently. 'Can you move your foot?'

Wincing, Lilith rotated her foot. 'It hurts, but I guess it's not broken.'

'Let me help you out of here.'

'I'm so embarrassed,' Lilith wept as I pulled her up until

she was leaning against me, her injured leg crooked behind her. 'I didn't want anybody to see this terrible house. Nobody will understand, and I can't explain.' Tears streamed down her face.

'Can you put weight on your foot?'

She tried it, yelped. 'Ouch!'

'Bad idea,' I said.

'No, I can do it.' She set her foot down experimentally, winced. 'Lend me a shoulder?'

With Lilith's arm draped around my neck and my arm around her waist, we hobbled toward the bedroom door with me kicking obstructions aside like autumn leaves.

'I smell smoke,' Lilith said. With her free arm, she pointed. 'Jesus, Mary and Joseph! Look!'

Tendrils of smoke drifted through the narrow opening I'd made between the door and its frame.

'Wait here.' I escorted Lilith to the bed, shrouded by mountains of clothing except for a small, semi-circular nest she'd dug out for herself. 'I'll be right back.'

Heart pounding, I eased into the hallway, stumbled along, following the smoke down the hall and into the kitchen.

'Jesus!' The passageway leading to the back door was engulfed in flames, the boxes it had contained burning brightly, buckling, collapsing in on one another. Flames licked greedily at the stove. Was it gas or electric? I couldn't remember.

On the floor near the refrigerator, a stray issue of *Life* magazine from December 1989 smoldered, its cover gradually blackened and curled, the image of a smiling Jane Pauley transformed bit by bit into a negative of gray ash.

Did Lilith have a fire extinguisher? I gripped the back of a kitchen chair and laughed hysterically. Of course she had a fire extinguisher. Maybe two, maybe a hundred! Somewhere under all this crap!

In the kitchen, the heat was intense. A wall of flame blocked the back door, our only exit. Somewhere in the basement, a smoke alarm began to scream.

Keeping my head low, I made my way to the bathroom, scooping up a couple of towels along the way. I tossed the towels in the bathtub and turned on the shower, soaking them with water. When they were thoroughly wet, I returned to the bedroom where I'd left Lilith.

'That crazy bastard set your kitchen on fire,' I told her, my voice urgent. 'Here, you may need this.' I draped a wet towel over Lilith's head, put one over my own head, then grabbed her by the hand. 'We'll have to go out through the front door!' I croaked, dragging her down the cluttered hallway after me. 'Keep low. Crawl if you have to.'

When we reached the perimeter of the living room, I dropped her hand so that I could use both of mine to shove boxes aside. 'Help me!' I yelled when I noticed that Lilith had simply plopped herself down among the ruins. 'We've got to get to the door!'

'That's my new coffee-maker!' Lilith moaned as I sent one biggish box flying into the piano. Seemingly oblivious to the smoke and the heat, she held another box in her hands and was gazing at it, looking morose. 'This is a tide clock!'

I knocked the box out of her hands. 'Lilith!' I screamed. 'Screw the tide clock! We have to get out of here!'

It seemed like hours, but it probably took only a few adrenaline-fueled minutes for Lilith and me to clear a path to the front door. It was then that I understood what Hoffner had been doing while he was crashing around Lilith's living room. He'd engaged the deadbolt. Stolen the key.

Son of a bitch!

I began searching desperately for an object I could hammer against the living-room window.

Maybe all of Lilith's junk was working in our favor, I thought as I floundered around, flinging boxes aside. I didn't know how long it would take for the fire to consume all the magazines and newspapers that were stacked in the back hallway, spilling over into the kitchen. What worried me was the smoke, swirling, growing thicker, gathering in a dense black cloud that pushed against the ceiling, descending more quickly than I thought we had time for.

'Lie down on the floor!' I yelled to Lilith. I yanked the drapes off the windows, grabbed a lamp, shade and all, and took a swing. The lamp shattered, but the window remained intact. 'Shit!'

From her spot on the floor next to the front door, Lilith coughed. 'Fireplace poker!'

'Where?'

With one hand covering her mouth, she used the other to point toward the far wall. With all of Lilith's goddam rubbish in the way, the fireplace and its tools might as well have been in Siberia.

My clothing clung to me, wet and hot. My skin smarted. I surveyed the room, eyes stinging, spotted what I thought might be a coffee table under a mound of quilts and thrashed my way toward it. I swept the quilts aside, pulled the table toward me and flipped it over. A cheap table, thank God, with screw-on legs. I wrenched off one of the legs and was crawling toward the window with my head protected by the wet towel when someone began pounding on the outside of the front door. 'Mother! Mother! Are you in there?'

'It's Nick!' Lilith croaked.

I didn't have a second to waste in wondering how Nicholas had gotten there. I pressed my cheek to the door. 'Nick! The deadbolt's thrown and we don't have a key. Can you break down the door?'

'Wait a minute!' Lilith cried. 'There's a spare key in the flowerpot!'

'Did you hear that, Nick?' I shouted. 'Spare key! Flowerpot!'

Nick heard. In seconds the deadbolt turned and the door flew open. A tsunami of air whooshed past us as we stumbled out of the burning house and collapsed on the brick steps, coughing until our lungs ached.

Supporting himself on a cane, Nick backed away from us, limping painfully, face sweaty and streaked with soot. 'We tried the front door, we tried the back! Burned my hand on the doorknob. Jesus, Jesus!'

'It was Hoffner,' I screamed, too preoccupied to wonder who 'we' were. 'He's crazy, Nick! He set the fire. Have you called 9-1-1?'

Nick wore a soft neck brace, held on by Velcro straps, so

he nodded with difficulty. 'I came in a cab. The cabby called it in.'

A metered cab all the way from Baltimore? How much did that cost, I wondered as I guided Lilith down the steps. I couldn't help it. Must have been my New England genes, frugal down to the last molecule.

After Nick had paid off the cab driver and insisted he be on his way, I said, 'Thank you, Nick. If you hadn't showed up . . .' I let the sentence die.

'I telephoned, Mother didn't answer, and I got worried. Hoffner'd been acting so squirrelly.'

Lilith and I staggered past Nick, across the driveway and on to the grass. With tears streaming down her face, Lilith watched her house burn. 'My things! All my precious things!'

I thought about all the 'precious' handbags, shoes and wicker baskets, all the indispensable toiletries, medical supplies and cross-stitch kits. The four Crock-Pots still in their original boxes, more than a dozen different flavors of Kraft salad dressing – from Asian Toasted Sesame to Zesty Italian – the sixteen-ounce bottles arranged on her kitchen window sill like mismatched chessmen. I grabbed Lilith's arms in case she took it into her head to dash back into the inferno to try to save them. I dragged her across the lawn, forced her to sit down against a tree, well away from the blazing house.

Out in the driveway, every door of Lilith's Toyota stood open; its trunk yawned. Hoffner had torn her car apart looking for the letters. Mercifully, he hadn't bothered with my Volvo.

I was rubbing sweat and soot off my face with the tail of my shirt, looking around, wondering where the bastard had gotten to. He had to be somewhere in the neighborhood, I knew, because his truck – GOTALAW – still sat at the edge of the drive not far from the tree where I had parked Lilith.

I wondered if Hoffner knew about Lilith's studio. No telling what he'd do to the studio – snap her brushes, squeeze paint out of the tubes, trash her paintings. If you had a giant yard sale, sold the entire contents of Lilith's house, you wouldn't equal the value of even one of her paintings, at least not in my opinion.

A sudden movement caught my eye, a flash of yellow at the perimeter of the woods. 'What's out there?' I asked Lilith who was eyeing Hoffner's truck with murder on her mind.

'A tool shed. Gardening stuff. A riding mower.'

'Keep an eye on your mother,' I told Nick. 'Don't let her anywhere near the house.'

I was glancing around the yard, looking for something I could use as a weapon, when Jim Hoffner stalked into view, bold as brass, heading for his truck and a quick getaway.

When he got within range, I flew at him like a banshee, attacking him with both fists, pummeling his chest like a jackhammer. 'You bastard! You set that fire on purpose! We could have been burned alive!'

Hoffner laughed, a manic, Halloween funhouse cackle that chilled me to the bone.

Infuriated, I cocked my arm, but before I could get off a good left hook to his jaw, Hoffner grabbed me by the hair, twisted my head painfully, and threw me to the ground. His right hand dived beneath his jacket and, almost before I could blink, I was staring up into the business end of what looked like a 9mm Glock.

'Bitch!' The arm holding the big black gun didn't waver.

'Hoffner, don't!' Nick yelled.

Hoffner's lip curled nastily. 'I have to, Aupry. Thanks to you and your big fat mouth, she knows.'

Lilith struggled to her feet, her eyes wild, wide. 'Stop! Is everybody *crazy*?'

Nick limped toward Hoffner. 'You can't, Hoffner! Hannah saved my life. She called the paramedics, she held my hand, she prayed with me, for Christ's sake, when we both thought I was dying.'

Sirens began to wail in the distance. With half my brain I willed them to hurry, with the other half, I prayed. *Please God, please, I'm not ready to go!*

It didn't seem to occur to anybody that if Hoffner wanted to weasel out of the mess he'd created, he'd have to dispose of three witnesses, not just one.

'What's that man talking about, Nicholas?'

Nick faced his mother. 'Hoffner believes your letters will

be worth a lot of money to a certain party who will pay anything to keep his dirty little secret.'

Lilith opened her mouth, but nothing came out. I could almost see the wheels going around, taking it all in. The 'dirty little secret' was Lilith herself.

'Tell him where the letters are, Mother. Nothing's worth getting shot over.'

Lilith stiffened. 'I put them in a safety deposit box where they can't do anybody harm.'

Suddenly the gun wasn't pointing at me, but at Lilith. 'I don't believe you! Let's go. Get them!'

Lilith folded her arms across her chest, set her jaw. 'No.'

Hoffner took a step in Lilith's direction. 'You're coming with me. Now.'

Without warning, Nick's cane shot out, knocking the gun out of Hoffner's hand. The gun landed on the grass at my feet. I snatched it up, cocked my arm and threw the gun as hard as I could, watching with pleasure as it spiraled into the flaming house.

'God dammit!' Hoffner bolted for his truck, gunned the engine and fishtailed down the drive. Before he had driven more than one hundred yards, the brake lights flashed red, the truck skewed sideways, and he leapt out of the cab. 'What's wrong with him?' I asked aloud.

Lilith held up a box cutter, shrugged. 'When he wasn't looking, I messed with his tires.'

'Lilith, how . . . ?' I indicated the box cutter.

'I picked it up when we were in the living room.'

I could have hugged her.

Hoffner bobbed like an apple, hesitating, caught between an oncoming fire truck on the one hand and an angry mob of three on the other, one armed with a box cutter, a second with a cane, and me with a rage so hot and intense that if I tore Hoffner to shreds with my teeth and bare hands, no court in the world would have held me responsible. Hoffner sprinted toward the woods, heading in the direction of Fishing Creek.

The pumper unit from the Church Creek Fire Company screeched to a halt at the foot of the drive, inches from Hoffner's front bumper. His truck was blocking their way.

A radio crackled. Permission apparently asked and granted, because seconds later the fire truck advanced, made contact with Hoffner's vehicle and shoved it, grinding and lurching, into a stand of trees where it sat, slewed sideways between two giant tulip poplars.

Hoffner's yellow jacket disappeared into the trees. If he continued in that direction, I worried, no way he'd miss Lilith's studio.

'Is everyone out of the house?' a fireman asked as he hopped out of the truck.

'Yes. We're all here.' I said.

'Good,' he said as his colleagues busily unrolled their hoses. The pumper roared to life and water began to play against what remained of the roof of Lilith's cottage, sizzling, changing the smoke from black to white as clouds of steam arose from the ashes.

'Injuries?'

Nobody spoke. Nick leaned on his cane, Lilith against a tree, leg bent, stork-like, at the knee. With the exception of the firemen who clearly had other priorities, I was the only able-bodied person in the neighborhood. If anybody was going to stop Hoffner, it had to be me.

'Nick, I need to borrow your cane.' With Hoffner's gun gone, I hoped the weapon would give me some tactical advantage.

Nick looked confused.

'Wait a minute,' his mother said. She uncurled her fingers revealing the box cutter cradled in her palm.

'My God,' I whispered, considering the implications. Slashing tires was one thing, but a living human being? I shivered. Yet Hoffner had just proved how dangerous he could be. I took the box cutter from Lilith, opened and closed it experimentally a few times, admiring the way the razor moved smoothly in and out of its casing. 'Just in case,' I told her, securing the blade and slipping the cutter into my pocket.

Then I sprinted into the woods after James Hoffner.

As I suspected, Hoffner had found Lilith's studio hideaway. When I charged through the door, his back was to me and he appeared to be studying 'Sailboat 23,' still clamped to Lilith's easel.

'The police are on the way, Hoffner. I'd blow this joint if I were you.'

He turned to face me, slowly, as if he hadn't a care in the world. He grinned malevolently. 'It's just you and me, then, Mrs Ives? Mano-a-mano?'

'Oh, for heaven's sake. Do you have to be so melodramatic? There's nothing here, as you can see. Lilith told you. She's put her letters into a bank vault. What don't you understand about that, Hoffner? No point in discussing it with me. Why don't you go away now and discuss it with the bank officers at BB&T?

'What do you expect to gain from the letters, anyway?' I pressed on. 'Chandler's not going to give in to blackmail. He'll simply acknowledge the affair and move on. Every public figure is having affairs these days. It's quite the thing. Lynx News isn't going to fire him because of a simple affair.'

Hoffner smiled dangerously. 'It isn't Chandler.'

'Dorothea? Don't make me laugh. She's known about her husband's affair with Lilith for years.'

'That's not what she told me.' With a swipe of his arm, he swept 'Sailboat 23' off the easel. Without taking his eyes off me, he stepped on the painting. When the canvas only sagged, he stamped on it repeatedly. 'Marriage! Reputation! Social standing! That's what motivates Doro Dearest.' A savage kick sent the ruined painting flying into the wall where it knocked over two others, like dominoes.

Several hundred yards away, Lilith's house was turning into a pile of ash. What remained in this studio was all she had, and I wasn't going to let Hoffner ruin that, too.

Hoffner's eyes narrowed and he opened his mouth, to threaten me, probably, but before he could utter a word, I heard sirens, supplemental fire trucks, I supposed, ambulances maybe, police. 'Hear that, Hoffner? I told you, we called the cops. They're coming for you.'

While Hoffner had been taking out his hostility on 'Sailboat 23,' I'd worked my way closer to the window and to the door that led out to the patio.

'You!' Hoffner snarled, turning away from the easel, backing me up against the chaise lounge. He reeked of gasoline. I hadn't smoked for decades, but I wished I still carried matches so I could strike one, set his jeans on fire.

The box cutter bulged reassuringly in my pocket, yet I hesitated to use it. Slashing another person's flesh, feeling their blood sluice over me, warm and red and smelling of copper . . . my stomach heaved.

I felt around for the afghan, found it where Lilith had draped it over the arm of the chaise, and tossed it over Hoffner's head.

'Goddammit!' It took Hoffner only a moment to shrug his way out from under the afghan, but it was time enough for me to wrench open the back door and escape through it, running hell-bent for leather in the direction of the main house.

Hoffner, mad as a bull, charged after me.

About fifty yards down the path I collided, literally, with one of two firemen dragging fire hoses toward the creek. 'Help! He's after me!' I panted.

The fireman looked puzzled. 'Who, ma'am?'

I turned, equally puzzled, in time to see Hoffner crouching at the end of the pier, untying one of the lines that held Lilith's motorboat to the dock. As the firemen and I watched, Hoffner stepped into the boat, tilted the outboard motor into the down position, stooped and squeezed the gas line bulb. His elbow shot out once, twice, three times as he yanked on the starter rope in an attempt to get the little engine going.

'Is there a problem, ma'am?' one of the firemen asked.

The distinctive roar of the outboard motor being revved up cut the breeze. With Hoffner's hand on the throttle, the little boat backed, turned and shot into the creek, leaving a rooster tail in its wake.

Hoffner had gotten away.

'No problem at all,' I told the fireman, mentally turning Hoffner over to the vicissitudes of the wind and the tide. 'I think my problem just solved itself.'

When I got back to what remained of Lilith's cottage, I was pleased to see that the Madison Volunteers had powered up their pumper and water from the creek was now reaching the blaze. A third truck screamed up the drive. The volunteers from the Neck District did their best, too, but by then it was mostly too late. The roof of Lilith's historic cottage had fallen into the shell of the building, leaving nothing but charred beams, blackened stone walls and an ancient chimney, standing erect and proud like a monument over the smoking ruins. Still the firemen remained, playing water on the house, chasing sparks and dousing flare-ups to keep the fire from spreading to the nearby woods.

Nicholas limped off to check on the damage Hoffner had done to his mother's paintings, while I remained sitting under a tree, watching the firemen and comforting Lilith, my arm around her shoulders. Quite suddenly, she shivered and all the color drained from her face. 'Lilith, are you OK?' I thought about the chaise in her studio. 'Do you need to lie down?'

Lilith shook her head, and slipped out from under my sheltering arm. 'Zan!'

I turned to see John Chandler, dressed in jeans and a polo shirt, striding in our direction. Eyes on the prize, he weaved up the drive, deftly navigating a path between fire trucks and fire hoses, seemingly oblivious to the chaos going on around him.

Next to me, Lilith struggled to rise, but before she could get to her feet, Chandler had broken into a loping run, closing the distance between them in seconds. He seized Lilith by the hands and pulled her up, catapulting her straight into his arms.

'You . . .' Zan breathed, crushing Lilith to his chest. 'I always . . .'

'Zan, why are you here?' Lilith asked when she came up for air.

'My wife received a disturbing phone call this morning. I had to make sure you were all right.' He stepped back, holding Lilith at arm's length, eyes on scan as if checking her for damage. Seemingly satisfied that she wasn't broken, he turned, noticing the firemen and the ruined house for the first time. 'I see I'm too late.'

Before Lilith could comment, I stepped out of the shadows and into a patch of sun. 'Her ankle's sprained, but otherwise—'

'You!' Chandler interrupted. 'Hannah Ives, isn't it?'

'Yes. It's me. Quite obvious now that you didn't tell me the truth when I visited you at your office.'

'I'm sorry, but I thought I was doing the right thing.' He paused. 'For my family.'

'At least you're here now,' I said. 'That's a step in the right direction. You mentioned a disturbing call.'

Chandler cleared his throat. 'Guy named Hoffner. He'd been pestering Dorothea. This morning my wife and I had a showdown. I found out that she'd actually agreed to pay him money in exchange for the letters I wrote to Lilith.'

'Hoffner doesn't have the letters, Mr Chandler. Lilith does. There were some photocopies once, but Nicholas destroyed them. Hoffner doesn't have anything to bargain with.'

'Is that why . . . ?' Lilith began.

Chandler's hands slid down Lilith's arms, found her hands and grasped them tightly. 'Perhaps I'm getting ahead of myself, darling. A couple of months ago, a young man shows up at Lynx, asks to see me. I was out of town on assignment – US troops were leaving Iraq – so my PA put him off. She told him to make an appointment, come back in a couple of days. Later, after Meredith disappeared, we were reviewing the Lynx security tapes, and the minute I saw him waiting at reception, I knew. I had my research people check him out, just to be sure. Nicholas Aupry, born September 27, 1987. He's mine, isn't he Lilith? He has to be.'

Lilith caught her lower lip between her teeth. Fat tears rolled down her cheeks.

'Darling, why didn't you *tell* me?'

'What good would it have done, Zan, except to feed your Catholic guilt?'

'God, Lilith. All these years.' He embraced her again, clinging to his former lover with quiet desperation, like a life preserver. 'You haunt my dreams, so, even in sleep, there is no refuge.' Looking at her again, drawing her in like a saving breath, he stroked her cheek with the back of his fingers.

'Remember Budapest? Eglise Matthias, Buda Castle, the view at night from Gellért Hill?'

Still weeping, Lilith nodded.

'Well, that's a pretty picture!' Nicholas had returned, his face flushed, whether from exertion or pent-up rage, it was impossible to tell.

Lilith started.

Keeping his arm firmly around his lover, Chandler turned. 'Son . . .'

'You haven't earned the right to call me that, Chandler!'

'Nicholas, it's true!'

'Shut up, Mother. I'm not talking to you.'

Nicholas advanced, paused, screwed his cane into the grass and leaned on it heavily. 'Where were you, Mr Chandler, when I lost my first tooth? Hit a home run? Graduated from college? Where were you when I nearly *died*?'

Chandler blanched. 'I didn't know, I swear.'

'Yeah, sure. I've seen the photographs. I've read the letters. You and my mother didn't keep secrets from one another. There must be another box of letters somewhere. Hell, a trunk full of letters for all I know. An affair like that. You don't just cut it off cold turkey.'

'Zan didn't know about you, Nicholas. I never told him.'

Nicholas scowled. 'Why not?'

'You wouldn't understand.'

'Try me.'

'It's too late now,' his mother said.

'I'll say.' Nicholas turned away from his mother, sneered. 'What will it do to your reputation, Chandler, if the world finds out that Mr Family Values has a bastard son?'

'Nicholas . . .' Lilith lurched toward her son.

Chandler grasped her arm, holding her back. 'No, Lilith. Let me handle this.'

The look Nicholas gave his father was pure venom. 'Bastard! That's what they used to call me at school. But *you* are the bastard, Chandler, not me!'

Nicholas swung his cane in a wide arc, striking Chandler on the temple. Chandler stumbled, his knees buckled, blood began to stain his white hair crimson.

'Zan!' Lilith screamed.

Nick staggered back, looking bewildered. 'I'm sorry, I'm so sorry. I didn't mean . . .'

Incredibly, Chandler smiled. He whipped a handkerchief out of his back pocket and pressed it to his head. 'Don't worry. It's only a flesh wound.' He caught Nick in a steel-blue gaze and held him there, saying nothing, until Nick slumped and averted his eyes. 'I understand, Nick. Completely. If I'd been you, I might have done the same thing.'

I wasn't inclined to similar understanding. I glowered at Nick. 'I think it's time everybody told the truth, don't you?'

'What do you mean?' Nick seemed genuinely puzzled.

'I didn't think much of that maniac you sent to my house, Nicholas.' I waved, indicating the patch of woods into which Hoffner had so recently disappeared.

'Hoffner?'

'Yes, Hoffner. He tore my house apart, looking for your mother's letters.'

'Christ! I didn't ask him to do that. How was I supposed to know he'd come unhinged like that? After the train crash, Hoffner tracked me down. Said he'd take my case, help me sue Metro and its board of directors. I was mostly out of it, drugged up and trussed up, so it was almost a week before I noticed that the bag with Mother's letters in it was missing. Hoffner showed up at Kernan with some documents for me to sign, so I sent him to the trauma center to see if he could locate the Garfinkel's bag. They gave him the note from you.'

'I couldn't very well come and get them myself, could I?' Nick rapped the cane against his bum leg where it rang hollowly in contact with the metal brace. 'Can't say I approve of his tactics, though. Never pick a lawyer off the Internet.'

'We have attorneys, Nicholas,' his mother said.

'Listen to your mother, Nick. You're going to need an attorney, aren't you? Do you remember what you told me?'

Nick gaped at me in confusion. 'Told you?'

'On the train. You said, "I think I killed somebody."'

Nick squinted, deepening the lines between his brows. 'I did?'

'You did. Just before you asked for your rosary.'

Nick sucked air in through his teeth. 'God, no. Not me. I must have meant Hoffner. Ever since he returned Mother's letters, I've had my suspicions. It's been eating me up, thinking that it's my fault he did it.'

'Who did Hoffner kill, Nicholas?' I asked, although I was certain I already knew the answer.

And so did Chandler. He'd done his homework, too. Before Nick could reply, Chandler said, 'Hoffner killed Meredith Logan, my production assistant. When Nicholas showed up that Friday armed with one of my letters to Lilith, Meredith had to have recognized the handwriting.' Chandler shot a glance at me. 'So when Hoffner telephoned on Tuesday intending to make a deal, the stupid girl arranged an off-site meeting.' Chandler cleared his throat. 'Meredith was in love with me.' He stole a glance at Lilith. 'One of those surrogate father things, I assure you. There wasn't anything she wouldn't have done to protect my reputation.

'Unless Hoffner talks, we'll never know exactly what happened at that meeting, but I think it's fair to say it went badly, and Meredith ended up dead.'

Chandler turned to me. 'I have good news. Capitol police caught Hoffner on a security camera, leaving Lower Senate Park via the parallel parking area on New Jersey Avenue not far from the Taft Carillon. There's a warrant out for his arrest.'

Balanced on her good leg, the other hooked up daintily behind her like a ballerina, Lilith reached up and touched Chandler's face. 'Zan, I'm so sorry. I'm sure she was a very special young woman.'

Chandler cupped Lilith's chin, tipped it up until he could meet her eyes.

'Don't look at me.' She burst into tears. 'My face is a mess,' she sobbed. 'And I'm still wearing my pajamas!'

Chandler simply smiled. 'After all these long years, do you think I care about a little soot?' He wiped her cheeks gently, one at a time with his thumb. 'Will you have me, my darling? I don't need to imagine life without you. It's been a purgatory of my own making.'

'But, but . . . what about Dorothea? Your girls?'

'One of your American naval officers had a saying for this, I think. "Damn the torpedoes, full speed ahead."'

Lilith bowed her head, as if accepting to share the burden. 'But your job, your show?'

Chandler tucked her hand into the crook of his elbow. 'Mike Huckabee has agreed to fill in for me on *And Your Point Is?* while I'm officially on assignment.'

Lilith grasped his arm. 'Assignment? What assignment?'

Chandler smiled the famous smile that launched his broadcasting career, the smile that stole the hearts of thousands of female viewers at nine o'clock every weekday evening. 'You, my dear.'

Underneath the veneer of soot, Lilith blushed crimson. 'But afterwards, Zan, what then? Will Lynx News take you back?'

Chandler laughed. 'Eliot Spitzer seems to have landed on his feet.'

Lilith looked confused. 'Who's Eliot Spitzer?'

'A former New York state governor who threw his career away by spending tens of thousands of dollars on expensive call girls,' Chandler explained.

I nudged Lilith with my elbow. 'He charged them on his VISA or something.'

'And he's now . . . ?'

'A primetime commentator on CNN. Go figure.'

While Chandler excused himself to telephone the DC police, I stayed with Lilith. In spite of the firefighters' best efforts, her cottage had been converted to a steaming, stinking, smoldering ruin. Hoffner had lost a gun to the flames, I'd lost another iPhone, and, except for her studio, Lilith had lost everything.

'Well, I guess that solves the problem of cleaning out the house,' Lilith joked. 'Bring in the bulldozers! I'm relieved that Zan will never have to see the mess I'd allowed my life to become.'

'Lilith,' I said gently, 'there are therapists who can help you deal with the hoarding.'

She waved me off, just as I had waved Paul off when he

had suggested I might seek outside help for post-traumatic stress. 'I watch reality TV, too, Hannah. I analyzed myself. Stuff was filling the emptiness in my life. I'd let Zan go, I'd turned my son over to others to raise, and I couldn't bear to let go of anything else. By the time I figured that out,' she added with a grim smile, 'the situation had gotten entirely out of hand. Just thinking about what needed to be done sent me into a state of paralysis.

'I didn't think it mattered,' she continued. 'What I bought, what I kept, what I didn't keep. It was nobody's business but my own. It wasn't hurting anybody.'

'It was hurting *you*, Lilith. That house nearly killed you.' I touched the knot on my forehead. 'And it nearly killed *me*!'

Lilith touched my arm. 'I'm sorry about that, Hannah, truly. And I can't tell you how grateful I am for your help. I lied, you know. Zan's letters aren't in the bank.'

'Surely you're kidding. Where are they?'

She pointed to the smoking ruins of her kitchen. 'In my oven.'

'Oh, Lilith!'

'It's all right.' She tapped her forehead. 'The memories, they're all right here. I know all of Zan's letters by heart, even the dopey poems. What do you think has sustained me all these years?'

'Love?' It wasn't really a question.

Next to me, Lilith nodded.

A sudden flare-up near the blackened hulk that used to be a refrigerator was quickly doused by one of the firefighters. I remembered its contents – champagne, caviar – and wondered if any of it had survived. Glancing sidewise at Lilith, at her beautiful face, radiant under all the soot, I suddenly understood. 'The champagne,' I said. 'You kept it for Zan, didn't you? Not *if* he came back, but *when*.'

'You are a perceptive woman, Hannah Ives.'

'Where are you going to sleep tonight?' I asked after a moment.

'Where I usually do. On the chaise lounge in the studio.'

Coming up behind us, Zan had overheard. 'I don't think

so. We need to get you to a doctor. Have him take a look at
that ankle.'

'I'll be fine. I've got some Ace bandages.' She paused,
giggled. 'I *had* some Ace bandages.'

'Like fifty of them?' I said.

Lilith blushed. 'Would somebody like to drive me to the
drug store?'

'How far can he get in that boat, Ms Chaloux?' Detective
Terry Hughes leaned against the fender of his white Taurus,
its hood still hot after the hundred-mile drive from
Washington, DC.

'There's a cup of gas, maybe two in the tank,' Lilith told
him.

The detective nodded. 'Out of Fishing Creek into the Little
Choptank, then. Maybe as far as the Bay. A few miles more,
then he's screwed.'

'Oars?' I wondered.

Lilith laughed. 'I'm not that well organized.'

The Coast Guard located James Hoffner six hours later,
floating in circles on the flats near James Island. He was cold
and he was hungry. A bos'n gave him a blanket and a granola
bar, which he ate huddled in the cabin of a twenty-five foot
RBS with his hands cuffed in front of him. Detective Hughes
was waiting for the boat in Cambridge, very pleased to take
delivery.

TWENTY-SEVEN

Paul was stretched out in a canvas lounge chair on our
patio, a bowl of mixed nuts balanced on his chest and
a Bloody Mary within easy reach on the glass-topped
table between us.

'Do you dream about your old girlfriends?' I asked, sipping
my rum and Coke.

Paul squinted into what remained of an early-November sun. "'Now that I am become a man, I put away childish things,'" he quoted.

'I sometimes dream about Billy,' I said, just to jerk my husband's chain.

'Billy?'

'I was ten and Billy was eleven. An older man!' I waggled my eyebrows. 'Billy was crazy about me. Snitched my winter coat during choir practice and hid it in the baptismal font.'

"'The course of true love never did run smooth.'"

'If you are going to speak in proverbs all night, Mr Ives, I'm going to leave you sitting out here and go watch TV.'

Paul grunted. 'So, who are you this time, Hannah Ives?'

The earth shuddered to a halt in its rotation around the sun. 'What are you talking about?'

Paul reached under his chair, pulled out a section of the *Washington Post*, folded open to the Style section, page seven, featuring a picture of me with Jeanette, Helen Sue and all the usual suspects. 'Splain, Lucy.'

I groaned. Everyone morning since that Talk & Tea at the Women's Democratic League, I'd been out on our doorstep early, intercepting the newspaper before Paul could get his hands on it, checking the social notices for any articles about the event. First, we'd been trumped by a star-studded premier at the Kennedy Center, later by a fund-raiser for the Children's National Medical Center, featuring a clown, a magician, and a jester who could twist balloons into animal shapes while standing on his head, an event not unlike your typical political fund-raiser, I thought at the time. Impersonating Lilith Chaloux was no crime, of course, but I didn't feel like explaining my motives to Paul, especially since I wasn't entirely sure exactly what had motivated me to slap Lilith's name tag on my chest in the first place.

'The devil made me do it,' I said at last.

'That's what you always say.' Paul took a sip of his drink, refusing to meet my eyes.

I got up from my chair and went over to him, tapped his outstretched legs with the rolled-up newspaper. 'Move over.' When he obliged, I sat down at the foot of the lounge chair and faced him. 'People were being murdered, Paul. Somebody had to bring the sonofabitch who was doing it down.'

'That's why we have policemen, Hannah. It makes me crazy when you go off half-cocked like that.'

'It seemed like a good idea at the time.' I laid a hand on his leg, squeezed. 'Besides, I don't do it all that often.'

'Oh yeah? How about the time you dressed up as a trophy wife and dragged your poor father along, forcing him to pretend he was a Texas oil millionaire?'

'String tie and all, as I recall.' I smiled, remembering how much Dad had enjoyed his part in bringing down the kingpin in a deadly life insurance scam.

'Seems I'm living with a chameleon.' Paul captured my hand, pressed it against his chest, closed his eyes against the last rays of the dying sun. 'I know I should be used to it by now, but I worry about you, Hannah.'

I studied his face, thoroughly in love with every crease, line, and wrinkle, wondering how many of them I was directly responsible for, rather than, say, Mother Nature.

'John Chandler's coming on in twenty minutes,' I reminded him, checking my watch.

Paul opened an eye. '"Come back. All is forgiven. Signed Lynx News?"'

'Nope. CNN called and John Chandler answered. He's got a new show. *To The Limit* premieres tonight.'

'What's that mean, *To The Limit*?'

'Extremes of all kinds. Religion, politics, sports. Individuals who push the envelope in order to succeed.'

'Can't wait,' Paul said, closing his eyes again. 'Like extreme paintball?'

'You're making that up!'

'I am not. Extreme paintballers are deadly serious individuals. Wannabe jihadists have trained at US paintball ranges.'

'America, land of opportunity,' I said. I reached out for my drink and polished it off. 'Tonight Chandler's taking on that whacko pastor in Florida who thought it'd be a brilliant idea to burn a Koran on the anniversary of 9/11.'

'Well, I'm glad Chandler's got work,' Paul said. 'What's happening with Lilith?'

'She's still in Woolford, rebuilding.'

'Her house or her life?'

'Both, I think.'

'And Chandler?'

'His wife left him. Rather publicly as it turns out, via a press conference on the steps of the Congressional Country Club.'

'Not a Stand-By-Your-Man kind of gal, huh?'

'Not at all. According to Lilith, Dorothea Chandler's been having a bit on the side with the tennis pro.' I shrugged. 'What's good for the gander is good for the goose, apparently.'

'My, my, my . . .'

We sat silently for a moment, watching the sun sink behind the wall that surrounds our garden. 'When's Hoffner's trial?' Paul wanted to know.

'It's scheduled to start in January.'

'What about Nick?'

'For once, he listened to his mother and hired a decent attorney, somebody who doesn't have to advertise in the *Yellow Pages*. The DA tried charging Nick with blackmail, but couldn't make it stick. The blackmail was Hoffner's idea, not Nick's. Nick just wanted Chandler to man up, admit to being his father.

'As for obstruction of justice, what did Nick know? He was hovering near death in intensive care when Hoffner murdered Meredith. If you'd *seen* Nick after the accident, Paul.' I shuddered. 'Pass his picture around to the jury and – *doink-doink* – case dismissed. Nick's testifying against Hoffner, though.'

'One thing I'm curious about. Did Hoffner attack those other two girls?'

'No, just Meredith Logan.'

Paul finished his Bloody Mary, then flipped his celery stalk into the shrubbery. 'I thought the police were looking for a serial killer.'

'That's what the *media* said, not the police. The police knew all along that Meredith's murder was the work of a different killer.'

'And you know this, how?'

'Dennis told me.'

Paul snorted. 'I should have known. Can you be more specific?'

'Nope. Dennis told me to hold my horses. It would all come out in the trial.'

Paul reached out and captured my hand. He squeezed it three times:

I

Love

You.

Still holding my hand, he asked, 'Would you ever leave me for a tennis pro?'

'You're forgetting, Mr Ives. I don't play tennis.'

'So I'm safe.'

'Perfectly.' And I squeezed his hand three times, too.